Driving My Obsession

Lauren Biel

Library of Congress Cataloging-in-Publication Data

Driving My Obsession/Lauren Biel 1st ed.

Cover Design: Pretty in Ink Creations

Editing: Sugar Free Editing

Interior Design: Sugar Free Editing

For more information on this book and the author, visit: www. LaurenBiel.com

Please visit LaurenBiel.com for a full list of content warnings.

It's not that we haven't learned our lesson about jumping into a car with a morally-black stranger. It's that we just really like them. To any reader who agrees, this one's for you.

Chapter One

Ambrose

Club lights strobe above me, their pinkish-purple array casting a warm glow on what little skin I've left exposed. My leather jacket covers my arms, but the scars on my head and face are still on display. The place smells like sweat, like the walls have been painted with the stuff. They probably have been.

A woman with raven hair stumbles onto the stage. Black panties hug her hips, and a black-and-white sequined bra covers her tits. I can't help but think of my mother as her hips begin to sway. As she gyrates along with the beat. She climbs the pole and hangs on by her thighs as she reaches back and unclips her bra, exposing one of the worst boob jobs I've ever seen. Puckered skin surrounds two huge bags of saline.

A topless blonde catches my eye, and she dons a soft, sweet look as she starts toward me. That expression fades when the lights flash and catch on my disfigurement. Disgust has a unique look to it. It's so hard to hide.

I take out a stack of money and wave it in front of her as she tries to sashay past me.

Her throat constricts as she gulps, probably swallowing the bile that rose into her mouth at the thought of grinding against someone who looks like me. "I would, but I'm on my way to another private dance," she says, looking toward the back rooms.

I lower my cash to my lap and allow her to think she's fooled me. As she nears the back room, I look away, knowing she'll glance back to see if I'm watching. Then the dirty little whore has the audacity to stroll to the bar and casually order a drink and sit down to talk to her coworkers. I hate liars. I'd rather you admit to my face that you don't want to dance for me because of how I look. Don't lie. Lying hurts worse.

She'd make a good target. That's why I'm in this shit-hole, after all. To find the vessel to receive all the anger that pours from me like a never-ending fountain. I don't get hard when I see these women with their goods on display. If anything, the opposite occurs and my dick tries to invert itself to get away from their filthy bodies.

The blonde walks by me again, as if I forgot about her lie. I pull her into me and she whimpers, but no one will hear it over the loud music.

I lean toward her ear. "I got these scars from surviving what should have killed me, you judgmental bitch."

I release her and she scurries away, looking back at me with wide eyes as she runs toward the back room. She probably plans to tattle on me, so it's time I make my exit.

I leave the club and get in my Jeep. I have somewhere I need to be, and I should have been there sooner, but my desire for revenge has been eating away at me recently. If I could resurrect the person who hurt me, I'd do what I should have done and pour my wrath into her. Since she's no longer an option, another whore will have to do.

When I pull up to the warehouse, I struggle to find a parking spot amongst the tightly packed cars. Stifling warm air engulfs me as I leave my Jeep behind and head inside.

I walk into a roaring crowd. Fists fly toward the stage as a fight rages on in the center of the room. Blood splatters across the makeshift ring's concrete floor, and bodies collide with the filthy ropes marking its perimeter.

I recognize one of the fighters. Boris is a Slavic beast. Despite his tiny stature comparatively, he's a monster in the ring. Had I been here earlier, I'd have had time to play the crowd for this fight. The fresh faces almost always bet against him, not realizing the power contained in that smaller body. They also don't realize he fights dirty. Darby, the club's owner, doesn't have any rules to break, probably because he thinks it makes for a more interesting experience when someone's fucking ear gets ripped off and spat onto the concrete.

It kinda does.

The bell rings, signifying the end of the fight, and Boris charges off the stage. His wide smile peeks through the blood coating his face like a gory mask.

He spots me in the crowd and heads toward me. "Beautiful fight," he says, a thick Slavic accent coating his words.

"Looked good."

"Felt good, too." He gives me a rough pat on the back before heading toward the locker rooms.

The sharp scents of blood and sweat fill my nose as I suck in a breath and weave through the crowd. They're focused on the two men readying to fight the next match, and that's fine with me. It gives me a chance to study their faces and find my mark. I don't want to screw up and swindle the same fucker twice.

I spot a new face in the crowd, his dirty fist gripping a wad of bills as he counts out what he's just won. The idiot might as well be waving a sign with my name on it. Judging by the smile on his face, he's already won a few others tonight. Sure would be a shame if he lost while he was on a streak.

"You got a bet on this fight?" I shout over the roar around us.

He offers a glance my way, then returns his gaze to the men.

I pull out a wad of money to rival his, and that gets his attention. "I'm willing to put everything on the underdog," I say. "If I lose, you'll get twice what you put in. You game?"

His eyes go to his winnings. He's weighing it up in his mind, and the bait is too tempting to pass by. The underdog in this fight hasn't won since he joined our little club eight weeks ago, but he's due for a win tonight. This guy doesn't know that, though. Only I know.

I set it up, after all.

"Tell you what," I shout. "I'll give you till the end of the first round to decide."

The man nibbles his lower lip and turns his attention to the ring. The fighters circle each other a few times before the bigger guy takes a swing and sends the underdog against the ropes. The one-sided beating continues for a few more minutes before the schmuck to my left eyes the fighters once more and shakes my hand.

"Pretty stupid bet to make. This guy is barely staying on his feet," he says.

I shrug and fold my arms over my chest as I catch the underdog's eye and wink. He turns back to his opponent and grips him in what looks like a hug. In fighting, this is known as a clinch. They use this move for a multitude of reasons, but this time it's so he can let his opponent know the deal has been struck and it's time to take a dive.

The underdog sends forth an uppercut when their bodies part, and the other guy takes it and goes down. The upset sends the crowd into a frenzy, and I take a moment to enjoy the look of shock on the man's face.

Ah, yes. Victory.

His gaze runs over my muscles, as if he's considering backing out on our deal and he wants to figure out if he can take me. He can't. Realizing this, he shoves his money into my hand, tucks his tail, and pushes toward the exit.

As much as I'd love to hang around and add a few more twenties to my stack, I won't be able to watch the main event. Especially since I *am* the main event.

I head to the back to prepare myself. I spend my time street fighting and ripping people off. Sometimes both at the same time. Well, it's less "street" and more "dilapidated building," but still. I bare-knuckle box, which is a fancy term for those of us that fight raw and dirty, without gloves between us. It's the most brutal way to fight, and it suits me well.

Before I leave the locker room, I check the roster. I like to know who my opponent is before I see his face. My finger scrolls down the chicken scratched list, and I release a sigh of relief because I'm not against one of the "Kursed" brothers. Gentry and Karson recently got back into the game after years away. Those two fight like bona fide psychopaths, and I'm not in the mood to earn a few more scars tonight. I heard they were hitmen before they became fighters, and while I don't usually put much stock in rumors, I believe this one. The bigger one is built for homicide, and the other looks crazed enough to do it for fun.

When I finish taping my wrists, I cut through the crowd and step into the ring to a wave of murmurs rippling through the room. Those disgruntled voices probably belong to the morons who just realized they were taken for a ride when I parted them from their money last night. If my boss paid me half a living wage, I wouldn't need to swindle people. If he didn't keep most of the money from those of us balls deep in the blood sport, I wouldn't have to work the crowd and my fellow fighters wouldn't be so willing to take a dive for a little extra cash.

The crowd transforms into a churning sea of screaming, chanting, roaring faces. Their fists pump the air as they demand more brutality. The audience is alive. I can feel the strength of it in my bones as I approach the ring. A woman in a bikini lifts a sign, panning it over the crowd. It's tacky. Putting someone pretty beside the ugly doesn't make these fights less ugly.

As we ready ourselves to begin the match, the roar of the crowd voices their disdain for the space between us. Makeshift stage lights and neon signs flicker above us and illuminate their red faces. Time to give them the show they came for.

I take the first swing, and blood slips from a split in my opponent's lip. He opens his mouth, turns his head, and spits out a tooth, which causes a roar of laughter and catcalls from the crowd. With a dazed look in his glassy eyes, he falls back into the corner, trying to recover. In a normal fight, this is where a ref would step in and call for a medical team to give us the go ahead to continue, but this isn't a normal fight. There is no medical team.

I charge toward him again, and he catches my jaw with

a surprise right hook. My teeth click together on the side of my tongue. The pain fuels me to hit him harder. His blood splatters on my cheeks and forehead like war paint.

My scarred body crashes into his as we take turns searching for soft spots. We're evenly matched in body size, but he doesn't have the years of experience I've gained. Or the anger. I don't have enough time to collect myself before he throws a punch to my face that sends me stumbling backward a step. Blood flows from my nose, and it hurts like hell, but it doesn't hinder me; it fuels me.

Thin scarlet ribbons drip from my chin, leaving little red stains all over the cracked floor. I lick the blood beads rolling down my lips so they fill my mouth with their iron tang. Nothing tastes better than blood drawn from pain— and there's something about tasting that pain.

The lights warm my sweat-slicked muscles, and I send my cut fist into his face. His scream echoes in my ears, and I revel in the power and violence. It's my love language. The crowd roars in approval, growing louder with each blow.

When he finally falls to his knees and clutches what must be a broken jaw, I let out a sadistic laugh. An audible crunch rings out over the cries from the bloodthirsty crowd as I prey upon that weakness and knock his head back once more. Blood sprays from his mouth and stains the concrete, and he doesn't rise to his feet again.

I win.

Nothing in my life feels right, but this? This feels right. When I'm surrounded by cheering crowds while covered in someone else's blood, knowing it will never be my life essence leaking onto the ground, I feel normal. And that's saying something. Not even the skin I wear feels normal. It's a tattered costume I can't take off.

I run a hand through my dark blonde hair. A few

strands fall into my eyes, and it looks almost brown from the amount of sweat woven through it. Red lights catch on my scars—tough strips of tissue lacing my body. I can hide the worst of them with clothing, especially the deep gouges I received on my abdomen, but I'm forced to show them to the world when I fight. It doesn't matter here, though. It adds to my persona and makes me seem like I've been through some shit.

They have no fucking idea what I've been through.

While I can hide the scars on my body outside of this place, I can't do shit for those on my face and neck. I keep the sides of my head shaved because it's patchy as shit if I let it grow. These marks keep me from blending into society, so I've given up on trying.

Who needs a fucking society that set free the monster who did this to me?

I look down at my beaten opponent and smile. Yeah, I win. It's what I do. Every time I step into that ring, I win. But I never feel like I've won as I leave—my body battered and bruised, my heart beating hollowly against my chest. On the outside, I'm un-fucking-defeated, but inside, I'm fighting to feel something more than numb. It's a place to push my constant anger.

But winning doesn't feel as good with no one in your corner.

The crowd quiets and begins filing out of the building. Everyone loves the scary, scarred-up fighter in the ring, but I'm dogshit on the soles of their shoes once it's over. Their eyes are no longer glued to me. Now they just want to look away. They cower from me or shield the eyes of their curious kids. Some of them know about my past. Some people even think I'm immortal. No little boy should have survived the damage flashed all over the paper and the six o'clock news. I'm the living embodiment of their worst nightmares.

I throw my shirt over my shoulder and head toward the makeshift locker room. The stench of men and unwashed towels fill the space, and I fling my shirt onto a metal bench against the wall. I stroll past a line of warped lockers and a dirty, cracked mirror, then groan as I run my hands beneath the sink's cold tap. Before I can even dry my hands, my "boss" storms in, his face contorted with anger. He raises his hand and sends his palm against the back of my head. The red rage spilling from his veins has now infected mine. I exhale, trying to keep from killing him.

"Why the fuck are you working the crowd like that, scar?" he shouts.

"It's none of your business," I say. I hate when he calls me that. I am not just my scars.

Darby's eyes narrow. "It *is* my business when you're doing it under my name. This whole thing is my business."

Darby lords over the fighters like a king, but I'm no one's property. He masquerades this business as legitimate when it's anything but. These fights are not only illegal but the last resort for those of us too desperate and broken to do anything else. We're the forgotten, abandoned by society and by the law. It's a shame that our only hope lies in this depraved, violent world he created.

He shoves his hand into my face. "Give me what you swindled off people or lose your spot next week, Mr. Sinclair."

My muscles tense as I fight the overwhelming urge to snap this man in half and leave him in a shallow, unmarked grave. But I know if I do, I'll have no future. Without this gig, there's nothing for me. With an animalistic growl, I reach into my pocket and fling the money near his feet. The cash flies into the putrid mix of pooling water, sweat, and urine.

"Oops, sorry," I say, though I'm not the least bit sorry. If I could whip down my jeans and add to the piss leaching into those bills, I would.

Darby reaches up to put a hand on my shoulder. "You know, scar, you're one of my best fighters. Piss-poor attitude, though." His voice lowers as he squeezes, and I'm about three seconds away from sending him across the locker room.

I shrug out of his grasp. "My attitude is what makes me a good fighter."

"You won't go far in this industry with it. Learn to be good without it."

The corners of my vision blur. He's hitting every last nerve I have. Does he see what I do to people's faces? He's coming dangerously close to being next.

Holding back is not my strength. It never has been.

"Get out of my face, Darby. Unless you want me to rearrange yours."

He juts a finger at my chest. "Thin fuckin' ice, scar."

The thinnest.

Chapter Two

Oaklyn

Nerves flutter in my stomach, spreading their wings and taking flight with every quiet moment. Once the music begins, it will pass. I'll find the tempo and move with it. I'll forget the people in the audience for a moment as the bass beats in time with my heart. The raised eyebrows and pursed lips will disappear as the song pulses through the speaker, and it's just me and the stage.

My body remembers this feeling all too well. It longs for it. Dance is so natural for me. It was the most important thing in my life before my life changed forever. My body remembers how to accentuate each note with a movement and make the most of every beat. As I step onto the stage, it doesn't matter what the patrons think of me. All that matters is what I think of myself. I may shed my clothes, but in my mind, I'm wearing the familiar outfits that gave me life.

I close my eyes, and the tacky neon lights shift into

elegant spotlights that shine down on me. I'm not half naked, dancing for a bunch of men. I'm in a costume, preparing for my debut on a stage.

The song starts, and I begin my show. The men throw money instead of roses. They demand a private dance instead of an encore. But I'm dancing, and that is all that matters at this moment. I lose myself to the song, which is better than what most of the other girls lose themselves to.

When the song ends, I'm brought back to my sweaty, half-dressed reality. No longer in top condition from hours of rehearsals, I'm winded and sore. The ache in my leg reminds me I'm not the person I used to be. That I'll never be that person again.

My skin itches from the sweat and glitter, and I fight back the urge to run off the stage and wipe away the icky feeling as I scoop the money from the floor. I avoid looking at the crowd as I lean over to pick up the last bill. Dancing isn't the most demeaning part of this job; it's the scrounging up the cash at the end that makes me uncomfortable. I can avoid their eyes, but I can't avoid their hoots and whistles and greedy hands. They reach for me as if they're owed a pound of my flesh for every dollar they tossed my way. My ankles wobble in my clear heels when I stand upright again. They always do by the end of the night, and the blisters between my toes don't help.

I hold the money to my chest and race off the stage to the safety and solitude of the dressing room. I lay the cash on my little desk in the back and slip off my shoes before I start to count it. No matter how much I make, I feel as if I'll never have enough for the car I so desperately need. Everything comes with a price in this life, and the cost of a ride is more than I'm willing to pay.

A deep groan comes from behind me. He'll notice the

look of disgust in the mirror if I react, so I keep my face stony and continue counting the bills. Jake's arms wrap around my waist, and I swallow the clawing urge to push him away and scream for him to never touch me again. He's the club owner, and he's taken a liking to me, as much as I wish he hadn't. His favoritism comes with the burden of unwanted advances instead of the perks of preferential treatment.

His fat hand rises to my chest and squeezes my nipple. My cheeks flush, not from arousal but discomfort.

"How's my girl?" he whispers in my ear. Alcohol dances on his sour breath, and my stomach twists.

"Tired," I say. I try to step away from him, but he's determined to hold me in place.

"You've been working so hard." He brushes back my red hair with his other hand. "If you give in to my offer, I'll give you a little something that will help you with your car situation. You'll make as much as a whole night, if you let me inside you."

My spine tightens. Even a shiny new Mercedes wouldn't be enough to get me to agree to sleeping with him. I may not have much left to my name, but I still have my dignity. People may think that removing my clothes for money makes me less than dignified, but they're wrong. I still have limits, and Jake is a hard no.

"Maybe another night," I tell him.

He gives my cheek a light smack. "Then you'll need another ride tonight."

"Really?" My heart sinks to my aching feet.

"You can't get something for nothing." He growls as he reaches down and squeezes my ass until it hurts.

Oh, fuck you, I think. I shrug away from his touch and wrap my long jacket around me, then stuff the money into my pocket and slip my feet into the flats I keep below the desk. "See you tomorrow, Jake," I say with the fakest pleasantry I can muster. I brush past him, but he stops me, reaches into my pocket, and takes out a large chunk of my money. I ball my hand into a fist at my side to keep myself from snatching back what belongs to me. "What's that for?"

"My cut. Now get going, sweet cheeks."

I can't respond, not because I can't think of something to say—I have *plenty* to say—but because I don't want to give him a reason to put me in a more precarious situation than I'm already in. Until I can afford a car, I'm stuck here. Each day chipping away more of my soul than the last.

He waves me off, and I head out the back door. I try to snag an Uber, but there aren't any available. Probably because of the sports game that's ending right around now. I consider going back inside and sucking Jake's dick for a ride home, but I can't.

Another dancer steps outside to smoke a cigarette in her car. She's almost done for the evening, so maybe she can give me a lift to my house if I wait around until her last dance. I shuffle toward her car and tap on the window.

When she looks up at me, her face shifts from friendly to disgusted. "What do you need?"

The other girls don't like me, and I wish I could say it's a problem of my own making. That would be easier than the truth. If I had some horrible character flaw, I could work to improve myself, but I can't fix the disdain they feel because Jake hovers over me like a fly on shit. They probably think I make more money, which would be a valid reason to hate me as much as they do, but that isn't the case. I probably make less than they do, especially on nights like tonight when I've pissed off Jake.

"Any chance you could give me a lift home when you

get off?" I ask. "I can give you a few bucks to cover the gas if it's out of your way." I happen to know it's not out of her way by much, but I hope my offer will sweeten the deal.

"Sorry, can't do it," she says with a flick of her cigarette. "My man is home with the kids, and I don't have time to travel all over town if I want to get back before they drive him insane."

Her shitty apartment is less than a mile from my trailer. That's hardly driving "all over town." But I don't argue. What's the point? "Oh, okay. Thanks anyway," I say.

I return to the road and throw my thumb into the air to flag someone down. Hitchhiking was surprisingly normal where I grew up. If someone needed a ride, you gave them a ride in the spirit of helping your neighbor. Here in New York, it's a different story. The cars just whiz by as if I don't exist at all.

A cool breeze bites at my thighs, and I pull my jacket tighter. When no one stops after fifteen minutes, I decide to wait a bit and see if the buzz from the game dies down. I walk back to the side of the building and slide down the wall. I watch as men and couples enter and leave.

With a deep sigh, I check the app once more and find no sign of a ride option anytime soon. The back door slams and Jake walks out, counting his money and pretending I don't exist. He's my only option, and I hate that he is.

When I don't speak, he finally looks down at me. "What? You couldn't find a ride?"

My cheeks burn. "No. Can you please take me home?" I hate begging. I'd walk, but my feet are so mangled, and it's far enough that I'd never make it. Not before I had to hitch another ride just to come back here.

"What will you give me for a ride? How desperate are you?"

I take some cash from my pocket and wave it near him. He understands the language of money, but it's not the language he wants to speak tonight. My eyes ease down his body until I land on the hard mass pressing against his jeans. I shiver.

"Can't you just be nice for once?" I ask. Nothing about his undersized palm-tree t-shirt and gold chains screams "nice guy," but a girl can dream.

"Here's the deal, sweets. A hand job will get you halfway home. Put your mouth on me, and I'll take you all the way."

He's just as desperate as I am, but he has the bargaining chip I lack: his fucking car. I refuse to put my mouth on him, but a hand job beats walking the entire way.

"Take me halfway," I say with a drop of my gaze.

He leads me to his BMW, and I get inside. The fancy leather sticks to the backs of my legs. The moment he sits down, his hands go for the button on his pants. He's not wasting any time, but I'm frozen in place, unable to move my hand toward his exposed dick.

"Well, come on. I want payment in full before we pull out of this parking lot."

I shake my head. "Not here, Jake." Not where we work. I don't want any of the other girls to get wind of this. It's bad enough they already think I've fucked him. That he favors me. I don't *want* that attention from him. I don't want *him*.

"Put your hand on my dick, baby, or get the fuck out of my car." The tone of his voice shifts, and the second half comes out aggressive and raw, as if the choice to leave isn't really a choice any longer.

I glance at the parking lot once more before I reach over and put my hand on his dick. The flesh there is warm and sweaty, like an armpit. A similar smell wafts toward my nose, and I nearly swallow my tongue as my stomach lurches. God, he's vile.

The moment I touch him, he groans as if he's been waiting for this. For any kind of touch from me. I stare at the rotating light tracing each letter in the Purple Lounge sign. My hand moves on his lap until he thrusts his hips up into my hand and calls me baby on repeat. Warm beads of come squirt from his head and dribble down my hand, and I look away. If I puke, he'll definitely fire me. I swallow the vomit creeping up my throat.

His sweaty hand winds through my hair. "Let's get you home, baby," he says, a satiated lilt to his voice. He has a more giving attitude once he comes, it seems.

I wipe my hand on a napkin I find on the floorboard and put my hands in my lap. Degrading acts are just something I need to get used to. For now.

Chapter Three

Oaklyn

I struggle at work the next night. As I wrap my hand around the pole climbing from the center of one of the smaller stages, I can't help but imagine Jake's skinny dick within my grasp. The hot skin burned my flesh and left a scar on my mind. At least he took me all the way home, though.

When I lower myself to the floor and arch my back, the men around the stage reach out to me, their sweaty hands accosting my chest. Fingers slide over my exposed skin, groping and squeezing things they have no business seeing, let alone touching. As they assault me, I have to smile. If the disgust shows on my face, I'll never make enough money to buy a car and begin to salvage my life. Thankfully, the dream I once had of dancing and acting in a theater has prepared me for this nightmare, and they aren't wise to the fake look of seduction on my face.

Without making it obvious, I raise my chest and rise to my feet. Their greedy hands recede like waves of toxic sludge, but no shower can last long enough or burn hot enough to wash away this film of dirt on my skin. It's inside me now. For feeling up my breasts, some of the men toss a compulsory bill onto the stage. It doesn't feel good. They might as well scream, "Here's your money, bitch!"

The song ends, and mumbles of conversation fill the silence before generic club music rushes into the gap. Sweat drips between my breasts as I lean over and pick up the money. The bills stick to my skin as I clutch them to my chest and scurry behind the curtain.

Back at my station, I stack the cash. I drag some of the crumpled rectangles along the edge of the desk to smooth them out, but it's pointless. They've been shoved in someone's pocket for too long, awaiting their chance to be thrown at my feet.

Speaking of my feet, they need a break. I slide off my heels and rub at my aching ankle. The bane of my existence. The sole reason I will never dance on any stage with clothes on again. I can handle a three-minute song, but anything longer than that and I'd probably fall on my face. Or worse.

I bend over to put on my sneakers, and the tough, tight fabric rubs against my blisters. My second shoe is half on as Jake's cologne wafts over me and turns my stomach. Before I can straighten my spine, his length presses against my ass and his hands move to my hips. This is the last thing I want at the end of a shift.

"Hey, baby," he says. He grinds against my panty-clad ass, and I try to step out of his grasp. "Don't be like that. You want a ride home tonight, don't you?"

I'm fucking sick of having a ride held over my head like this. Being down on my luck shouldn't equate to being down on my knees. And that's what he'll expect tonight. A hand job was enough to get by last time, but he'll up the ante.

One of the other girls enters the dressing room and clears her throat. Jake releases me, and I fall forward onto the desk. My cheeks burn red, and I'm sure the other girl thinks I look like a naughty schoolgirl who got caught bending over her teacher's desk for a good grade. That couldn't be further from the truth. His unwanted advances make me sick, and I don't keep quiet about them to get a leg up in this business. I'm not trying to one-up these other women. I'm just trying to survive.

Through my mirror, I glance at the other woman. She's at her station, busying herself with her outfit for her next dance. I can't be the only one he sexually harasses. There's no way.

Without waiting for Jake to solicit me for sex again, I throw on a cami and shorts and top it off with my long black jacket. He realizes he's not getting anything from me, so he snatches the stack of cash from my hand and strips half my money before walking away. My heart sinks. He didn't earn that money. His breasts didn't get fondled. But there's no arguing with him. Instead, I throw my leftover cash into my pocket and head out the back door.

As I step into the night air, I count the money he's been nice enough to leave in my possession. An Uber will take an even larger chunk out of my meager earnings, so I trudge toward the bus stop with anger-fueled steps. A chill wind bites at my bare ankles and legs as I get to the bench and check the time on my phone. I missed the last bus of the night by five minutes. Fabulous.

With no other option, I throw my thumb into the air as the rare car drives by. Their headlights glide over my skin, but they keep driving. I'm tired. I'm cold. I'm angry. My rage only grows with each passing vehicle.

How can an entire city of people be so blind to the needs of their neighbors? I'm not some scary man mumbling to himself on a street corner. I'm a woman with aching feet and a sharp pain in my leg. I pose zero risk.

I raise my thumb again as headlights peek around the bend. Instead of speeding by, the Jeep slows and pulls to the side of the road. I've accomplished the first task, which is getting someone to stop. Now I just have to hope the driver doesn't harbor the same expectations as my shitty boss.

If I walk to the driver's side, I'll be standing in the middle of the street, so I step up to the passenger-side window. It lowers, but I can't see the driver's face in the shadows. "Can I get a ride home?" I ask. I should feel ashamed for begging like this, but when the alternative means fucking Jake inside the building, I feel little more than grateful for the opportunity to beg at all.

"Where about?" the low voice says from the driver's seat.

"Just outside the city. Off Jones Avenue."

He flicks on the dome light and dips his head as he moves a duffle bag off the passenger seat. When he sits up and the light lands on his face, I nearly gasp at the sight of him. Scars cross his face and neck, and even more occupy his right arm. My eyes land on a dark patch of blood on his knuckles, and I gulp back my discomfort.

"Sure, get in. But judging by the way you're looking at me, I'm guessing you won't."

I take a step back and pull my coat tighter around me. "I don't usually get in cars with strangers, especially not when they have—"

"Scars?"

"No," I say, shaking my head. "You look like you've . . . been in a fight." I almost said he looks like he's murdered someone—or a bunch of someone's—but I caught myself.

The man looks at his hand. "You aren't wrong. I *was* in a fight, but not the sort of fight you're thinking of. I do bare-knuckle boxing down at the warehouse off Jensen Avenue. And this is nothing."

I look back at the club. At the empty bus stop. Getting into this Jeep with this stranger is better than returning to the club and begging Jake for a ride. I can't afford his fee.

I open the passenger-side door and take a seat in the car. The man eyes me as my jacket spreads a bit in the front, his gaze crawling over my fishnet stockings and the glitter-covered shorts that ride up my thighs. He looks at the club, putting two and two together.

The man throws the Jeep in drive. "You work at the club?" he asks.

"Yeah."

He scoffs. "You're too pretty to be a whore."

I don't even know how to respond to that. This back-handed compliment is borderline offensive. I'm not a whore. If I was, I'd have fucked Jake for the money by now.

I cover myself with the skirt of my jacket. "I'm guessing you won?" I ask, pointing toward his hand.

"I always win."

"I see you're quite modest." I fidget with my jacket. "What's your name?"

He swallows, as if this question is wholly unexpected. I suppose most hitchhikers don't reach for pleasantries. "Ambrose," he says. "What's yours?"

I consider lying, but I'm too tired to fabricate something on the spot. "Oaklyn."

"Is that your real name or your stage name?"

"My real name." God, he's a dick. "You're being kind of rude," I tell him.

A hauntingly handsome smirk slides onto his face and twists the thin scar beside his mouth. I should ask him about his face. It's only fair. But I push the question down in my gut and leave it alone. It's none of my business, and I don't want to piss him off, even if he's bordering on that with me.

Like a ship drawn to a lighthouse on a rocky shore, his dark eyes keep drifting to me. He looks at me as if he's imagining how my shift went. In his version, I'm probably bouncing on dicks all night. He couldn't be more wrong, so he should keep his eyes to himself.

He turns onto my street, and I sit up taller. "You can drop me off here," I say. I'm not a complete idiot. If he doesn't know where I live, he can't storm into my house and murder me.

"Don't be ridiculous. If I want to know which place is yours, I can just sit here and watch which home you enter."

He has a point.

I take a deep breath. "It's that gray trailer on the right, just past the house with the basketball hoop in the driveway."

He pulls against the curb in front of my trailer and puts the Jeep in park.

"Thanks for the ride," I say.

He doesn't respond. When I've closed the car door behind me, he throws the Jeep in reverse and leaves me in front of my trailer without waiting to see if I go inside. But at least he didn't kill me and put my skin on a blow-up doll, so that's a plus. As his taillights fade and disappear, I wonder if I'll ever see him again.

Probably not.

Chapter Four

Ambrose

Anger simmers, boiling within my veins. I shouldn't have picked up a girl like her outside of a place like that. I let her out and hightailed it out of there before I did something I'd regret. Or that I wouldn't regret at all. She seemed like the perfect victim for my plan, but I haven't thought through all the details yet. I need more time to come up with the perfect way to exact my revenge. That's why I let her live tonight. I'm not yet ready to unleash this black monster inside me.

I don't know why it has to be her, but it does. It's not her fault the other dancers ignored and avoided me as if my skin imperfections were contagious. She wasn't the one who pushed my money back toward me like it was soiled. But she still wears skimpy little outfits and dances for men much worse than me who just look more normal. Close enough.

Fucking. Whores. Just like the woman who carved me up with a butcher knife.

I drive toward home, stewing in my frustration with

every mile marker I pass. I rub at my cut knuckles and anticipate a hot shower to wash away the dry, sticky blood. When I pull into the apartment parking lot, I take a deep breath before getting out of my Jeep. The late-night stragglers milling about outside turn and stare. Their judgmental eyes go from my face to my hands and back to my face again. I bark at them as I pass, and they look away. They didn't care if they made me uncomfortable, but the moment the shoe slid onto the other foot, they got to feel that pointy rock of discomfort grinding against their sensitive skin.

I begin pulling off clothes the moment I step inside my silent apartment. My leather jacket. My shirt. My shoes. The undershirt I put on after my fights. My fingers work open my jeans, and I step out of them without missing a beat. By the time I reach the bathroom, I'm down to my boxers. Such simple tasks seem so monumental when my body is racked with this much tension. I'm always tense after a fight, but that girl made it so much worse. The familiar scent she emitted sent a lead weight into the pit of my stomach. Like sweat and old liquor. Stale.

They all have that smell.

I turn on the shower as high as it goes and climb beneath the spray. The hot water attacks my skin and matches the heat in my veins. The caked blood dissolves from my hand and circles the drain, but I wish there was so much more. I stare at the white porcelain until I can almost see a rush of red instead of the pale pink tinge. I imagine rinsing off my body after picking up a woman like Oaklyn. My brain conjures up fantasies of what I'd have to do to her to coat myself in that much blood. It lands on my favorite imagining: a butcher knife carving up skin. She would beg for me to stop, but I wouldn't. My attacker didn't stop, either.

Then I see Oaklyn's face in my mind. Terrified, tear-filled eyes. Mouth moving as she asks why. I only have one answer for her.

Because someone has to pay.

She seemed different, though, and that gives me a moment of pause. It doesn't derail my desires, but it slows the train to a crawl. I rationalize that it's not *me* who would commit such a heinous act. It's the big, black, ominous creature lurking inside me. One that my mother recognized in me so long ago.

One that I'm forced to silence now.

I close my eyes and wash the sweat from my hair, and flashes of that girl pass behind my eyelids like pictures in a photo album. Dark red hair flows over her shoulders, and the familiar lifelessness dims her big green eyes. The pictures begin to move, and I see her in a grocery store or a bank instead of twirling on a pole. Something about her seems to belong to those places more than a club.

Then my mind's eye roves lower, and I catch a glimpse of the scars on her thigh as her jacket spread. My fingers graze similar ridges of pink flesh on my inner thigh, and I drop my head back and let the water drown me for a moment.

The moment I turn off the shower, steam rises from my reddened skin. I wrap a towel around myself and head toward my bedroom. Beside my bed, I lift the towel from around my waist and run it through my hair before dropping it to my feet. Too tired to worry about my clothes strewn through the apartment, I crawl into bed and cover myself with the sheet.

Every time I close my eyes, I think of that girl again. This isn't ideal. I don't need anything more stirring up my shitty brain.

But I can't stop myself. I think of her and the way she looked when she had her thumb in the wind and the defeated glint to her eyes as she asked a stranger for a ride and sealed her unfortunate fate. Though I try to keep that image of her in my mind, my brain would rather fabricate other images. Now she's topless, coming off the stage after a dance, and she's walking toward me instead of avoiding me. When I offer money to her, she doesn't recoil in disgust. She smiles and takes my hand, leading me toward the back.

My cock hardens to these dirty thoughts, and I rub my hand along the length of my dick, toying with the piercings on the underside of my shaft. My fingers graze the barbell in my frenum piercing, then stroke down to the lorum barbell at the base. Apparently I wasn't scarred enough and needed to add more.

I crush my cock in my grasp, sending a shot of pain through my groin. This is wrong. I shouldn't beat my dick to thoughts of her. I release my cock and put my hands above the sheet.

Don't even think about doing that. Whores are not worth my pleasure.

Ashamed of myself, I roll onto my side and force my mind back to thoughts of revenge. The whore doesn't deserve my come. She only deserves my wrath.

And I'll make sure she takes all of it.

Oaklyn

Driving My Obsession

A CRACK RUNS through the center of the full-length mirror hanging from my bedroom door. The placement splits my reflection in half. In more ways than one, this is a fitting way to see myself. A broken woman stares back at me, the two halves not quite matching up.

I strip off my jacket and hang it on a hook in my barren closet. The cami comes off next, and my breasts relax as my arms lower to my sides. The tight, sweat-coated shorts cling to my skin, and I breathe a sigh of relief as I peel them away. After removing my stockings, I'm finally naked. It feels good to be exposed within the safety of my home, where no one can grope me with their hands or eyes. When I'm naked at home, I don't look like the woman at the club. I look like the person I am—a sad creature who misses her old life.

That's not entirely true. There are many parts of my old life that I wouldn't return to, even if someone held a gun to my head and tried to force me through a door to the past. My parents weren't supportive when I chose to pursue a career as a professional dancer, and I wouldn't want to relive any of the moments when they tried to talk me out of it. Soon the talking turned to a personal attack on my character. They couldn't understand the joy I felt when I prepared for a show and took the stage. They refused to support my dream of broadway lights and cheering crowds. Unable to see the merit in being part of an ensemble of talented individuals, they told me to call them when I failed.

Instead, a doctor called them to let them know their daughter's life hung in the balance. It was all downhill from there.

I push those memories from my mind, unable to relive them right now. Their vicious words still bite at me, even after all this time, and the man who drove me home didn't help matters. His attitude toward my current profession reopened those festering wounds. Despite what he said in the car, I'm not a whore. I haven't had sex with *anyone* since I started working at the club six months ago, and I've made a special point to sidestep all advances, especially those from Jake. If I could let go of my dignity and fuck him, I'd probably have a car by now. A few times with Jake and I could probably afford a better place to live, too.

I shouldn't say that.

The trailer was my grandma's, and she was the only person who still accepted me when she found out how I earned a living after my accident. She even let me move in. She died shortly after and left the trailer to me, much to my surprise. It's nothing fancy but it was hers, and now it's mine. I should be grateful I have a place to live at all, even if the power is finicky and the roof leaks every time it rains. My parents wanted nothing to do with me, though they viewed me as a failure long before I stepped into a pair of platforms and grabbed a pole.

My hands graze my thigh, rubbing over raised scar tissue. I started cutting long before my career ended, but I slashed shallow gashes into my hip instead of these deeper gouges on my thigh. The cuts on my hip hid behind my costumes, but when I had to change the sort of stage I danced on, I didn't care who saw my pain anymore.

I pull a razor from the nightstand and sit on the edge of the bed, rolling the glinting metal between my fingers. This will give me the release I need. Instead of turning to drugs or heavy drinking, I find comfort in creating an outlet for my pain.

It's been a while since I've cut, but as my life spirals out of control, it feels like the only logical thing to do. Maybe

Jake will stop wanting to get between my legs if I paint them with blood and scars.

Blood and scars.

That makes me think of the man who gave me a ride home. He said his name was Ambrose, but I just keep thinking of him as "the man." He seemed more concerned about the marks on his skin than I was, and his definitely weren't self-inflicted. His haunting brown eyes appear in my mind, and I almost drop the razor. I recognized the emotion there. The anger. Everyone has a little anger in them, I guess.

I close my eyes and bask in the pain as my skin spreads around the metal. Warm blood rises within the wound and races down my leg in a steady trickle. I rub my hand through the blood and write the word *whore* on my pale skin. Just like the man who dropped me off said. Just like my parents believe.

In a way, I am a whore. Dancing and removing my clothes don't make it so, but I've been a whore for a long time. I sold myself for a dream, only to wind up in a nightmare. I'll wake up eventually, but not today. Tomorrow isn't looking too good either.

Chapter Five

Ambrose

Rain taps against my bedroom window as I sit on the edge of the bed and stare into the darkness. I'm not scheduled to fight tonight. Usually I'll go work the crowd and make some side cash when I'm not slotted for the ring, but my mind is on other things.

Like that girl from the club.

I've tried my best to think of anything other than her red hair and porcelain skin, but she invades my mind like a virus. Thoughts of her multiply at an alarming rate, over-taking rationality and making me feel sick. She's the vessel that will hold all my rage. I can't allow her to consume me. Without even trying, she takes bites of my sanity and spits them at my feet, chewed up and coated in saliva. I have to do something about this. These feelings need an outlet.

I grab my keys and jog through the rain until I reach my Jeep. The parking lot lights make the asphalt glisten like a black canvas with miniscule diamonds tossed across it. I pat my pocket when I sit behind the driver's seat, ensuring I have what I need, and a smile spreads across my face when I feel the little objects rattling against each other. This won't be as satisfying as choking the life out of her and running a blade across her skin until she comes to, but it's close.

After a short drive, I pull into the club's parking lot. When she comes out, I'll use the rain as an excuse. I'll say I just wanted to make sure she had a way home. Then I'll slip my little gift into her pocket or her bag when she isn't paying attention, and the mind fuck can begin.

I've decided it isn't enough to just kill her. Like a cat with an injured mouse, I want to toy with my prey before I rip out its entrails.

The clock on my dashboard marches toward midnight, and I worry I've missed my opportunity. Maybe she isn't working tonight. Maybe she's already gone home. I don't enjoy the idea of stepping foot in that filthy club again, but my curiosity wins out and propels my feet toward the door.

I enter the dimly lit strip club, struggling to draw a breath when a heavy cloud of alcohol and cigarette smoke descends on me. The haze obscures the patrons and gives the illusion of secrecy. Music pulses in my chest, heightening my senses as I walk through the maze of dark corridors to get to the main floor.

I scan the walls. The vibrant mixture of crimson paint and gold accents creates a seductive glow on everyone inside, including myself. The place reeks of allure and temptation. I hate it. The flashing lights and gaudy colors only veil the evil inside this place. It disguises the flaws of the whores who creep along the floor like cockroaches searching for a crumb. Mirrors line the walls, reflecting fragmented images at me. Naked women writhe and grind, their glittering outfits casting bright rays of light at me. It's infinite. It's sickening.

Driving My Obsession

A diverse cast of characters fills the dirty seats in the main room, from clean-cut businessmen to dirty old men. Actually, they're all dirty old men. Their hushed conversations and smothered laughter blend with the sultry melodies.

The bar along the back wall calls to me like a beacon of light. When the club environment chokes me, a stiff drink is my only source of oxygen. The prospect offers a momentary escape from the pain growing like a disease inside my body, but my sobriety nags at me. Instead of reaching for air, I search for a place to sit down and suffocate. Alcohol almost ended my fighting career, so now I force myself to stay sober.

I choose a seat near the entrance to the private rooms and the back of the building. An electric candle flickers in the center of the table, casting intimate light across my scarred face. I study the little device until I find its off switch, letting darkness wash over me when I snuff it out. I don't want to be seen for multiple reasons.

The stage is mesmerizing, even for someone like me. It's bathed in a spotlight that draws my eyes, and the crimson curtain separating the stage from the back area looks like a waterfall of velvet blood. I fixate on the woman swirling her hips in the middle of the main stage, but I don't watch her the same way as the other men. Hatred fills my gaze, not lust. Each sway raises my blood pressure and increases my heart rate. Plenty of shit stiffens on me as she removes her top and reveals her breasts—my jaw as my teeth clench, my fists as they form tight balls in my lap—but not my dick. Never my dick.

The whore finishes her half-hearted performance and leaves the stage with her money tucked inside her flimsy underwear. Generic rock music fills the silence as she exits through the curtain and by the end of the song, I'm ready to leave. I haven't seen my fire-haired target since I sat down, and I figure I've chosen the wrong night to begin my work.

Another song starts, and the curtain parts. Heads bob like buoys in the sea, all turning toward the woman stepping into the spotlight. She is a goddess among mortals. Oaklyn glides across the stage, her red hair cascading over her shoulders. My eyes lock on the sequined bra pushing her tits to her chin. I'd rather see them relaxed, but the bright, flashy fabric hugs her body and gleams with an ethereal light. She hardly looks real.

A cyclone of emotions tears apart my insides. The round muscles at the hinges of my jaw tighten until I'm certain they'll explode. Instead of titillating me, her beauty ignites a burning rage I struggle to control. She's tearing me apart.

This club is a theater of desire, where fantasies overtake reality. Where you leave your coat of morality at the front door and put it on when you leave, cloaking your naked desires once more. Though Oaklyn stands there in little more than her own skin, something about her doesn't belong. Unlike the other women who work here, she doesn't engage the crowd. I worried she might spot me, even after I shut off that stupid candle, but she doesn't even see us out here. As she grips the pole and leans back, she's lost to something else. We don't exist.

I observe her from my dark corner. The natural seduction that comes from seeing a beautiful woman's nearly naked form contrasts with the dark undercurrents born of my obsessive hatred. Within this intoxicating realm where sexy meets loathing, my obsession thrives, drawing me deeper into a game that blurs the line between sanity and madness.

A man near the stage leans forward and waves a handful of cash at her. With her eyes closed as she moves to the music, she doesn't even notice him. She slides down the pole and removes her top to an onslaught of hungry hands. The men reach for her breasts and thighs, and I envision breaking each finger that nears her body. A low growl rumbles in my chest, but I force my ass to stay planted in this cheap chair. I close my eyes and take a breath. When I open them again, I see my mother on that stage instead of Oaklyn. My fists clench into tight balls and drive my nails into my palm. The pain clears my head, and I can see clearly again.

But the anger and need for revenge have been renewed.

I stop focusing on Oaklyn's looks. Her beauty doesn't negate the rest of the deplorable shit in this place. It can't. I haven't spent most of the last thirty-five years of my life hating this club and the whores within it for something beautiful to come and lighten up the darkness I've shrouded it in. It's ugly and disgusting, and she can't change that.

Oaklyn's song ends. With a curl of my lip, I watch her grab the money from the floor. How degrading. Soon after she disappears into the back, another set of tits replaces her. No shortage of whores, I guess. This one is a haggard ghost, with dark, choppy hair that comes to an abrupt halt near her jawline. Black makeup circles her lids like it's trying to escape her watery eyes. She looks like she could be anywhere between twenty and thirty-five. The lifestyle seems to age them in weird ways.

I drop my gaze when I hear someone come out from the back area. I don't have to turn around to know it's Oaklyn; I can tell from her scent alone. Defeat with a touch of vanilla. When I'm sure she's walked past and won't notice me, I turn to watch her walk away. She's traded her heels for a pair of low tops. Interesting choice of footwear for a woman like her. A cami strap slips down her arm, and her shorts hug her ass. She drifts to the bar as if she has the weight of the club on her shoulders, then plops down on a leather stool. Her hand rises, and she flags down the bartender. I can't hear what she orders, but I know it's a Moscow Mule when the bartender delivers her drink in a copper mug.

Now that I know she's occupied, I can put my plan into place. I slip out the door without her noticing me—hopefully without *any*one noticing me—and look around the parking lot. I'll head to my Jeep and drive back and forth in front of the building until she steps outside and needs a ride, then I'll swoop in and leave her with a parting gift before she exits my car in front of her trailer. I get nearly to my vehicle when I hear a door open near the back of the building.

Curiosity gets the best of me and I turn around, spotting the dancers who were on stage before and after Oaklyn. The women walk with their arms hooked together. How chummy. As they climb into a car together, I wonder why these women never offer Oaklyn a ride home. Can they sense how different she is?

They back out of the parking lot, and my eyes swivel to the door near the back of the building. The door they conveniently left slightly ajar. With no one else in the parking lot to witness it, I walk toward a new plan.

The door creaks as I ease back the thick metal and peer inside. Seeing no movement, I take a step into the small room lined with mirrors, makeup, and lockers. My heart quickens as I imagine my mother back here, getting ready for her moment on the stage. Or getting railed by her manager. I wouldn't be surprised if that was my shitty origin story.

My eyes land on the heels Oaklyn wore on stage. They're tucked beside a desk, between the wall and what I assume is her area. I'm drawn to her property, entirely overcome by an intense desire to get my hands on her stuff.

My hand runs over the tabletop. A brush teeters on the edge, and I lift it and examine the red strands of hair woven through the bristles. A palette of green eyeshadow gleams up at me. Instead of coating her lids in darkness like all the other whores, she chooses a color that accentuates her eyes. I fucking hate how different she is.

Pictures of children and boyfriends adorn the other mirrors in the room, but her spot is devoid of any personal touches. It doesn't seem like anyone would even miss this girl.

Which is good.

A black bra hangs over the back of the chair. The sequins stitched into the stiff cups catch the fluorescent lights and shimmer beneath my fingers as they glide over the material. I lift the heels, dangling them in front of me like I'm holding a dead animal. They're just as disgusting. I hate these excessively tall and needlessly skanky shoes.

After sitting in her chair, I unzip my fly, pull out my cock, and hold it against the soles of her slutty stilts. I look back at the curtain that separates this room from the rest of the building and hope no one comes in as I stroke myself against the same material that's been against her skin. I don't know why I'm scared someone might come in. I probably blend in with the creeps that frequent this place. There's no way I'd be the first masturbating maniac they've had to chase from this room. And that's what I'll go with if someone catches me.

I'm just a crazy, crazy guy.

I stroke myself faster, trying to think about anything

other than her full tits straining against that bra. My mind reaches for anything other than the way the light hugs the curve of her ass when she bends over and rocks her hips.

Fuck it.

Just because she's killable doesn't mean she's not fuck-able too. I explode to some convoluted thought of squeezing her throat while the walls of her pussy squeeze my dick. Beads of come shoot into her heels, and I love that she'll step all over it the next time she slides her feet inside. I hope it's still wet and sticky. I hope she's disgusted.

I reach into my pocket and pull out one of the little gifts I've collected for her. After I place it on her desk, I zip my fly and make a hasty retreat. I'd give anything to see the look on her face when she discovers what I've done, but I can't risk getting caught. Not when I have so much in store for her.

Chapter Six

Oaklyn

Heads turn toward me when I step onto the bus. Some of the frequent flyers know what I do because they watch me get off at the stop in front of the club several days a week. A few keep their judgments to themselves, but I don't miss the curled lips and avoidance of the others. The old woman who likes to sit up front does her usual thing. She grips her massive carpet bag of a purse and places it beside her on the seat, silently telling me I can't sit with her. I wouldn't want to anyway. Her musty baby-powder perfume assaults me from here, and the tiny whiff makes my head hurt.

I choose an empty seat toward the back and stare through a dirty window. I hate riding the bus, but I wish it ran later at night so I had a reliable way to get home after work. The heavy scent of exhaust creeps into my nose and intensifies my growing headache. My workday is just starting, and I already have visions of crawling into bed and returning to sleep.

The bus pulls to a stop in front of the club, and I make my way down the center aisle without crying. It's a feat. I'm burned out, defeated, and my ankle aches like an absolute bitch. On top of all that, I have to do a walk of shame just to get on and off a bus so I can earn a few measly dollars while avoiding sexual assault for the rest of the night.

I can't take much more.

An invisible cloud of smoke drifts from the main room, and I can't understand why it's so hard for the other girls to remember to put on the goddamn fan when they come in for the early shift. I don't care if people smoke, but I don't want to smell it when I have a jackhammer pounding behind my right eye. It's also as hot as Satan's asshole in this room. I go to the window and flick on the shitty box fan.

As I turn toward my station, I pause. Something small and brown sits on my desk, right on the corner. It's some sort of nut. At least . . . I think it's a nut. I pick it up and look at it.

It's a fucking acorn.

"Ha, ha," I mutter under my breath. "You girls are so funny. How original to mock my name like this." They must have rubbed their two collective brain cells together for a week to come up with this shit.

I drop the acorn, and it rolls across the floor until it hits the wall. It can stay there and rot or grow a tree for all I care. I hope one of those bitches steps on it in bare feet. Better yet, I could slide it into one of their shoes to ensure they step on it.

But I don't. While it would feel good to give those catty bitches what's coming to them, I've never been a mean girl and I don't intend to start today.

I slip off my sneakers and pick up my heels. Something white and flakey coats the inside, and now I've moved from annoyed to pissed. I'm definitely being fucked with. I look around the room, trying to figure out who has whatever goo this is. Hair gel? Fucking glue?

Bitches.

The song before mine ends. I brush off my shoes to remove what I can, but it's really stuck to the material. Without another option, I slip them onto my feet with a grimace and pull off my jacket and sweatpants. I dressed for work before I left the house because the bus schedule conflicted with my call time.

Psh, call time. You can force the girl out of the theater, but you can't force the theater out of the girl.

I rush to the curtain just as my song begins. I chose a slower number today. My ankle has been giving me fits since the rain last night, and I don't want to strain it with a fast song that's loaded with tricks. I'll have to rely on the pole a bit more than usual, but my body needs a break.

Using my arms and thighs, I climb the pole, hook my leg around it, and ride down to the stage. I focus on the music instead of the incessant cat calls. I pretend I'm in the ensemble of a production of *Chicago*, my black silhouette cast upon an opaque wall in front of me as the leads sing about how horrible men are. What a treat for the audience.

I wouldn't have had to remove my top in a production like that, though. This is where the fantasy ends and it becomes harder to pretend I'm living my dream. This is no one's dream.

With my breasts fully exposed, I move closer to the edge of the stage and smile. The smile is fake, but even the ensemble needs to have acting skills. Per Konstantin Stanislavski, there are no small roles, only small actors. I wonder if he ever frequented strip clubs.

Probably not.

I purposely avoid scanning the crowd. What is there to see aside from unhappy husbands and misogynists? At least we get some young couples on the weekends. People who aren't so hard on the eyes. People who are desperate for a new experience, not these perverts who are only here to fill their mental spank banks.

But someone in the corner catches my eye.

The leather jacket looks familiar, and I swear I see bandages on his hands. The shadows shield him from view and the lights flashing over my face make it more difficult to make out details, but I think it might be the guy from a few nights ago.

I mentally shake my head. *Can't be. Can it?*

I spin around the pole and try to get a better look, but a man waves a bill toward me and begs me to focus on him. Needing money more than I need to satisfy my curiosity, I lean toward his outstretched hand and offer him a bright smile as I relieve him of his cash.

It's a twenty. Shit. Jake has rules for us by denomination. The more they pay, the more we must play.

I sit on the stage in front of the guy, spread my thighs, and tuck the twenty into the crotch of my panties. I bring his head down and let him snatch the money with his teeth. It's hard to control the roll of my eyes, but I manage. I lean over and take the edge of the bill between my lips, then spit it onto the floor behind me as I stand up. I don't let it touch my tongue. Not after it's been graced by God knows how many pussies, tits, and assholes.

The song ends and I look toward the dark corner of the club. The mystery man is gone. I must have imagined him or, at the very least, it wasn't the same man who gave me a ride. That guy would never set foot in a place like this.

I gather my money, leave the stage, and head toward the

back. After stowing my money in my bag, I throw on my cami—sans bra because my tits need some air—and head out to the floor. We're allowed one drink per shift. Right now, with the taste of dirty money lingering on my lips, I need it.

I go to the bar and sit on one of the stools, and the fake leather grips the backs of my thighs. The bartender, a sweet girl who also dances on occasion, walks over to me. Her black hair wobbles on her head in a high ponytail.

"What can I get you, Oak?" she asks. She's not the usual bartender. If she was, I'm sure she'd know my drink.

"Moscow Mule." I reach toward the bar and touch her hand. "And make it strong, please."

She nods and rushes off. I notice something on the edge of the bar, so I lean toward it and pick it up. It's a fucking acorn. My mind goes back to what I found on my desk.

What the fuck?

Despite being named after the tree that produces them, I've rarely seen the things. Now I've seen two. In one day. In places they shouldn't be. This isn't a family park or a hiking trail; it's a goddamn sin den. I run my fingers along the acorn's rough top, wondering if it's even real. It is, and that's more concerning. Unless there is some weird shop that sells bags of acorns, someone has taken the time to collect these little things so they can leave them around for me to find. Then again, you can buy anything online.

Maybe it wasn't one of the girls after all. It's probably a man who's gotten obsessed after a dance. It happens more often than any of us care to admit.

Sudden realization hits me.

The white substance.

I fucking gag and snatch my heels off my feet. *Fucking pigs!* I toss the stupid acorn into the overflowing garbage can by the bar. I'd throw my heels out too if I could afford another pair. Since I can't, I'll just have to soak them in hand sanitizer.

The bartender places my drink in front of me, and I take a sip. Vodka punches the back of my throat and makes my eyes water. It cleanses my mouth and calms the panic in my chest at the thought of some man obsessing over me enough to come all over my heels. But that's part of the job. They pay me to be their obsession.

I nod my thanks to the bartender and down the drink to drown my disgust in the bottom of the copper mug. By the time the cup is empty, the liquor has worked its way through my body and I feel a little more at ease.

I carry my heels to the sink in the back and run scalding water over them. Each pass of my soap-covered hand over the material makes me see red. I feel fucking violated. What happened to creeps beating off outside your window while you undress? Now they come in people's shoes and leave fucking nuts lying around? Make it make sense.

Jake meanders around the back room, sexually harassing the others for once, and I wonder if he's the culprit who jizzed in my shoes. But that wouldn't explain the acorns. He's not smart enough to know they come from oak trees.

I sneak out the back before he can see me. I'm not in the mood to work the floor or shrug off Jake's advances. Even though I could be walking right into the arms of my weird stalker, I'm calmer once I'm away from the building. No matter what monsters lurk out here, it's better than staying inside to be preyed upon.

Raindrops hit the pavement in front of me, then the night sky opens and it begins to pour. Great. My cloth shoes absorb all of it until I feel like I'm walking on sponges as I head toward the bus stop to call for an Uber. The overhang shields me from the bulk of the rain as I pull my phone out of my jacket pocket. It's soaked too.

"Fuck," I whine.

Painted the color of a storm cloud itself, the silver Jeep slows to a stop in front of me. He rolls down his window, and I swallow at the sight of his face. Not the scars, though. The purple hue to his swollen bottom lip is what takes me by surprise.

"Your fight didn't go as well this time, huh?" I ask as I lean forward.

"This?" He rubs his lower lip. "The other guy looked much worse."

We stare each other down. My stomach tightens at the thought of accepting a ride from him again, but the cash in my pocket slaps back my hesitation. I didn't make very much today—the slower numbers usually don't—and I'm loath to part with any of it.

"Are you getting in or what?" he asks.

I look back at the club before opening the car door and getting into the passenger seat. As soon as I close the door, the air shifts with an electrified tension that isn't entirely uncomfortable. But it *is* weird. Is saving forty-something dollars really worth this risk? The moment when I opened his car door, it was. But now that I'm beside him . . .

I'm not so sure.

Chapter Seven

Ambrose

I can't believe she got into my Jeep again. What part of our previous interaction made that seem like a good idea? I said if I ever saw her again and she was stupid enough to get in my car, then I have no reason to hold back that demon inside me. But my plan disintegrates the moment I see how defeated she looks. She probably wouldn't fight me off if I tried to kill her right now, and that's no fun.

The scent of the club clings to her body and hangs like smog in the Jeep. She smells like sweaty old men and cheap perfume. Now it haunts my car, and no amount of air freshener will exorcize the stink from the upholstery.

My eyes glide over her body. Heavy makeup cakes her face, and the rain and sweat have smeared it in some places. Glitter glimmers on her chest, accentuating the curves of her breasts as they bulge above the neckline of her low-cut camisole. She's not wearing a bra, and her nipples press against the thin fabric and beg for my attention. My eyes roll downward, stopping at the tiny shorts over her fishnet stockings. A vision pops into my head. In it, I'm cutting those slutty, stringy stockings away from her skin.

I force my mind to shift the image to one where I'm cutting away her skin instead of her clothing. That's better.

I look away and throw the Jeep in drive, heading toward her home without saying a word. If I speak, I'll say something that will make her hop out before I can do what I need to do. As we travel in silence, my thoughts wander to how fragile her throat would feel in my powerful hands. Maybe I could cover her red hair with a blonde wig, further elevating my revenge fantasy. Make her look like the victim I need but can't have.

Thinking about her red hair was a mistake. Now I want to know what it feels like when it's wrapped around my fist as I force her pink lips over my cock and fuck her face. That thought hardens me, and I put my arm on my lap to hide it. Guilt rolls in my gut because of my shameful erection. Despite being the beacon of sexuality, a whore like her shouldn't arouse me.

I hate that I want her. It pisses me off.

"Why do you do what you do?" I ask. My voice spears through the silence, and she's taken off guard by the abrupt question.

Her full lips spread as she tries to formulate an answer. "I need the money, and I was born to dance," she says, toying with the hem of her shirt.

"Born to dance on the laps of disgusting men?"

Her eyes widen, and her chest rises and falls as her breath quickens. "I . . . I . . ."

"No one is born to be a whore," I elaborate.

She scoffs, then finds her voice. "Until six months ago, I danced professionally. Not like this."

"Why'd you change streams? Seems like you'd want to go from a dirty pond to clear waters, not the other way around."

"It wasn't my choice," she says, her eyes staring out the window. "But I choose to dance, even if it's lewd. It's what I was made for."

Her words tempt the corners of my lips to rise, but I sober. No matter what brought her to that club, it doesn't negate the fact she's there. That she's one of them. She's tainted now, and no amount of soap can wash away the dirt and decay.

I force my eyes away from her and remind myself why I picked her up after watching her do her filthy dance. That evil side of me hungers to take my knife and rip her apart. Eviscerate her. Fuck her heart while it's still beating. Cover my imperfections with her skin. Wear her.

A low growl leaves my throat, and I hope she doesn't hear it. My hand drops to the knife between the seat and the center console, and I toy with the metal blade between my fingers. Killing her has become a fantasy—sick, twisted, and erotic as fuck. I'm close enough that one swipe of my arm could plunge the knife into her neck. It's exciting.

My eyes fall on her again. The sweet face attached to the body I want to desecrate gives me pause. I hate that she's a walking contradiction. Her clothes and body advertise her slut status, but that face . . . It makes me weak. I fucking *hate* being weak. Instead of lashing my anger outward, I internalize it. I boil myself alive.

I'm on fire.

I want to kill her. I need to. I never had the chance to make my mother pay for what she did to me, but I have the opportunity to send this whore in her place. The overwhelming desire is becoming harder to resist.

But tonight isn't right.

The buzz of doubt in my gut whips back the beast that wants to rip her apart and feed on her sin. How much longer can I deny its hunger?

Oaklyn

THE AIR SHIFTS BETWEEN US, seeming to grow hot and stale. I try to ignore the heaviness as I shift in my seat. Why would he offer a ride when he seems to hate me so much? I should have told him no thanks and called an Uber.

Ambrose pulls his Jeep to a stop in front of my house. He doesn't even bother pulling into my driveway. He can't wait to dump me onto the concrete.

"Get out," he says. His taut muscles tense further as his fingers tighten around the steering wheel. The twist in his expression wraps a coil around my chest, squeezing until I can't draw a breath. Sweat beads along my hairline.

"You don't have to be a dick," I say as I pull my bag against my chest.

He scoffs. "Yes I do. Go."

Once I'm out of his Jeep, I slam the door behind me. Fuck him. I smack the passenger window as he slams on the gas and throws a thick spray of rainwater into my face.

"Dickhead," I mutter under my breath.

This shouldn't bother me. I deal with plenty of assholes when I'm at work, and my skin has thickened considerably because of it. But it does bother me. *He* bothers me. Something brews within him, and I certainly don't want to meet it head on. Even without adding his shit to the pile, I have enough darkness in my life.

Like the hands that explore my body despite the "no touch" rule. Or the boss that tries to assault me on a daily basis. Fucking Jake. Then there's the overwhelming sense of failure every night when I come home, and it's only made worse when I have to rely on the kindness of a man like Ambrose.

I won't allow him to take me home again, even if he smiles and asks nicely, I tell myself.

It's a lie. His obvious dislike for me grinds my gears, but I feel a weird pull toward him. Even with the scars on his face, I find him alluring and attractive. What the fuck is wrong with me?

When the spray of water settles, I peer into the darkness surrounding my trailer and throw my bag's strap over my shoulder. Trees tower over either side of the quaint single-wide, illuminated only by my weak-ass porch light. There aren't any streetlights out here. From the corner of my eye, a dark shadow stalks around the side of one of those trees. I'm probably imagining it—a fear unlocked after realizing some creep from the club is stalking me. Though I know it's probably not real, I can't stop the fear from climbing up my throat.

I rush toward my front porch and reach under the little decorative bench by the door, my fingers scrambling blindly for the key tucked beneath the seat cushion. Since I don't have a car, I don't see the need for a keyring. I also don't take it with me because I worry about what would happen if a creep from the club found my house key. Namely Jake. I can't imagine what that fucker would do if he could enter my house. Well, I can, but I don't want to. The thought makes my whole body shiver. I unlock the door and tuck the key beneath the cushion before going inside.

My grandma's small, manufactured home doesn't offer me much, but it's more than what I would have had if she hadn't taken me in. My parents have a sprawling four-bedroom home on several acres, but they pushed me out of their oversized nest when I chose to chase my Broadway dreams and pursue what I loved. Dancing was bad enough, but dancing for men? Too far. They cut off all communication when I made *that* choice.

My grandma loved me, though. She was so proud when I told her I'd aced my audition shortly before my accident. She was my only form of support, but she loved so hard that it was all I ever needed. When I told her my parents wouldn't help me after my accident because I'd chosen to dance at the club, she didn't bat an eye. She just helped me bring my things inside and said she was proud I wanted to keep working after what I'd been through, no matter where I worked.

But now she's gone, and I have no one.

I go to the bathroom, flick on the light, and wipe away the heavy mascara stains around my eyes. I never wear makeup like this because it shrinks my eyes and makes me look much older than I am. But "daddy" Jake wants us to wear our makeup a certain way. I'm his doll, and he wants to dress me up to his liking. It's the last thing I want to be, but what choice do I have? My aspirations become unreachable if I don't play along, and I refuse to give up. Buying a car is such a tiny goal, but it's one that I need for my own sanity. To show myself that I can do it. That I don't need to lie down for Jake to make it in this city.

I have other goals, but those are too lofty to reach for right now. They're hidden deep within my heart, buried so that I can't even see them. I know they're there, but having them at the forefront of my mind would destroy me. Like putting a five-course meal in front of a starving woman, I'd lose my mind if I focused on what I'll probably never have. But these dreams aren't impossible. I'd just have to start over somewhere else.

But to do that, I need a fucking car.

Chapter Eight

Ambrose

I sleep most of the next day and finally pull myself out of bed once the sun goes down. There aren't any fights tonight, so I have nowhere to be. No purpose. What else is new? After scarfing down some leftover Thai food, I sit in front of my computer and turn it on. The screen sends a splash of blue light across my face, illuminating my skin in the darkness. I don't fuck around on the computer often, but I have a very specific mission tonight.

To find out more about the girl from the club.

She made the mistake of giving me enough details to dig a little deeper into her background. While I don't know what I'm looking for just yet, I'm sure I'll figure it out as I go. And then I'll decide how to use it against her. The acorns were just the first step in my rousing game of mental tennis. There are many more heats to go.

I type her first name and our city into the search bar, but I only get articles about how the trees do in our climate.

Maybe she hasn't been in this area long enough to draw any results. I'll have to try something else.

Oaklyn dancer.

Results populate, but it's nothing to do with the girl I'm looking for. I try again.

Oaklyn professional dance.

This search brings up a large, blue headline.

`Professional Dancer's Career-Ending Injury`

I click it and a news article comes up.

Alcohol contributed to the crash that cost a professional dancer her career this weekend. Jaws of life were needed to extricate Oaklyn Grey from . . .

My eyes move away from the words and fall on the image attached to the article. Stage lights shine on Oaklyn, but they aren't the seedy low-budget lights from the club. She's bathed in an actual spotlight as she's frozen in time with a look of sheer concentration on her face. Her arms lock in a graceful pose, stretching to the side as her torso defies gravity. One leg stands below her, the toe of her shoe the only point making contact with the ground. Her other leg stretches behind her and creates a nearly straight line from her foot to her shoulder. Red hair winds into a tight bun on her head, elongating her neck. A pale pink leotard clings to her skin, every curve of her body visible. While it provides more coverage than what she wears when she strips, it's somehow more alluring. Less isn't always more.

My mind places the image beside the woman I've seen with my own eyes—two distinct versions in two very different situations. The mental depictions merge until she straddles the line between two different worlds.

As I study the picture on the screen, I forget the dirty version of Oaklyn Grey and focus on this clean, beautiful creature before me. I've seen her nipples in person, but seeing the way they cast the slightest shadow beneath the fabric of that pink leotard hardens my dick in a way her straightforward nudity never did.

I look around the empty apartment before I lower my gray sweatpants and pull out my dick. My mind wanders, and I imagine this sweet, green-eyed creature in the crowd as I fight. She cheers me on and likes what she sees because I don't have any scars. In this fantasy, I look normal and she doesn't look like a whore. I stroke my cock to the idea of landing a winning blow and bursting through the crowd. Rushing straight for her, I toss her body over my shoulder and head toward the locker room so I can pound my post-fight energy into her pure cunt.

I run my fingers across the screen as I keep stroking myself with my other hand. I touch the juncture between her legs. The skintight fabric hugs her mound, and I envision spreading that material and using her until I've fucked the fight out of my body.

I tap the keyboard, and the printer beside my desk roars to life. After the wheels spin for what feels like an eternity, her picture slides onto the tray. I grip the warm paper with my free hand and place it below my dick. My hand strokes harder and faster to the person Oaklyn was before she became a whore.

I come, spilling beads of pleasure across her picture and smearing the fresh ink. As soon as I've ridden out the waves of release, anger brews in my gut. Hatred swirls with attraction. A need to kill her collides with a need to make her mine. I'm obsessed with the girl she was before she became what I hate. In more ways than one, her life is such a tragedy.

Now she's my tragedy, and she needs to pay.

Oaklyn

I'M RUNNING LATE for work, but it's not my fault the bus arrived fifteen minutes past its usual time. When I burst through the back door, a whoosh of humid air blankets my face. Would it kill Jake to turn on the air conditioner? He probably likes to see us covered in sweat.

One of the girls enters the dressing area and curls her lip at me. I'm accustomed to their bitchy attitudes, but that doesn't mean I don't get sick of it. I'm Jake's little obsession, and that doesn't sit well with them. They were his prior playthings until he moved on to someone else. Until he moved on to me.

She glances at the wall beside her and rolls her eyes. I follow her gaze to a picture taped to the painted concrete. A picture of . . . me? I step closer and recognize the image depicting the last time I looked happy. I looked alive.

My heart sinks into my stomach. This picture brings horrible memories to the front of my mind; it's the one the local news outlets plastered all over the internet after the accident. My ankle throbs while my heart aches to go back to the time in my life when nothing mattered but pursuing my lofty goals. Now my goals are sad. Pitiful. Pathetic.

Just like me.

Driving My Obsession

I turn toward my station and find more pictures taped to the mirror. Tears threaten to stream down my face as I rip the long-forgotten images from the glass and crumple them in my fists. When crumpling isn't destructive enough, I shred them until I can't see my smile or my lively eyes. My arms and legs ache for the familiarity of those dance moves. They call to me like an old language I can no longer speak. An empty void remains where my heart used to beat as I'm forced to see how much my life has changed. I've been taken from the top of the world and driven beneath the soil. Now I'm rotting, decaying a little more every day. I breathe, eat, and sleep, but I'm dead inside.

The other dancer turns her nose up at me as she wraps her hair into a bun and heads for the floor. How the fuck can I step onto the stage and dance after seeing what my life was before it became what it is? Who the fuck is deranged enough to do something so cruel? One of these girls really wanted to hurt me by rubbing my reality into my old wounds, and I hate that they've won. Tears cloud my eyes, but I wipe them away before they can fall. They may have won, but I refuse to give them the satisfaction of seeing the pain cutting a path through my makeup.

Jake enters the dressing area and pauses at the picture taped to the wall. He's the last person I want to see, and he's definitely the last person I want looking at images of me in my element. He pulls the picture from the wall and runs his fingers over my figure.

"You look like a little Barbie," he says. "How did a Barbie like you end up on a pole?" The way he studies the picture sends a chill up my spine. His gaze shifts to me, and my lungs refuse to draw breath as he steps closer.

I turn away, but he doesn't stop until he's pressed against me with his hard cock grinding into my lower back.

"Please, don't," I whisper, not wanting to draw attention from the front of the house by speaking louder and telling him off.

He crumples the picture in his hand. "That isn't you anymore, and it will never be you again. Accept what you are and stop fighting it."

Tears burn the backs of my eyes as his hands raise my skirt. He pushes my chest to the desk and throws the crumpled picture at my head. It bounces off the side of my face and rolls to a stop at my feet as he lowers his fly and pulls his dick from his slacks. Hungry fingers grope for the edge of my panties, then he pulls them aside with a grunt. I go to scream, but his sweaty hand covers my mouth and nose. My tears finally fall, lacing through his ringed fingers as he silences me.

He pushes into me and I drop my full weight onto the flaking black paint. My makeup smears. My vision blurs. I scream into his hand and beg him to stop, but nothing will deter him now. His sweat slips into my mouth and burns my lips. My stomach clenches and I retch. I consider opening my mouth a little wider and sinking my teeth into his hand, but I still need this job. Even after he does this to me, I still need this job.

The metal door behind us crashes shut and fills the room with glorious sound. I watch in the mirror as Jake panics and pulls out of me, rushing to put his cock back inside his cheap pants. His eyes search the room, then he rushes to the door, opens it, and peers outside. He must not see anyone, because he returns to me. I can only hope he's too shaken up to try again.

He leans over and brushes my tear-soaked hair away from my face. "I always knew that's how I'd end up inside you. You had so many chances to give yourself up your own way." He slaps my cheek three times before grabbing his gun from his office and rushing outside to hunt down the source of the interruption.

I lower my skirt and drop into the chair. My chest rises and falls faster than it should, and I'll hyperventilate and pass out if I don't regulate my breathing. I close my eyes and force myself to take controlled breaths. I've never been assaulted like that. Most of my life was spent in a cushy environment that kept me overprotected and far away from villains such as Jake. Now I've been abandoned by those who once shielded me, and I'm doing a piss-poor job of protecting myself.

This job blurs the lines of consent. People can reach out and betray every ounce of your personal space for a fucking dollar. Maybe ten if you're lucky. To people like our patrons and Jake, I'm just a thing to use.

I wipe away the tears and makeup stains, then slide my heels onto my feet. The thought of dancing tonight literally hurts my soul and sends phantom pains throughout my entire body, but if I'm still here when Jake returns, he'll finish what he started.

Whoever slammed the door saw what was happening to me and while I feel so many emotions, the one that prevails is embarrassment. What a stupid emotion to feel right now. Anger lurks somewhere in my mind, but the shame over-whelms it. Regardless, whoever it was, I'm thankful for them. Even though it was probably my nutty—in more ways than one—stalker. If I ever find him, I'll be sure to thank him before I call the police. That's if Jake doesn't find him and kill him first.

Chapter Nine

Ambrose

A cold sweat collects on my brow and slicks my palms as I pull my Jeep around the corner of the building. The back door flies open, but I don't stick around to see who opened it. I slide into traffic, then turn around and head back to the club. Pulling into a parking spot, I chuckle to myself. The greasy fuck who had his hands on Oaklyn stomps through the parking lot and peeks into cars, but he's too dense to realize the source of his outrage sits less than ten feet from him. As far as he knows, I've just arrived.

Emotions cyclone inside me, crashing into each other in a shower of sparks and chaos. The pictures I plastered around the dressing room netted the anguish I hoped for. As she ripped apart those little pieces of paper, her pain enthralled me and left me nearly breathless. Peering through the slender crack between the metal door and concrete wall, I could almost taste the torment, and it was fucking delicious. I wanted to hurt my little tragedy, and I did. I really did. But so did whoever the fuck that was inside that back room.

That's where my emotions and rationality collided, locking into a battle fiercer than any fight I've ever been part of. I loved every moment of the emotional catastrophe I created, but Oaklyn is *mine* to torture. That piece of shit had no right.

So I stopped him.

I shouldn't have, but my hands gripped the door and slammed it shut before my mind could register what was happening. Oaklyn is a whore, and she was getting the whore treatment she deserved. What my *mother* deserved and what I was probably born from. So why did it bother me so much?

Anger swells like a tidal wave inside me. It crashes against the destructive cyclone and turns my emotions into a tornadic waterspout. As much as it pains me to do so, I'm forced to admit that jealousy played a small part in slamming the door, but that wasn't what bothered me most. It was the face I saw in the mirror. It was the way her hands clenched into fists that couldn't fight back. She didn't want him to touch her, and that goes against everything I believe about her. If she isn't a whore, she isn't my target. I'll just need to wait a little longer before I make a decision I can't take back. I have to be sure.

I stare at the club entrance. The black doors call to me even though I never want to set foot in that place again. It's like walking up to a tragic car crash and knowing what I'll find as soon as I pry the doors apart. Deceptive agonal breaths may trick others into believing there are signs of life, but those women are already dead inside. They're martyrs for their chosen profession, willing to die for enough cash.

Pathetic.

I switch off the ignition and head inside, unable to stop myself from complying with the magnetic pull. I have to know the truth. I have to know if Oaklyn is who I believe her to be.

A large crowd packs the main floor, which isn't surprising for a Friday night. I blend in with a sea of other men. We become faceless to the women on stage, I'm sure. These men are an ocean of skin, ebbing and flowing with cash, and the dancer on stage is the moon, pulling them toward her by an unseen gravitational force. I'm not one of them. I'm a goddamn island, and I won't be moved.

The sensual music fades as the dancer ends her show, and generic pop music filters through the rising sound of conversation and drink orders. The whore cleans up the cash littering the stage, then rushes through the curtain with her earnings. A hefty bouncer climbs the riser on the lip of the stage and wipes at the pole with a rag, though I don't see the point. The stained piece of cloth appears just as soiled as the pole itself, if we're being honest here.

I sit up in my seat when I see the signature red hair bobbing through the crowd. I expected her to appear on stage, to dance for me, even though it's not for me at all. She's probably too shaken up by what happened earlier and chose to work the floor instead of performing. If that's the case, she needs to put on her game face. No one will request anything from her with her lips drawn down in a permanent frown. Then again, they aren't paying to stare at her mouth, and a man proves that point when he waves his hand and flags her down.

The frown dissipates and a smile slips into the vacancy it leaves behind. Either she's a very good actress or a very good whore. Maybe she just disliked the guy in the dressing room and this guy is more her speed. A whore can still be choosy, I suppose.

Her full breasts spill from her skimpy top and rest on the man's shoulder as she eases her ear toward his mouth. A renewed rage floods my system.

I regret helping her earlier. I had it right the first time.

She's a whore.

After a nod of her head, she grips his hand and leads him toward the back of the building. The private dance section. The place I've never been led to like that. I stand out of instinct, my feet determined to follow them behind that velvet curtain, but the bouncer standing at the doorway to the promised land makes me think twice. They let people get away with a lot of shady shit around here, but there's no way he'll let me into that area without a whore on my arm.

A strung-out blonde fumbles past me, and I take a step toward her and grab her wrist. Maybe the copious amount of alcohol running through her system will blur my scars. She smells like she bathed in Everclear. If someone lit a match in her vicinity, she'd likely become a human Molotov. The image puts a smile on my face, which is good since I want her to see me as likable enough to take into the private area.

She turns to face me, but her deadened blue eyes seem to glare straight through me.

"I need a private dance," I tell her.

She stumbles and licks her lips, her lids dropping and rising again in the slowest blink I've ever seen. When her eyes pinch together in a tight squint, I know she's finally focused enough to see me because her muscles tense.

Yeah, I know. I *know*. I'm fucked up, but I'm not the worst looking guy in this place.

If I'm being honest, however, she may be the worst

looking girl in this place. With her stringy blonde hair and the stink of desperation and one-too-many oozing from every pore, she should be glad I've even asked for her company.

This realization appears to dawn on her as well because she gives a slow nod before taking my hand and leading me toward the curtain over the doorway. The bouncer waves us in, seemingly oblivious to her inability to make safe decisions in her current mental state. Actually, he probably doesn't care. He doesn't get paid extra to be a voice of reason, after all.

The moment we cross the threshold, the ambience shifts. Instead of body odor and aftershave, I'm engulfed in a cloud of vanilla and spun sugar. The floor stops fusing to my shoes in a sticky death grip. Low lights set the mood, and soft music plays overhead as the thumping bass from the main floor becomes a distant memory. This is the money room.

Tall partitions separate the space into four separate sections, probably to keep others from stealing free glances. This is very much a pay-to-play area. Purple curtains drape from brass rods above each doorway. Three are open, but the one on the very end has been pulled shut.

Found you, tragedy.

The woman on my arm guides me to the first booth, but I keep walking toward the one on the end. Too drunk to argue, she follows. We reach the third sex stall and step inside, and she nearly rips the curtain down as she stumbles while closing it. The blonde zombie rights herself, regaining what little composure she has, then stumbles toward me. I have absolutely no interest in a dance. I just needed to get back here. In the same room as *her*.

Because I'm not done hurting her yet.

I want to break Oaklyn's soul before I break her body. It will make my revenge that much sweeter when I finally end her.

The blonde turns around and puts her ass on my lap, doing her best to grind against me in the least graceful fashion I've ever seen. She spins around and her arms flop over my shoulders like two dead fish. When her sour breath infiltrates my nose, I've had enough. I grip her chin between my fingers and squeeze to keep her head from wobbling. She whimpers, taken off guard by my rough touch.

"Get out," I tell her through gritted teeth.

She stops her pathetic grinding and blinks a few times as her eyebrows pull together. "You can't be back here without me." The words come out slurred together, and it takes me a moment to work through the mushy syllables.

"Make up an excuse. Go get me a drink or something."

"But . . . but you told me you'd buy a dance."

I pull out a stack of bills and hand them to her. "You're paid. Now get the fuck out."

That seems to satisfy her need to follow the rules, and she finally climbs off my lap. "What do you want to drink?" She's not the brightest in the bunch, and I don't think she can pin that on the alcohol.

"I don't actually want a drink. I want you to get your drunk ass out of this booth, and I'll be gone before you get to the bar."

"Okay," she whispers, walking out on wobbly legs with the wad of money clutched in her dirty fist.

The moment she closes the curtain behind her, I exit my booth and hover outside of Oaklyn's. Soft moans filter through the purple fabric hanging inches from my face. She's clearly faking her arousal, but the dude beneath her probably believes every fabricated sound that leaves her perfect lips. I need to know what she's doing. I need to see it for myself so I can throw more meat to the angry beast snarling in my gut. Feeding my anger will strengthen my resolve. Seeing her for what she is, what she *truly* is, will banish any doubt from my mind.

I turn on my phone's camera and aim the lens through the crack between the curtain and the doorframe. When I see her pale skin captured within the frame, I look away. I can't watch what she's doing to him. Not right now. If I look at that screen, I won't be able to stop myself from rushing in there and beating them beyond recognition, and that isn't part of the plan. I record for as long as I can before I get the fleeting feeling that I need to get the fuck out of here. I tuck my phone into my leather jacket and rush out of the club.

The moment I slide into the safety of my Jeep, the phone and its secret video begin burning a hole in my pocket. I pull out the device and stare at the dark screen. Unable to wait until I get home, I push play and hope I captured what I need.

Black panties flash before my eyes, the thin material hardly covering her pussy. I must have bent my wrist a bit while recording because the camera angles away from her lower half and focuses on her tits in some dude's face. She swings her deep red hair off her shoulder, giving the camera a glimpse of her face. I pause the video and stare at her. My gaze moves from her half-closed eyes to the seductive way she's biting her lower lip. She almost looks like she's enjoying it. It's seductive and slutty. It's vile.

And it's making me hard.

I'm not aroused by what I see before me, though it's arguably one of the sexiest things I've ever seen. I'm aroused by the idea my mind has conjured while watching Oaklyn whore herself out—a new step in the plan to bring about her demise.

Lost inside a mental maze of nervous energy, I drive home. It's similar to what I feel before a big fight, when all the tension grows inside me and seeks an exit. A release. I've come up with an outlet for this feeling, and the explosion will be euphoric. The destruction will rival goddamn Hiroshima. The drive home is a blur, and I don't even care about the glares and sideways glances as I jog through the parking lot and head for my front door. Let them get a good look tonight. I'm too excited about what I plan to do to give a single fuck about their judgment. Once I'm inside, I connect my phone to the computer and begin porting the video over to my hard drive.

I dabbled in a bit of video editing not long ago when Darby wanted me to cobble together a few promos to draw interest online. Putting my recently acquired skills to work, I craft a clip that shows Oaklyn in all her dirty glory, complete with slowed shots and closeups of her face so there is no denying the veracity of what this video contains. I consider throwing some cliche porno music over the top to really sell it, but I want the recipient of this video to take it seriously. I want them to hear each moan and sigh that comes from Oaklyn's filthy mouth. As a final touch, I throw a clip art acorn into the corner. Like a serial killer, I've developed a signature, and I want my name on my work.

I craft a burner email account, find the recipient's email address, and send the video on its merry way. Energy and anticipation brew and bubble inside me, coming to a rolling boil as I envision the ripple of repercussions this will cause my little tragedy. I rip my pants open, not able to wait a second longer to spill my load to her impending misery and unequivocal embarrassment.

I click on the attachment after I send it, filling my screen with Oaklyn's body. Fantasies of her devastation fuel each stroke. I only wish I could be there to see her face when she gets the call or the text or the email once her dirty little secret has been pushed into the light of day. Disappointment is too weak for what they'll feel when they see it.

I stroke myself faster.

And I come to her misery.

When I finally reach hell one day, what I have done will have me sitting on Satan's lap like he's Santa. But this is just the beginning. I have so much planned, and it's only going to get better from here. Well, better for me. For Oaklyn, it will be much, much worse.

Chapter Ten

Oaklyn

The worst part about being assaulted at work by your own boss? Facing him every day afterward. At least he hasn't tried to proposition me again, which I'm glad about, even if I don't understand what changed. Maybe he's moved on to one of the fresh-faced eighteen-year-olds who doesn't have a care in the world. Those impressionable young girls probably enjoy his attention. Puke.

Speak of the devil, Jake slinks into the dressing room as I'm sliding my arms into my jacket so I can get the fuck out of here. "You had a good night tonight," he says, as if congratulating me on a winning game.

I have nothing to say to him. I don't even want to look in his direction and give him the satisfaction of my undivided attention. He doesn't deserve to breathe the same air, so I grip the door handle.

His hand shoots toward me and wraps around my arm. "No hard feelings, right?"

The casual lilt to his voice ping-pongs inside me, and it takes every ounce of strength to keep my composure. No hard feelings? I have the hardest of fucking feelings. He's lucky I need the job. If I didn't, I'd punch him straight in the throat and then stomp on his dick when he's on the ground. The idea brings a smile to my face, and I guess he takes that as "no hard feelings" because he releases me and leaves.

I throw my bag over my shoulder and escape into the warm night. A truck rumbles by, and a cloud of oil smoke explodes from the exhaust, ruining the clean air. My chest seizes when I try to draw a breath. I'm so sick of this dirty city. Filth greets me everywhere I turn and no matter how many showers I take, I never feel clean. I long for the life I lived before the accident, before I made a stupid decision that upended my soul. If I had a time machine, I would go back to the night of the cast party and beg myself to get a cab or an Uber.

But I can't think about any of that. Time machines aren't real. This miserable life is my reality, and I need to stop wishing for the impossible.

I pull out my phone to call for an Uber, but a glint of silver in the distance catches my eye, and I lower my hand. The familiar Jeep pulls in front of me with perfect timing, and the window begins to lower.

"You need a ride?" he asks.

I nod. I don't know why I keep torturing myself by getting into a vehicle driven by a man who finds my line of work so beneath him, but here we are. Doing it again. Fear of assault is the furthest thing from my mind because I doubt he'd let his dick anywhere near me for fear of picking up all the STDs I don't fucking have. I fear his disappointment more.

Driving My Obsession

What the fuck is wrong with me?

Probably a lot.

I should be more concerned that a stranger would assault me, but I've only been assaulted once in my life, and he wasn't a stranger. He was the most familiar person at my job.

I lean over to fasten the seat belt, and he pulls away from the curb without looking at me. He doesn't even speak. Honestly, I don't mind the silence. I'm embracing it after the deafening din inside the club.

My phone chimes and I pick it up. A name comes across the screen that I haven't seen in a while: Mom. My stomach rolls against my insides, and I grit my teeth to bite back the nausea creeping up my throat. Since I announced my intent to attend a school of dance instead of medical school, she's only texted to let me know when someone has died. I have no grandparents left, so that only leaves my dad. Though we're estranged, he's still my father, and I don't want him to pass away before we've had a chance to reconcile. I've tried in the past. I've reached out. And I've been met with an unending silence.

Moving my dry tongue across my lips, I open the alert and scan the text.

> Do you not have a shred of dignity left in you, Oaklyn?

This message sends me into another sort of panic, denying me the sigh of relief my body craves. She argued her point about the frivolity of dance for months. She spent less than a week cursing the day I was born when she found out I had turned to stripping. What else have I done to earn her disapproval?

> What are you talking about?

> Don't act naïve. I got an email from you.

> I haven't sent you an email.

The furious tap of my fingers across the keyboard and the pings of response fill the silence in the Jeep. I'm so fucking confused. I've made as much effort to contact her as she has made to contact me. I have *not* emailed her.

She sends a screenshot of an email, and I blink a few times when I see the sender's address. That's my name, but that isn't my email.

> That's not me.

Another screenshot follows, this time showing a still frame from a video. I can't deny this one.

It's me.

Giving a lap dance.

With my bare breasts shoved into a stranger's face.

My hand flies to my mouth, and I suck air through my nose to calm the explosion of panic inside me. I'm a firework store, and someone has just lit a fuse in the building. I'm imploding. I spot the acorn in the bottom right corner of the screen, and I realize who has struck the match. My stalker. It has to be. He went from coming in my fucking shoes to ripping open old wounds and pouring rubbing alcohol over the raw flesh. He held a flashlight to the keyhole in my closet and exposed my skeletons to my family. Though they know what I do, they've never had to see it firsthand.

An invasion of heat scorches my cheeks. My stomach rolls again, and my abdomen lurches inward. A cold sweat pops onto my brow and lower back. I want Ambrose to pull over so I can vomit what I just saw onto the side of the road, but I don't want him to ask any questions. How would I even explain that my mother just saw me shaking my breasts in some old guy's face? Or the stalker who's hellbent on destroying what little sanity I have left?

As I dangle on the verge of hyperventilation, the voice from the driver's seat cuts through the darkness.

Ambrose

"WHAT'S THE MATTER?" I ask. Bright red patches paint her cheeks and chest, and she dry-heaves behind the hand pressed over her mouth. I pull to the side of the road. Not in my fucking car.

She just shakes her head, her hand glued to her face. The wheezy gasps through her nostrils slow, and she finally speaks. "I got a text from my mother, that's all."

My stomach tightens, and I swallow so hard that I can hear the click of my throat. No fucking way. No. Fucking. Way. "Is everything okay?" I ask.

I know it isn't. Her world is a glass globe that has been flung from a skyscraper, and I'm here to witness the glorious destruction as it collides with the concrete and shatters at my feet. What are the chances her mother would respond to my email while she's in the car with me? Probably about the same as the chances of a baby surviving the onslaught of a psychotic, knife-wielding mother, and I beat the fuck out of those odds.

Maybe I'm lucky after all. I should go to goddamn Vegas after this.

Invisible steam rises from her palpable anger, and I take a deep breath and inhale it into my lungs. I would strip to nothing and bathe in her torment if I could, but then I'd never see her again. And I need to see her again. I have so much more planned for her.

She wipes away the tears that have slid down her cheeks and collected on her chin, and that's such a waste. I want to drink them. "It's this fucking asshole from work," she says. "He's doing crazy shit to me."

Not many stalkers get to sit in the car with their stalkee and listen to them bitch about the stalking. They don't get to hear the anger and disgust lacing every heated word. My cup runneth over. "Care to elaborate?" I prod.

I want to hear more.

I want to hear everything.

Give it to me, Oaklyn. Tell me how evil and horrendous I really am. Tell me how my actions made you feel.

She shakes her head. "No."

Way to ruin the fun, tragedy.

She swallows. "I'm just going to go home and hate myself more than I already do."

Do I want her to go home and hate herself for what I've done? Yes. Absolutely. I want her to eat, sleep, and breathe this feeling for the rest of her days. I only wish I could keep watching once she leaves my car. I'll just have to log her look of despair for later.

A seedling of guilt struggles to spread its thready roots in the soil of my heart, but I crush it beneath my heel. Everything that's happening to her is *her* fault. If she hadn't chosen this disgusting profession—the same line of work my mother chose—this wouldn't be happening. I wouldn't be obsessed with a person I want to kill and fuck in equal measure.

Satisfied she won't soil my interior with her puke, I pull away from the curb and continue toward her trailer. I don't rush to get her home, though. I take my time. Every second she's in my car is a second longer I can enjoy her pain.

I get an idea. I want more access to her, and I know how I might achieve that.

"Maybe I should give you my number," I say. "It's probably not a good idea for you to hang around outside that club at night while you wait for a ride. Anytime you need a lift, you can give me a call and I can come get you. Your stalker might think twice if they see a man picking you up. Kind of like how girls do at the club when they pretend they have a boyfriend to get the creeps at the bar to leave them alone."

She nibbles at her bottom lip and stares at the phone in her hand, running her thumb along the screen. "Okay," she finally says.

That was easy. I give her my number, and she punches it into her phone. I expect her to send a text so I have her number as well, but she doesn't. That's okay. The fish has nibbled the bait, and it's only a matter of time before I sink the hook into her jaw.

"Thanks," she mumbles. Her gaze shifts to the window, and I bask in the despondent way she peers into the darkness rushing by outside. Her sadness is like sunshine.

I'm miserable when I see her porch light break through the shadows in the distance. All good things must come to an end, but like a spoiled child who doesn't want to wait in line for another turn on the slide, I'm annoyed. I want more. And I want it now.

As she climbs out of the car and trudges to her front

door, I'm struck by another idea. It's incredibly risky and could crash the plane before it even leaves the runway, but I'm on a hot streak. I peel away from her driveway, my courage building inside me at a rapid rate. My dark eyes narrow to slits, not seeing anything through the windshield as I turn the Jeep around. A sly smirk spreads on my face.

Yeah. I'll take my chances.

Chapter Eleven

Oaklyn

I grab the key from beneath the bench cushion and step inside as he drives away. He's such a confusing man. He didn't berate me like he normally does, instead choosing to be almost . . . supportive? But I don't have time to sit and wonder about the bipolar stranger who opted for kindness tonight. I'm still focused on the screenshot my mom sent me as I pull a bottle of vodka from the kitchen cabinet. The events of that lap dance rush through my mind with a clarity that turns my stomach. I know what she witnessed.

My actions.

My sounds.

His sounds.

Oh god.

I need a drink, but I need a shower first. While I usually feel dirty after work, knowing my mother has seen me grinding on a man makes me feel absolutely filthy. A hot shower won't do shit to scrub the feeling away, but I sure as fuck plan to try. I place the vodka on the island in the kitchen and scurry to my room, stripping away my sin-laced fabric at the door. When I kick off the last piece of clothing, I feel a bit better. Until I look at myself in the mirror.

Black mascara and eyeliner ring my eyes, reminding me who I am. Who I can't run from. The girl whose breasts bounced in some old guy's face while a stalker videoed the whole ordeal from the shadows. The girl whose mother saw it all.

God, I'm sickened.

If she didn't hate me before, she definitely does now. I don't know how she could believe I sent it to her. Clearly it's someone out to hurt me. Shouldn't she show an ounce of concern? I'm still her daughter, after all.

But I guess that's not entirely true. Her daughter is dead to her. She buried me when I didn't choose a career she could brag about to her rich friends. Any concern she feels isn't directed toward my safety. She's probably only worried my unauthorized porno will end up in the hands of someone in her social circle. God forbid I become the topic of the gossip mill during brunch.

I turn on the shower and run my hand beneath the water, ready to wash away the grime of the day. The touches. My shame. Not even scalding water would be hot enough for that. I step over the lip of the tub and shut the curtain. With closed eyes, I tilt back my head and let the heat massage my scalp, then part my lips beneath the stream and let it fill my mouth. I scrub my skin until it's red and raw. After plopping a healthy dollop of shampoo into my palm, I wash a pound of product from my hair and rinse myself off. The water slows to a trickle once I flip the handle, and the pipes rattle within the wall. I get out and towel my hair, then wrap the damp fabric around my body.

These mundane tasks don't cleanse me of everything, but they wash away enough to allow me to feel a little different for a while. I'm a little normal, giving me some space from the line that separates me from my life before the incident.

Sometimes after a good shower, I indulge myself and pretend I'm preparing for a big show. I'll wake up in the morning and head to a rehearsal that will last for hours. My fellow cast members will watch as I practice my solo. They'll cheer me on when I land a flawless cabriole.

When I look down at my discarded clothes, it thrusts me back into my reality. My ankle couldn't withstand hours of rehearsal time, let alone a cabriole. I'll never prepare for a show again. Well, not that kind of show. No one cheers me on as I perform. It's just me, myself, and I, and we all hate our life now.

I step into my pajama pants and pull a black cami over my chest. My legs run on autopilot and guide me to the vodka bottle that sits on the island. The cap twists right off, and I pour a hearty dose into an old plastic cup. I tilt back my head and swallow it in one smooth gulp. Some people hate the taste of vodka, but I love it. It's the first alcoholic beverage that my mother let me drink. She always used to say she'd rather I drink responsibly at home than anywhere else.

I hate how right she was.

If I'd stayed home that dreary fall evening, my life would be so different. My fantasy of preparing for a show would be my reality. I'd have gone to bed two hours ago so I could rest up. I'd be happy instead of miserable. My life would still be the one I had molded since I was a little kid.

From the time I was small, I knew I would carve out my future in a pair of dance shoes. If my mother had known what an impact those dance classes would have on me, she wouldn't have ferried me to so many of them. She wouldn't have sat in the audience and beamed with pride during my first solo. When I made a B in sixth grade science, she threatened to take away those dance classes because she thought I was destined for greatness in the medical field. I never made less than an A- after that, but it had nothing to do with a drive to follow in my father's footsteps. I was more inclined to binge films starring Ginger Rogers than a marathon of *Grey's Anatomy*.

This is called a sign, Mom.

I toss back another shot and wipe my nose. The alcohol opens my sinuses, soothing the inflammation from hours spent in a smoky room. An emptiness fills me as I turn the bottle in my hand. Loneliness creeps up on me like a cat in a dark hallway, weaving around my feet and sending me to the ground. Or maybe it's always there and I just don't acknowledge it. Yeah, that's probably more accurate.

I have no friends. People who I considered friends hung around my hospital bed for a while after the accident. They brought flowers. They offered condolences. Then our paths split. The song didn't end for them. They had a stage to return to while I struggled through rehab and depression. I learned to walk on my busted ankle, but I never got over the unending sadness. Even the girl who I considered a close friend—the girl who walked away from the accident with bruises instead of broken dreams—hasn't reached out for months. I wonder what she's been up to . . .

I pull out my phone as the alcohol nestles into my gut. There's a warm glow inside there, and I find myself feeling drunk after only two shots. It's probably because I haven't eaten since lunchtime.

I flop onto the couch and search for any news about the girl who drove the car that fateful night. A few articles pop into the feed, but they make me feel worse instead of better. She's currently touring with a show. Good for her.

My head drops onto my closed fist, and it feels like I'm holding up a giant stone. My whole body feels heavy, actually. Disconnected. The hand holding the phone trembles under the insignificant weight, and a dizziness overtakes my brain. A rolling blackout barrels toward me.

What. The. Fuck.

Since when have I ever gotten drunk from such a small amount of vodka? Tipsy, sure. But this? This isn't a buzz; it's a clap of thunder on repeat right beside my ears.

I lie back, letting the couch cushion's synthetic fibers caress my back. The moment my head hits the balled-up blanket behind my head, the whole room spins. Hard. My stomach clenches, but the overpowering exhaustion trumps the discomfort. My heavy eyelids refuse to stay open, but my chest is heavier, as if there's a weight above me. Becoming one with me.

I release my body's tension as it fights the desperate need for sleep. Then I give in.

Chapter Twelve

Ambrose

Oaklyn's hand falls from the couch and sends her phone to the floor. I back away from the window, unable to contain the smile on my face because my impromptu plan has gone off without a hitch. Originally, I thought I would just lurk outside her bare windows and watch her sadness unfold, but when she brought out the vodka bottle and left it unattended while she took a shower, I knew she'd be back for it. Using the key she keeps under the bench cushion, I let myself in and dropped a little surprise into the bottle. I would hardly call it breaking in, though. She practically asked for me to come inside when she so blatantly showed me where the key was. Now I can snoop to my heart's content while she sleeps.

An odd silence greets me when I step inside, and I'm shrouded in a sense of unease. When a stranger enters someone's home, a symphony of screams and breaking glass should announce their arrival as the homeowner tries in vain to steer the intruder away from their safe space. It's so quiet in here I could hear a mouse piss on cotton.

Shaking off the eerie feeling, I creep through the attached kitchen and enter the living room. I want to rummage through her closets and drawers to find all her dirty secrets, but I'm drawn to her body. It pulls me with the same magnetism she possesses when she's dancing, but for a different reason. She looks so fucking clean. Innocent. Little cats dot her pajama pants, and the strap of her black cami hangs off her shoulder. Her bright red hair looks almost brown because of the water still clinging to the straight strands. I miss the red waves.

My fingertips move toward her, itching with a need to feel her skin. She'll be soft. So soft . . .

I pull my hand away. I need to do what I came here for.

Her bedroom is at the very back of the house. The bathroom stands right beside it, and its open door allows the mouth-watering scent of her shower to fill the backside of her home. I peek inside, but continue to her bedroom when I don't see anything of interest.

My lips form a tight line as my gaze falls on her unmade bed. Rumpled blankets and random pillows lie across the mattress. How does she not feel like her mess of a life isn't more so when she climbs into this travesty each night? I roll my eyes.

After scanning the rest of the room, I stop at the closet door. When I open it, it's just as messy as her bed. I flick the racks down the rod and find a few nice shirts, but most of the options are skanky and scandalous. The nauseating amount of sequins and glittering fabrics burns my eyes. And fuck me, they stink. Not even an acid bath could rid them of the stench of that club. I rip down every shirt and bra set that has so clearly been designed to display her body. My knife blade emerges with a flick of my wrist, and I slice through the fabric. Straps, sequins, and clasps fall to my feet in a heap of glorious destruction.

She'll have nothing to dance in tomorrow. I cut the whore off at the head.

I spot a garment bag near the back of the closet and pull it into the light. I unzip the side of the bag and remove its contents: a pale pink leotard and a tutu. The leotard is familiar. It's the same one she wore in the photo attached to that article about her. My hand reaches for the blade I've tucked back on my hip, but I stop myself. Cutting this into pieces would probably hurt her, but I know what would do even more damage to her psyche.

I take a hanger from the closet and use it to attach the leotard to the back of her bedroom door, right over the mirror. She's sure to see it here. When she does, it will be another reminder of her fall from grace.

I toss the empty garment bag on top of the destroyed slut suits and make my way to her dresser. Makeup and hair products litter the smooth wooden top. More mess. Pulling open a drawer, I discover a treasure trove of panties. My fingers run through the river of lace, silk, and mesh in search of something more alluring. I find what I seek near the bottom—a pair of simple cotton panties that are more akin to shorts than the stringy offerings surrounding them. I imagine the way the fabric would hug the curve of her ass, hiding more than it shows. Nothing slutty about these panties. I tuck them into my pocket.

Finding nothing of interest in the remaining drawers, I return to the living room to bid farewell to my target and leave her a parting gift. As I kneel beside the couch, I notice her phone beside my foot. I pick up the device and turn it on. It asks for her fingerprint, which is easy enough. I press her limp thumb against the screen, and it springs to life.

To the gentle sound of each breath rolling past her parted lips, I scroll through her texts, reliving the turmoil she experienced in my car. I swell with pride over the bitter anger woven through her mother's words—venom meant to maim. If she didn't like her daughter before, she probably hates her now.

I close the text message screen and open the internet browser, immediately pulling up an article about a theater production. Scanning the text, I spot a familiar name, though I can't place it. Then it dawns on me. This is the girl who caused the accident that sidelined Oaklyn. It looks like my plan has worked better than expected. She's been digging at her own wounds.

Guilt nibbles at my insides, but I ignore it. I have no reason to feel guilty. She's not worth it.

I read the text messages one more time to remind myself of the joy this brings me, then I place the phone on the coffee table and turn my attention to her. She looks so sweet compared to how she looked in that video. Without the makeup, the dead-ness in her eyes, and the slutty fucking outfits. When she can't make those whore noises. I breathe in her scent. It's nothing like the club. It's fragrant, almost fruity. My fingers wind through her hair, parting the silky strands. Having dried, they've taken on the red glow again. My cock hardens against my zipper.

I swing her arm over my shoulder and lift her from the couch. She doesn't stir and if it weren't for the gentle rise and fall of her chest, I'd wonder if she were dead. A wobbly bar stool nearly tips over as I carry her toward her bedroom. I catch it with my foot and right it before it hits the floor. When I reach her bedroom, I lay her on the strewn blankets and sit beside her. I don't intend to fuck her, though. I intend to kill her.

Her skin—just as soft as I imagined—presses against my knuckles as I bring the blade to her throat. I could end her so easily right now. But it'd be *too* easy. She wouldn't fight or flail or feel any of the gashes I'd paint on her flesh. She'd be as innocent as I was when my mother attacked me. I thought I'd like the ease of her being asleep, but it's not what my little black heart wants.

It's just not enough.

Or maybe that's just what I'm telling myself.

Ending her shouldn't be this difficult for me, but I find a reason to stay my hand at every turn. Something about her makes me reconsider. What is it?

I study her face and lean over to brush the hair from her cheeks. Warm skin meets my fingertips. Thick lashes frame the seams of her eyelids. If they were open, would I see the dead stare she wears when she's in the club? Or would they come alive?

Every breath raises her chest before letting it fall once more. I'm mesmerized by the motion. Even though I've seen them, I long to pull down the thin cami and expose her breasts. My hand moves on its own and pulls down the neckline. Her tits are even more beautiful when they aren't coated in sweat and glitter. When wandering hands aren't exploring them.

A low growl leaves my throat, and the sound catches me off guard. Why should I care who touches her? I sure as fuck don't want to.

That's a lie. My cock isn't throbbing like this because I don't want to touch her. The naked truth is that I want nothing more than to wrap my hands around the tits I weaponized against her in the video to her mother. I want to touch her. I want to—

Don't, I scold myself. *We don't fuck whores.*

Maybe I can pretend she's not the thing I hate.

Or . . . maybe I'll fuck her exactly like the thing I hate.

I pull my cock from my pants and stand up. Once I've stripped the clothing from the lower half of her body, her perfect pussy makes me forget all about her profession. I toss her pants to the side and hook my hands around her thighs to pull her toward me. My cock twitches against her slit. I lean over her and fill my hands with her tits, reddening the skin as I squeeze. Unwilling to respond to my touch, her nipples remain flaccid. Her nerve endings are as oblivious as she is, unable to register that I'm touching her at all. I drop one hand from her chest and push my fingers inside her pussy. She's not wet, but I don't need her to be. The warmth is enough.

"I should use a condom because you're a whore, huh?" I ask, even though she can't answer. And even though I have no plans to put a barrier between us. I want to know what she feels like. I rub my cock—the only part of my body that is free of scars—along her slit. "With you out like this, you can't judge my scars. You can't judge me at all."

It's been so long since I've fucked someone. Their silent judgment makes it almost impossible, and it's not something I'm imagining. They all want the man in the ring until the man in their bed becomes the grotesque figure they can't look in the eye. But my tragedy can't judge me. She's painfully vulnerable to my carnal desires.

My hatred.

My hands slide over her hips and rake the scars on her thighs. The hum of understanding vibrates through the rough tissue, each mark a permanent memory etched into us.

I draw back my hips and push inside her. Though I'm met with resistance and friction, I don't stop. I tear my tragedy in two, ripping her apart physically this time. A feral groan leaves my lips because I'm wearing the embodiment of my anger on my dick and fucking the painful memories of my past.

And fuck if she doesn't feel like heaven within my mental hell.

I lean forward and wrap my hand around her throat as I pound into her. Pressing harder, I cut off her breath. She still doesn't wake. I could kill her right now, but there'd be absolutely no fun in that. She wouldn't even know what happened or what I'd done to her body while she slept. I loosen my grip and allow her to draw a few breaths before I toy with her some more.

"Such a dirty whore," I growl as her tits bounce against my chest. "Your pussy will be sore tomorrow. Ripped open by me. Your stalker. The man hell-bent on destroying you." My words are met with silence, but it still feels good to spill each anger-soaked syllable.

By doing nothing at all, she's going to make me come. Just by being a receptacle for my pleasure, she'll draw every ounce from me like the whore she swears she isn't. I grip her hips and my fingertips dig into her flesh. I fuck her harder, knowing this would hurt her if she were awake right now. When I pull out to my tip, blood streaks my cock.

I love that she'll think about me tomorrow when she wakes up, sore and used. Well, she'll think of her stalker, but we're one and the same. As she struggles through her shift at work, she'll ache with each movement and remember that someone was inside her. All without knowing who that someone is.

What a mind fuck.

Goddamn.

That's tragic.

The thought tightens my balls with a sudden shock of pleasure that I feel in the base of my spine, but the risk of coming inside her without knowing what kind of protection she's on worries me. I wouldn't want her to have a child from a night she wouldn't want to remember. Breeding a whore means hell for the spawn that is created. Whores like her—whores like my *mother*—aren't good moms.

Even though the risk is high, I can't help myself. An unwavering desire to fill her dirty cunt, her tainted pussy, her whore's hole, overtakes me. I want to use her for what she's meant for. From graceful dancer to desperate cumslut, she has no choice but to take what I desperately need to give her. I fill her, coming deep inside her with a groan that conquers her silence. Like a doll, she remains motionless.

A pretty little fuck doll.

I pull back slowly, watching the white residue of my pleasure mix with the red of her pain. The feelings swirl and blend into a pink hue until I can't tell the difference between the two emotions. A thin line drips from her, and I gather it on my fingers and stuff it back inside her. I don't want her to lose a drop of me. She needs to bask in my come until she wakes up. Before I go, I leave her with a little gift that ensures she'll know exactly who was inside her.

Her stalker.

The unknown man who haunts both her nightmares and her every waking moment.

I zip up my pants and drag her toward the pillows, then throw the blanket over her. A smile tugs at my lips as I admire my handprint around her neck. The marking blazes a bright red across the pale skin. I've accomplished a lot tonight, but it's not enough. I need something more. I lean over her, gather saliva in my mouth, and drop it between her parted lips. The thought of her waking up with an ache in her cunt and my taste on her tongue is almost enough to get me hard again. But I can't stay and play.

On my way out of her room, I look back at her once more before flicking off the light. I fully intend to leave more devastation in my wake before finally ending her suffering. Until then, she's my pretty little tragedy.

See you soon.

Chapter Thirteen

Oaklyn

A hammer pounds behind my forehead and rattles against the base of my skull. I open my gummy eyelids, struggling to recall what I can from last night. I fell asleep on the couch after two measly shots of vodka, but I somehow ended up in my bedroom. My sandpaper tongue scrapes across my lips, and my head swims as I try to fully wake up. I didn't drink that much. Not enough to cause this. I lift my hand to my face, wiping sweat from my overheated skin. When I shift onto my side, I suck in a sharp breath as pain spears through my abdomen and between my legs. It's like nothing I've ever felt—like someone has torn me apart and poured lemon juice inside me. I rip the blanket away and find the lack of pants concerning because I put them on before I went into the kitchen to drink.

I slip my hand between my legs and cup myself. The pain intensifies, but it's not just the burning sensation. A deep ache rushes toward my fingertips whenever they land on my skin, similar to the way a fresh bruise feels. When I try to sit up, a different sensation plagues me. Something moves between my legs. Inside me. A blinding wave of emotions narrows my vision. Ignoring the bruises I've just spotted on my thighs, I turn my attention to the hard object that is definitely *not* supposed to be there.

The torn skin along my opening screams for me to stop as I put my fingers inside myself, but I whimper through the pain and keep going. Something slick and hard meets my fingertips, and I finally get a grip on the foreign body as I fight through the pain and bear down. I bring the object into the light. As I release a scream, the acorn falls from my hand and lands between my legs on the mattress.

I scramble out of bed to get away from it, wincing with every painful twinge of my muscles. The acorn rolls around and drops off the bed as if it's trying to chase me, but I can only stare as it comes to a stop by my toes. I finally gain the strength to pick it up, then freeze again when the slickness coats my palm. It wiggles in my hand, and I realize I'm shaking.

My stalker was inside my room. Worse, he was inside *me*.

My brain can't accept this.

I refuse.

Jake's assault degraded me, but this? This is terrifying. Someone entered my home while I slept and took something from me that I can never get back. Judging by the way my body feels, it was a violent attack. So why didn't I wake up? It was only two shots of—

He drugged me.

My hand releases the acorn as if it sank sharp teeth into

my palm. Overcome by a powerful wave of nausea, I race to the bathroom and rid myself of whatever remains in my stomach. All of it. My forehead drops to my arm as it drapes over the toilet seat. Sweat drips from my temples. Vulnerable and half naked, I squat over the tile floor.

I pull myself together because there's nothing else I can do. Reaching out to the police isn't an option. I'm a sex worker. My report would get shoved to the bottom of the stack and eventually forgotten. As far as most of society is concerned, I got exactly what I asked for. That couldn't be further from the truth.

I didn't ask for any of this.

When I stand up, my eyes catch on my reflection and I struggle to breathe. Rows of bruises line my neck on one side, and a single mark stands out on the other. I place my hand over it. Fingers. A thumb. I've been strangled, and I have no recollection of it. And that's the scariest part.

I go back to my room and rush to put on my discarded pajama pants so I can conceal the parts of myself that feel too vulnerable and exposed. That's when I spot the dried blood lingering within the creases of my thighs. Each new discovery leads me further toward insanity as I uncover just how violently I've been attacked. Because I can't remember any of it, it feels like this happened to someone else. But then I feel the pain. See the bruises. Run my fingers over blood. Pull an acorn from *my* fucking body. And I can't deny the truth. This happened to me, and someone wants to hurt me, possibly even kill me.

As I pull my pants into place to cover what I no longer want to look at, my eyes are drawn to the strewn clothes inside my closet. When I look closer, I realize these aren't my clothes. These are *pieces* of my clothes—more specifically, the outfits I wear at work. I kneel beside the pile and lift the tattered rags. They've been ripped to shreds. Glancing at what remains on the racks, I see that none of my everyday wear has been touched.

Then I see it. Hanging from my bedroom mirror, obscuring my face when I stand, is my leotard from my last production. It's a slap in the face. After everything else this psychopath has done to me, it wasn't enough. He had to do more. He had to remind me I will never be more than what I am.

I drop to the bed before I can collapse, then put my head in my hands. I don't know what I did to deserve this. Hasn't enough bad shit happened to me without an unhinged stalker adding to it?

Tears stream down my face, but I raise my eyes to the doorway as a thought crosses my mind. I've been too upset to consider it, but now the alarm bells scream in my ears and rival the sound of my heartbeat.

What if he's still here?

I creep toward the door, looking around my room for a weapon and settling on a broom tucked beside the dresser. I'm not sure how well this flimsy thing will protect me if I find him, but I *need* to know if he's still haunting my home after violating me. I swing the broom against my shoulder and step through the doorway.

The lights are still on in the living room, and the brightness unsettles me because it's another reminder of the break in my nightly routine. I always turn off all the lights before bed. I can't afford the power bill otherwise, and I prefer to let the sunshine do all the work during the day. Sunlight doesn't cost a thing.

Swallowing my unease, I tighten my grip on the broom

handle and do my best to clear the house the way I see cops do it on fucking television. I swing the broom around each corner and expect to connect with a body each time. By the time I reach the kitchen, I'm confident I'm alone.

My shoulders fall and a war of emotions rages in my chest. On one hand, I wish he'd been lurking somewhere in my trailer so I could finally put a face to the monster under the bed. I'm also disappointed I can't take a stab at him. On the other hand, I'm relieved as fuck. Sometimes it's better to keep away from the monster and leave it a mystery.

Maybe you already know who it is.

That thought is the most unsettling of all. I've likely seen this person, and they sure as fuck know enough about me. They even made a point of leaving my final costume hanging on my bedroom door. And they knew about that costume because they searched my history online and pasted my past all over the club's dressing room. How did they gain access to the back room at the club? How did no one see him pasting the pictures everywhere?

My blood freezes in my veins.

Jake.

It all makes sense. He has more of a reason to carry such a vicious vendetta against me than anyone else I know. I've turned him down on a nightly basis for months, and his fragile ego probably couldn't take it anymore. He probably stopped trying to sleep with me after his foiled assault attempt the other night because he planned to do much worse to me when the time was right. And who else could get into the private rooms to video the lap dance that ended up seared into my mother's brain? Fucking Jake.

I can't stay here. If I can't go to the police, I have to get the fuck out of town before my stalker comes back. I sure as fuck can't go to work tonight. Even if my muscles didn't feel like pudding, I don't want to be anywhere near the creep who's trying to ruin my life. I don't even want to be in the same city.

I return to my room and toss the broom to the ground as I step onto the worn carpet. I reach beneath my mattress and pull out the money I've been saving for months. The money that was supposed to go to my future and will now have to go toward a momentary escape from my stalker. I have to return eventually, but what do I have to return to? If Jake has taken things this far, I can't return to the club tonight. Maybe not ever. There are other places I can dance, but I have no way to get there. Buses don't run that far out of this city. It's heartbreaking. No, it's worse than heartbreak. This whole situation has done so much more than hurt me. It has destroyed me. Handing over my hard-earned money to escape my deranged stalker is the last straw.

I'll have to figure this shit out later. Once I've gotten to safety.

I pack a bag and stuff the money inside, then grab my phone from the coffee table in the living room. When the screen comes to life, I'm greeted by the volatile text messages from my mom. Which means he looked at my phone. He *enjoyed* reading what he's done to me. Sick fucking psychopath. He's probably so proud of himself.

My stomach tightens and threatens to send me back to the bathroom for another vomit session, but I don't have time for this. The bottle of vodka glares at me from the kitchen island. I'd normally take a swig to quiet my nerves, but I'm almost positive that's how my stalker drugged me. I storm toward the offending vessel of unconsciousness and pour it down the sink. My hand longs to smash the bottle and vent some of my pent up frustration, but I don't want to clean up a mess when I come back.

Speaking of cleaning up messes, I need to let Jake know I won't be in for a few days. If my suspicions prove incorrect, I'll still need a job when I return. Actually, who am I fucking kidding? Even if I find proof that Jake has been sabotaging me at every turn, I'll have to continue working for him. If I want to keep dancing, if I want to continue pursuing my passion, if I want to reach for a dream that seems to be slipping further from my fingertips with every day that passes . . . I don't have a choice.

I send a message saying I need to visit a sick aunt in Florida. I don't have an aunt, in Florida or otherwise, but I can't tell him where I actually plan to go. Without knowing how much he knows about my past, I don't want to give anything away. He doesn't need another bullet for the gun he's aimed at my skull.

With shaking hands, I search for the first bus back to Wisconsin. Just seeing the name of my home state brings back a flood of memories. Most are good, which is the saddest part. My eyes nearly bulge out of my head when I see how much a ticket will cost, and that's just one way. A round trip will eat a significant hole in my savings. As my thumb hovers over the button to confirm an immediate reservation for the first ride out of town, I rack my brain for any other way to get to Wisconsin. But I have no friends. If I call my family, they'll tell me to pay for a ride with my dirty money. Even if I tell them the dire circumstances, I'll be met with, "You wouldn't have had this problem if you'd just gone to medical school." I can think of no other option . . . until one slithers to the front of my mind.

I close the browser on my phone and type out a text message to the only person who might be willing to help me. It's a Hail Mary play, but it's all I have left. What else do I have to lose? Before I can talk myself out of it, I hit send, lock my front door, and grab a butcher knife from the knife block. I don't know how long it might take to get a reply and the sun is already starting to set, so I'll need to be safe while I wait. My stalker could return at any moment. If he does, I'll be ready. He won't get the jump on me again.

Chapter Fourteen

Ambrose

The crowd sings my praises as the ref raises my hand, declaring me the victor in the first fight of the night. I don't usually like being the opening act, but it's the only way Darby will allow me to fight twice in one night, breaking the one-fight rule he imposes on everyone else. And I needed two bouts tonight. Pummeling someone's face keeps my mind off that fucking girl.

Since I sank into her last night, it's all I've thought about. I long to get inside her again, but I need to pace myself. The next time I fuck her will be the last time. There'll be no going back for either of us after that. We'll get the release we deserve. I'll dish out my ultimate revenge, then I'll free her from her tragic life. Like putting down a deer that's still breathing after its entrails have been strewn across a desolate highway, it's the humane thing to do at this point.

I jog back to the locker room and grip the tape around my wrists with my teeth, pulling it away from my hands until they're bare. Once my hands are free, I flex my fingers and allow the blood to rush toward the sore spots. A pleasurable ache greets me with each movement. I towel the sweat off my skin and dress in casual clothes so I can work the crowd until my next fight. Grabbing my phone from my locker, I spot a notification. Someone sent me a text while I was in the ring.

My eyebrows pull together as I read the message.

> I need to get out of town for a few days, and I need to leave as soon as possible. I know this is a huge ask, but is there any way you could drive me to Wisconsin? I can pay for gas and food, and you can stay in the extra room at my family's cabin.

A smile curls the edges of my mouth. Last night produced results I never could have expected. She's decided to run from her stalker, not realizing she's running right into his waiting arms. And we'll be traveling to a cabin? Hopefully that means it's a secluded spot, which would be the ideal location for what I need to do. If everything falls into place, the final act of this tragic play will come sooner than I wanted, but all good things must eventually come to an end. I can't let this golden opportunity pass me by.

I fire back a text and tell her I'm on my way. After slipping into my leather jacket, I grab my bag and throw it over my shoulder. The door whips open as I reach for the handle, and Darby stands on the other side, his eyes widening when he spots the bag.

"What the fuck, scar? You've got another fight tonight. You can't leave."

I shrug my shoulders. "Emergency. Gotta go." I try to push past him, but he sidesteps into my path, his eyes narrowing into dark slits.

"What do you mean? The only thing you *gotta* do is fight."

My frame towers over him as I step closer. "I'm leaving. Call the fight or slide Boris into my slot. I'll be back in a few days. Maybe a week."

"A *week*? What about your—"

"Figure it out." My fists clench into tight balls at my sides. I don't have time for this shit. I have a date with my red-haired destiny.

"I could ruin you, scar. Keep you from ever fighting again!"

I glare down at him and smirk. "But where's the money in that?"

His shoulders deflate and he steps aside. Checkmate. The crowd pays good money to see me fight, and he knows it. That's why his panties are in such a twist. If he strikes me from the schedule for a few nights, he'll lose money until I make my grand return, but firing me means losing his cash cow for good. He'd offer me higher pay before he'd fire me, but I wouldn't accept it. It wouldn't be fair to my fellow fighters.

I push past him, then stop and shout a parting shot over my shoulder. "Call the Kursicki brothers. Maybe if you offer them fair pay for the fights, they'll agree to fill my spot while I'm gone."

Those two would fight for free, but I can't miss an opportunity to take a dig at how underpaid we are.

Satisfied I've made my point, I head toward my Jeep and get into the driver's seat. I feel for my knife between the seats and find the hefty handle. I'm glad I waited for the right moment to take her life, but I worry some semblance of buried morals has kept me from doing what needs to be done. I'll just have to throw more dirt on the pile and bury them deeper. Nothing can stop me from making someone pay for what happened to me, and that someone has to be Oaklyn.

The drive toward her trailer passes by in a blur of trees and street signs. I'm wrapped in a state of euphoria. Anticipation crawls along my spine at the thought of seeing her face, and I allow myself this guilty pleasure because it's almost over now. I can't deny that I find her beautiful, and I won't try to chase away those thoughts any longer. This is as close as I'll allow myself to get, however. If I venture much nearer to admiration, it'll be harder to take her life. I'll be too tempted to keep her around so I can repeatedly take her cunt.

I pull in front of her home, and she rushes from the doorway, looking in every direction as if someone might spring from the trees and drag her to hell. I have no need to drag her. She's stepping into hell on her own.

A tight tank top hugs her curves, and her red ponytail swings over her bare shoulders as she jogs toward the Jeep. I want to wrap that thick tendril of hair around my hand and pull, but am I slitting her throat or fucking her from behind as I reveal her pale neck? My mind struggles with the indecision, but then I smile. It can be both.

She tosses her bag into the backseat and flops onto the passenger seat in a breathless heap. A light sweat glosses her skin, making her shoulders and forehead shine beneath the dome light. Her chest heaves up and down, and she tilts her head as she pulls her ankle into her lap with a sharp wince. The light moves to the marks I left on her neck. She tried to cover them with makeup, but they peer from beneath the translucent smudges. Or maybe I only notice them because I made them. Either way, it hardens me.

"Close the door," I say, wanting the darkness to hide my shame.

She does as she's told, and the light clicks off. "Thanks for helping me," she says. "My stalker broke into my house last night, and I need to get away for a few days while I figure out what to do."

I wish she'd tell me more. I want to hear how my actions have destroyed her—those little details would be a symphony to my ears—but she doesn't offer anything else. That's okay. We have a long drive ahead of us, and I'm sure I can get her to open up along the way.

"I need to know where we're going," I say.

"Oh, right." She rattles off the address, and I punch it into my phone. "It's my family's cabin, but no one should be there. It's a pretty long trek, so we can take turns driving if you want."

I shake my head and pull onto the road. No one drives this Jeep but me. "What do you hope to accomplish while you're away? Your stalker will still be here when you get back."

She shrugs and looks out the window. "Maybe I won't come back."

"Where would you go?"

"I don't know." She picks at the side of her nail and nibbles at her bottom lip. "I don't exactly have a lot of great options. That's why I'm working at the club. To give myself more options."

What a lame-ass excuse. She's working at the club because she's a whore who likes to let men use her body in exchange for cash. I won't let her tell me this lie. "Why not work a normal job like everyone else? You'd be less of a target for stalkers if you worked a desk job."

She turns her head toward me and stops clawing at her

finger. "Are you victim blaming right now? Seriously? People don't get stalked because of their profession. People get stalked because there are too many men and women running around with a screw loose."

Shots fired. But she isn't wrong. My mother shook a few screws loose when she sank a knife into me more times than the doctors could count.

"Don't get me wrong," she continues. "If I could go back to the professional dance world, I would, but that just isn't possible. I was in a wreck six months ago that destroyed my ankle, and the professional dance world demands more than what the plates and screws can handle. I can manage a few minutes on stage at the club, but that's about it."

"Do you have to dance?"

She returns her gaze to the window. "Do you have to fight?" When I don't answer, she knows she's made her point. "It's the same thing. Sometimes we're created to do something, and we can't deny the drive to do it. I was meant to dance. It's the one thing that brings me any happiness, and I'm not willing to give up the only shred of joy I have left in life."

A sign marks the interstate, and I ease the Jeep onto the on-ramp and merge with the trickle of vehicles heading the same way. Headlights cut through the darkness and illuminate her face for a moment. A single tear slithers through her makeup.

"Don't you have any aspirations?" I ask. "You aren't happy in your current career, so what's the end goal?"

A soft laugh springs from her throat. "I can't look too far ahead. Whenever I try, things seem impossible. Right now I'm focused on getting a car so I can find work at a nicer club outside of our shithole town."

The speck of sympathy I felt for her blows away on a

puff of air. Instead of seeking a way out of her slutty situation, she only desires a nicer place to spread her legs. Which is fine. The last thing I need is for her to give me doubts about ending her life on this trip. Her little admission has only bolstered my conviction. She's the right target, and the right time is just around the bend.

Then she speaks again, and what she says next drives a chasm through my resolve.

Chapter Fifteen

Oaklyn

It's not easy to open up to someone I don't really know, but I'm trying. Since I have to be around him for several days in the middle of nowhere, I might as well be a bit more personable, especially when he's been kind enough to drive me there. Is it the kindness I find myself so drawn to? His good looks certainly help. He's insecure about the scars on his face, but I see more than that when I look at him. Those marks don't affect his strong jawline or the way his tongue runs over his full bottom lip when he's thinking. They certainly don't detract from his dark eyes.

Maybe it wouldn't hurt to tell him about the impossible end goal.

"I have bigger dreams, but I haven't spoken them aloud to anyone because they feel so silly," I finally say.

His hands adjust on the wheel, and his shoulders seem to tense. The shift is nearly imperceptible, so maybe I've only imagined it. "Are you trying to make it to a whorehouse somewhere in the western part of the country? Is that the real reason you need a car?"

"No, but even if that was the goal, who are you to judge me? Who are you to judge anyone? Sex work is still work." I regret even opening my mouth at this point. Maybe I should have stayed behind and taken my chances with the stalker. "Never mind."

His jaw works his muscles into a tight ball, the skin at his temple writhing with every grit of his teeth. "No, go on. What's your big dream?"

I won't give him everything. I haven't spoken of this plan to anyone, and I won't start with him. But I'll give him a taste. "I eventually want to stop stripping. Not because I think it's a dirty profession"—I give him a pointed glare—" but because I just have other aspirations."

He shifts in his seat and clears his throat. "That's . . . admirable."

It pains him to give this compliment. He struggles to speak the word, as if he's just forced a shard of glass from his throat. It doesn't cut me, though. It's the first genuine compliment I've received in months that didn't pertain to my tits or my ass, and I drink it like wine. I'm left with a warm, fuzzy buzz. If he thought the idea was stupid, he would have said as much. He's had no problem offering rude remarks thus far. This gives me hope. Maybe my idea isn't as far out of reach as I imagined. Let the compliment cut him. It's giving me life.

The miles stretch out behind us as we travel in silence, and the gentle hum of the tires rolling over the pavement pulls me toward sleep. I've been drowsy since I woke up. Whatever drug was used on me must have been a powerful one. I rub my thighs together, and the ache between my legs reminds me of the hell I endured while unconscious. Yes.

That drug was powerful as fuck. My hand goes to my throat, but I pull my fingers away before they can press into the bruises on my neck. I almost forgot I'd covered them with makeup to avoid any questions. Even though I don't have a reason to feel embarrassed, I can't stop the shame from welling inside me. I wrap my arms around myself, providing the comfort I crave.

"Are you cold?" His voice cuts through the darkness, and he reaches to turn on the heat.

I place my hand over his and shake my head. He recoils from my touch, and my stomach sinks. Does he actually view me as a filthy creature? He probably rubs the seats down with bleach every time I exit his car. How can he go from being concerned about my comfort to disgusted in the blink of an eye? This is torture for both of us. I can't fathom why he'd agree to this when he can't stand the sight of me.

I've had enough.

"Turn the car around," I say. "I'll pay for the gas and your time, but I think it's best if I just go home. This was a terrible idea."

He grits his teeth and cracks his neck, rolling his shoulders to release pent-up tension. He has no reason to be so tense. "No, I'm taking you to the cabin. What's the problem?"

"Since you snatched your hand away like I have the plague, I can only assume I'm the fucking problem. I'm not dirty, Ambrose."

"Sounds like you're projecting," he says with a smirk. "Don't try to pin your insecurities on me."

"Why else would you pull away like that?"

He pushes his hand toward my face, flipping it back and forth in front of my eyes. "Do you see these scars? Did you ever consider that *maybe* I don't want you to see or feel them?"

"Did you ever consider that *maybe* I don't fucking care about them?" I scoff and push his hand away. "Now who's projecting?"

That shuts him up. He tightens his grip on the steering wheel and goes back to grinding his teeth. If he isn't careful, he'll end up with dust for molars.

"How'd you get the scars, anyway?" I ask.

"Story time's over. Take a nap or something."

Fair enough. I guess we all have things we don't want to share. I go back to staring out the window and wondering why his bad attitude hurts my feelings. It's not like I like him or anything. Yeah, he's attractive. Yeah, he's brooding and mysterious.

Yeah, I might have a problem.

Ambrose

SHE DOESN'T GO to sleep, but at least she's quiet now. It gives me a moment to finish mulling over what she said. It shouldn't have changed anything, but it does. The two opposing sides of my mind grip the rope of indecision and dig in their heels.

She's a whore, which makes her the perfect target.

No. She has dreams. She wants to make something more of her life.

She's still a whore. Now she's just a whore with dreams.

I steal a glance at her. Would this be easier if she wasn't

so beautiful? Maybe I should have picked a Tuesday-after-noon stripper. A girl who didn't have such full lips or a perfect nose or a single dimple that pops onto her right cheek when she smiles. I should have picked a girl with the fake tits I can't stand instead of full, natural breasts that make my mouth water.

I need to stop. Thinking about how seductive she is only makes things worse, and by things, I mean the ache in my balls. I need to kill her sooner rather than later, but I have to feel her around me one more time before I do. That's all I'll allow myself. Any more than that and I'll be too tempted to keep her around.

"Oh, can we stop at the next exit?" she asks. "There's a really good diner that makes the best burger I've ever had, and I haven't eaten since yesterday."

I want to say no. We still have a ten-hour drive ahead of us, and I want to finish this play before the sun sets on tomorrow. But maybe it won't hurt to let her have the last meal she wants. Granted, I doubt she'd pick a greasy burger from a roadside flytrap for her last meal if she knew she'd never eat anything again, but this is the best I can do. I ease the car onto the exit ramp and turn to her for directions.

She points and guides me down side streets with an excited gleam to her eyes. It's almost endearing. When we pull up to the building, it's not at all what I expected. From the animated way she directed me, I figured we'd end up somewhere nice, but this place is a dump. Save for the N in the massive DINER sign perched on the roof, the neon lights have abandoned their stations. The busted parking lot looks as if it was paved when asphalt was first invented, then never touched again. Trash tumbleweeds roll past.

"Are you sure this is the right place?" I ask. We're more

likely to get a hefty dose of food poisoning than a good burger here.

She nods and opens her door, then leans back into the car when I don't move. "Aren't you coming?"

With raised eyebrows, I stare at her. She can't be serious.

"Suit yourself," she says with a shrug.

Dirty windows line the diner, giving me a clear (enough) view as she waltzes inside and chooses a booth seat right in front of me. Without even sparing a second glance in my direction, she lifts a menu and runs her finger over it. A man at the bar turns on his stool and eyes her with a grin. He whispers something to his burly friend, and that's enough to get me out of the Jeep. I head inside before they can descend on her like vultures.

Despite how decrepit the place looks, the interior has been kept clean. The tables would gleam if their varnish hadn't been worn down to a dull finish. My feet don't stick to the floor, which means they mop the checkered tiles on a regular basis. Maybe it won't hurt to grab a bite.

I drop into the seat in front of her, and the men at the bar turn away, their smiles evaporating from their faces. Mission accomplished.

"So you decided to join me?" she says with a smile as she lowers the menu. Smug satisfaction lights her face and accentuates the dimple in her cheek.

"You said you were paying for the food, and I'm not one to turn down a free meal."

"If you order the most expensive thing on the menu, it's still cheaper than a bus ticket."

"Is that why you picked this place?" I ask. "Because it's cheap?"

The smile drops from her face. "No, I chose this diner

because I used to come here with my parents. We'd drive to New York for dance competitions a few times a year, and we'd always stop here on our way home. It was a tradition."

A waitress approaches our table and asks for our drink orders. I order a Coke, but Oaklyn requests some special blackberry concoction from their vintage soda fountain. When the waitress delivers it to our table, I hardly have words. The glass is twice the size of mine, and I don't know where she plans to put all that liquid.

With wide eyes, I motion to her drink. "You don't plan to drink all that, do you? We'll have to stop nine times before we're even out of Pennsylvania."

"I'll use the bathroom before we leave. I have a strong bladder." She pulls the monstrosity toward her and takes a massive sip through her straw. "Besides, when will I have the chance to come here again? Probably not for a very long time."

Probably not ever, I think. Guilt rears its ugly head once more, and I shove it down. It's getting more difficult to deny what I'm feeling for her. How fucking disgusting.

"Let's make this quick," I say. "We need to get back on the road."

We have to reach the cabin so I can finish the job before this girl makes me question my plan. The goal isn't to fall in love and run off into the sunset. Even if I wanted that, she'd never accept me for who I am or what I look like. I don't want her, either. I hate her because she's so much like the woman who took a knife to my body. If I'm not careful, my tragedy will take a knife to my soul. But not if I can strike first.

Chapter Sixteen

Oaklyn

We're almost an hour from the cabin, but I can't hold my bladder any longer. It would be impressive if I'd held it this long, but I've already asked him to stop several times since we left the diner. Four times, to be exact. I squirm in my seat, pressing my thighs together and counting the cars we pass on the interstate to keep my mind from wandering to the pulsing pain in my abdomen. A slight whimper escapes my throat, and Ambrose's head whips toward me.

"Again? Jesus fucking Christ." He aims the Jeep toward the offramp and searches for the nearest gas station. "I told you this would happen."

"I'm sorry for my very normal need to piss," I mutter.

"Pissing is normal, yes, but not every five minutes." He pulls up at a rundown gas station and throws the car into park beside the pumps. "Make it quick."

With a huff, I get out and slam the door behind me. A metal bell rings when I enter the gas station, and the atten-

123

dant behind the counter leers at me as I head toward the back of the store in search of a place to relieve myself.

"You gotta go around the back of the building," he calls. "You also gotta buy something. We ain't running a charity here."

I snatch the first thing I see from the rack beside me—a bag of chips that are probably as stale as this man's soul—and rush toward the counter. My hand works into my pocket, and I pull out a five. I'm almost desperate enough to leave the change and the chips behind, but every dollar counts right now. It's a good thing I waited, because he slides a key attached to a long stick back to me, along with my change.

"Thanks," I say. I gather everything into my hands and shuffle out of the building.

Late-morning sun beams down on my skin, and cotton clouds hang in the sky. A lone sparrow pecks at a few soggy french fries lying in a puddle on the pavement. I open the bag of chips to toss it a few as I rush past, but it flies off. I dump them near the ground by a trash can and throw away the bag. Hopefully the little bird will come back and enjoy the dry snack I've left it. I'm only sorry I didn't have more time to put them somewhere a bit cleaner.

I round the corner of the building and nearly collide with a couple of drunks hanging out on the sidewalk. For someone who isn't running a charity, the station owner sure doesn't seem to mind the two brown-baggers hanging around the bathroom door. I guess they bought the booze inside. The acrid scent of spilled urine claws toward me as I swing open the door, and I make a mental note to bathe twice when I reach the cabin. I go to lock it behind me, but there's no way to turn the deadbolt on this side.

"Fuck, fuck, fuck," I whisper as I scramble to unbutton my shorts. I'll just have to be quick.

Hovering over the filthy toilet seat, I breathe a sigh of relief as the pressure in my gut lessens. The feeling is only second to a really good orgasm. My eyes drift shut until I've completely emptied everything in the tank, then I reach for the toilet paper in the little silver holder to my right. A cardboard roll brushes against my fingertips. More whispered curses explode from my lips, and I search around the bathroom for something to wipe with. Men have it so easy. They only need to shake the dribble away. I wiggle my ass to see if I can achieve the same effect, but it doesn't work. Not wanting to sit in piss-damp panties for the rest of the drive, I groan and hobble toward the paper-towel dispenser with my shorts around my calves. I don't enjoy the thought of dragging that stiff crap through my crotch, but it beats the fuck out of the alternative.

As soon as I've pulled a few of the rough sheets of brown paper from the dispenser, a sound catches my attention and I freeze. Footsteps. They crunch across the gritty sidewalk outside, and the shuffling gait nears the bathroom door.

"Someone's in here!" I shout as I run the paper towel across my tender skin with a grimace. It feels like sandpaper, especially when it grates against the tears between my legs.

The footsteps stop outside the door, and someone raps against the metal.

"I'm almost done!" I call. I yank up my shorts, flush the paper towel—because fuck this guy's plumbing—and turn on the faucet to wash my hands. I don't know why I expected soap, but I'm still disappointed when I don't see any. The disinfectant spray on the back of the toilet tempts me, but I settle for water alone. As I grip a few of the useless paper towels to dry my hands, my heart refuses to beat.

The door's reflection glares at me from the dirty mirror. It's only open a crack, but an unmistakable eye peers through the tiny opening. Fine hairs rise along the back of my neck. A panicked cramp squeezes my stomach.

The eye blinks, and it's enough to break my frozen state. I move toward the door and put my weight against it, wedging my sneaker at the bottom in a desperate bid to keep the hunk of metal from opening again. I close my eyes and hope I only imagined it; maybe my stalker issue has caused me to see something that wasn't there.

Then the door moves. Whoever is out there is very real, and they want to get inside.

I press my shoulder against the cool metal and scramble to keep my feet planted. I've used my good leg against the door, but my busted ankle cries out any time I'm forced to rely on it as backup. Fear grips my lungs in a chokehold, and I struggle for every breath. I can't keep this up much longer.

"Help!" I scream, but I don't know who I expect to come running. Ambrose is too far away to hear me, and I doubt he'd come to my rescue anyway. But what other option do I have? "Please! Ambrose, help me!"

Each terrified sound only seems to fuel my attacker's need to get to me. The door rocks against me with renewed force. Adrenaline rushes through my veins, leaving me light-headed and weak. I gasp for air between cries for help. But it's no use. I'll have to make a run for it.

I step away from the door and allow it to open. Then I come face to face with my attacker.

Ambrose

WHAT THE FUCK is taking so long? Either she has no concept of time or she needed to do more than piss. Whatever the reason, I'm sick of waiting. I lock up my Jeep and jog toward the back of the building, the way I saw her head when she left the gas station with a bathroom key in her hand. As soon as I round the corner, her muffled screams reach me.

I rush past the wino perched on the sidewalk, knocking him onto his back as I barrel by. The brown bag falls from his dirty fist and sends a spray of booze across the pavement. His garbled curses fall on deaf ears. I can only hear the sound of scuffling feet behind the bathroom door. Someone is trying to take what belongs to me, but it sounds like my tragedy is giving them one hell of a fight.

I take a step back and aim my shoulder at the door before ramming against it. The metal hinges squeak, and a thud resounds in the tiny space as the door collides with someone's back. They move away, and I'm able to push it wide open.

Sunlight fills the bathroom, and I spot Oaklyn. She's backed against the wall. Tendrils of red hair fall from her disheveled ponytail, and she grips a long stick in her shaking hand. Her chest rises and falls as she sucks air through gritted teeth. A wild look blazes in her green eyes. I have never seen something more fierce and beautiful in my life.

The man turns to face me, and I'm overjoyed to see the long scratches carved into the side of his stubbled cheek.

Beads of blood dot the red lines. His glassy eyes blink slowly as he takes me in, his gaze running over my frame. He can't see the taut muscles beneath my jacket, but he doesn't need to. My size is enough to make him think twice. Too bad he doesn't have a choice. When he touched my tragedy, he lost the right to walk away. He'll be lucky if he can ever walk again when I'm finished with him.

My hand shoots forward and grips the front of his shirt. He tries to argue, the words tangling around his tongue, but I refuse to give him a chance to speak. I raise him up a bit before I bring my other fist around in a jab that rattles his jaw, then I snatch him out of the bathroom. His head clangs against the metal doorframe as I swing his body into the sunlight. A deep groan pours from his mouth, and his eyes roll in his head. I've dazed him, which is a shame. I want him to feel everything I'm about to do to him.

Oaklyn emerges from the bathroom as I continue to pummel his face with my fist. I expect her to run for the Jeep or beg me to stop, but she surprises me when she steps behind him and brings up her shin in a swift kick to the man's groin. My stomach tightens because I've seen how defined her legs are. That had to hurt.

"You fucking creep!" she screams into his face, but I'm pretty sure he doesn't hear her because he's close to passing out at this point.

Blood gushes from his nose and busted lip. His right eye has begun to swell, and I'm almost certain I've freed two of the yellowed teeth from his mouth. But it's not enough. I need more. I release my grip on his shirt, and he collapses to the pavement in a limp heap. His hands rise in a feeble attempt to cover his face, but that's not what I'm going for anyway. I'm a fighter. I know how to work someone over and leave them with something more than a few superficial facial wounds and a concussion.

Like a wild animal, I pounce on him and rain blows to his rib cage until I feel a satisfying crack. Rage flows from my fists in an invisible flood, and I want to drown this fucker in it. As I continue my mindless attack, a mantra plays like a song in my head.

She's mine.

She's mine.

She's mine.

How *dare* he touch her.

Hands close around my arm, and I look up to see who's been stupid enough to stop me from collecting the debt I'm owed. It's Oaklyn, and she's trying to pull me off of him. I snatch my arm away and raise my fist once more, but she pleads for a ceasefire. Her words finally register.

"The station owner is going to call the cops. We have to go."

As much as I would love to keep laying into this piece of absolute shit, I'm not a stupid man. I have no desire to deal with the police. I rise to my feet and send a final kick into the man's rib cage before I turn for the Jeep.

"You don't think they have cameras here, do you?" Oaklyn asks as we pile into the car and pull away from the gas station. She searches the building's roof.

"A dump like this? Doubtful." I eye her as she repairs her ponytail. "He didn't touch you, did he? I mean . . . he didn't—"

"No." She doesn't look at me when she answers.

I don't ask anything else. If she doesn't want to talk about what happened, I won't force it out of her.

Blood darkens the tip of her finger. She broke a nail in the struggle, and it snapped off low enough to expose the quick. I'm struck again by how hard she fought to keep that man away from her. She didn't want him inside her. She didn't want the man from the club either. My brain refuses to admit that she might not be who I've made her out to be in my mind. That she might not be a whore.

Because she *has* to be. For any of this to work, she has to be. The alternative is too horrible.

"Thank you," she says as we pull onto the interstate. "I don't know what would have happened if you hadn't shown up. I didn't think you'd hear me yelling for you, but I guess I'm louder than I thought."

"You called my name?"

She shrugs her shoulders. "Well, yeah. Who else could I call for?"

No one has ever depended on me like this before. What would she think if she knew her protector was also her tormentor? I can't let her find out. Not until the end. If she isn't who I think she is, if she isn't the perfect target I've built her up to be, I'll have to let her go. But if she is . . .

There's only one way to find out. I need to test her.

Chapter Seventeen

Ambrose

A slight thrill runs through my bones when she directs me to turn onto a dirt road ahead—I don't get many chances to test the Jeep's off-road skills in the city—but the feeling is short lived. The red dirt has been packed to smooth perfection without a mudhole in sight. How fucking boring. Even the curves in the narrow path were drawn into the countryside with ease of travel in mind.

We eventually turn off the main strip of dirt and meander down a gravel driveway for nearly a mile. Trees choke out the light, casting dark shadows over the path, even though it's daytime. We're in the middle of nowhere, and it's perfect.

The forest breaks apart, and the house comes into view. Her parents must have an endless store of money if they can afford this property, especially since it sits on the edge of a massive lake. It seems to be the only house in this slough.

I've never seen anything like it, which isn't surprising. None of the foster parents I've lived with had enough money to stay in a place like this for a night, let alone owning such a cabin. Well, maybe they had enough money, but I certainly never saw any of it. I was lucky to receive a sliver of the allotment the state paid them for my care.

I park near the wooden front porch and get out of the Jeep, grabbing my bag from the back before following her to the front door. She pulls a key from beneath the doormat, and I roll my eyes internally. No wonder she was dumb enough to keep her house key beneath the bench cushion at her trailer. She inherited the bad habit from her parents.

Judging by the stuffy air when we step into the cabin, this place hasn't seen a visitor in a very long time. After adjusting the thermostat, Oaklyn leads me up a creaky stair-case and down a hallway. Instead of family pictures, only works of art line the walls. How goddamn pretentious.

She motions to a door near the end. "You can stay in there," she says. "It's the guest bedroom. We don't have wi-fi or cell service out here, but you can always watch television if you get bored." She looks around. "Well, if my parents still have the satellite connected."

I nod, but I have other plans regarding entertainment while I'm here. And all of them involve her. I don't want her to get too comfortable here. Aside from the test I've planned, I need to remind her that her stalker could be anywhere. She needs to remember she's never safe if I want things to work the way I've pictured. I pull a switchblade from my pocket and push it toward her.

"What's that?" she asks. She turns the handle between her fingers.

"Protection," I say. "If your stalker has a way of tracking

you, he might know you're here. We won't be in the same room, so this might buy you some time if he gets to you before I can."

Her eyes widen as she processes what I'm saying, and it takes every ounce of strength in my body to stop the laughter from rising out of my chest. Her stalker didn't need to track her when she literally called him for a ride. It's too perfect.

"Thanks," she mutters. Gripping the blade in shaking hands, she turns for her room.

I step into the bedroom I've been assigned and flick on the light. A lazy ceiling fan churns above the bed. I open a window beside the dresser, but I'm not only interested in getting some fresh air into the room. I need to find a silent way to get to the lower floor, and I'd prefer to avoid those loud-ass stairs. A half roof slopes a few feet below the window. Perfect.

After placing my bag beside the bed, I lie back and wait for nightfall. If I want my plan to have any chance of working, I'll need the darkness. Oaklyn knocks on the door to ask if I want any food from the pantry—dry and canned goods are our only option until we can visit a nearby store—but I tell her no thanks. I'm too excited to eat. Tonight will finally put any doubt to rest. Either she deserves to be the outlet for my long-awaited revenge or she doesn't. And I don't know which one I want it to be.

I have carried this anger for my mother for far too long. It's a bag of bricks on my shoulders, and each time I think about what that woman did to me, I add another to the growing stack. When my mother fashioned her bedcovers into a noose and ended her own life, she piled on a few more and denied me the chance to take the revenge I'm owed. The burden is too much, and I'm ready to shed this weight.

But I'm not ready to say goodbye to Oaklyn.

My stomach sours with this admission. If she hadn't planted this doubt in my mind, I wouldn't find her so alluring. She's a whore. She removes her clothes and allows men to feel her up for money. Her reasons for doing so are compelling, but they aren't good enough. Still, I can't stop this nagging feeling that I've gotten something wrong, and I can't move forward until I know for sure.

I mull these things over until the sun has slipped far below the horizon. By the time it grows dark enough to get started, I'm nearly frothing at the mouth with anticipation.

I ease out of the open window and creep to the edge of the slanted half roof, then drop to the ground. I'll use the ladder I spotted near the matching outbuilding to get back up there if I can't manage it on my own.

Before I enter the downstairs, I go to my Jeep for the little bag of acorns I've stashed beneath the driver's seat. If everything goes how I think it will, I'll need to leave a little souvenir behind for her. I grab my knife and tuck its sheath into my pants. The thought of her panic when she realizes her stalker has followed her all the way to this cabin—when she realizes her stalker is *in* the fucking cabin and he drove her here—sends a rush of adrenaline straight to my brain.

Using the key beneath the mat, I let myself in through the front door and search for the breaker box. I find it in the laundry room and cut the power to the house. Now it's a race against time.

Even if a home seems silent, it's never as quiet as when all power has ceased to flow through its walls. That silence is loud enough to wake even the lightest sleepers. I can only hope she tries to talk herself down from panic before coming into my room to ask for help. I guess I should also hope she comes to me for help. Otherwise, my plan was for nothing. She seems like a pretty independent woman, bound and determined to do things for herself, but she's also in a precarious situation. I've planted enough fear into her heart, so she'll likely be too terrified to search for the source of the problem on her own.

I exit the house and lock the door, then slip the key beneath the mat. As I race around the side of the building, I consider grabbing the ladder but decide to try pulling myself onto the roof via a jump first. My choice is the right one because I reach the roof's edge with ease and pull myself onto the rough shingles with minimal effort. My muscles are good for more than throwing punches.

Back in the bedroom, I stash the bag of acorns within my bag and flop onto the mattress. I try to slow each breath that pours in and out of my lungs. A light sweat slicks my back and forehead, but I can blame that on the temperature. Then again, if I'm so overheated, why would I still be fully dressed? I rip off my shirt and pants and toss them to the floor.

And I wait.

Oaklyn

My eyes spring open. I try to blink away the wave of disorientation, but a wild panic squeezes my chest in a vise grip. Where am I? *The cabin in Wisconsin.* What am I doing here? *Escaping your psycho stalker.* Why is it so quiet?

My inner voice has no answer.

I feel around the side table for the bedside lamp and find the switch, but nothing happens when I click it back and forth. Thinking the bulb has gone bad, I get onto my knees on the mattress and reach for the cord attached to the ceiling fan. I'm met with more darkness. The power is out.

Goosebumps born of fear prickle my skin. I've never been afraid of the dark, even as a child, but having a stalker can certainly change your outlook on things. It can make you feel unsafe in situations you would normally breeze through. This would be one of those situations.

I grab my shorts from the bedside table and slide them over my legs, then feel my way through the dark until I reach the door. I grab the knife from the top of the dresser, but after seeing the way Ambrose beat the living shit out of that man, I don't think I'll need it. He's my weapon, and I need to get to him.

"Ambrose?" I call into the hall. When he doesn't answer, I tiptoe to his door and knock. "Hey, are you up?"

His feet shuffle toward the door, and it swings open. I can't see him, but his masculine scent rushes toward me on a puff of night air breezing through the open window behind his silhouette. Black leather. Some sort of exotic spice. A twinge between my legs replaces my fear for a moment.

"What's going on?" he asks in a husky voice, and I feel awful because I've clearly disturbed his sleep.

My eyes begin to adjust to the darkness, and I look at anything other than the way the moonlight catches on the defined muscles carved into his shirtless chest. "I'm not sure. The power seems to be out. Could you check the breaker box?"

"Maybe Mommy and Daddy forgot to pay the power bill." He starts to close the door, but I wedge my foot in the opening.

"Look, I'm not usually the type to get scared shitless from a power outage, but considering the reason I've come to this cabin, it would be really nice if you could help me. Please?" I place my hand on his, remembering his disdain for my touch only once my fingers graze his slick scars. But he doesn't pull away.

He lets out an exasperated sigh. "Okay, fine." He grips my hand and pulls me into the room, then leads me to the bed and pushes me backward until I'm sitting. "I'll check the breaker box in fifteen minutes if the power hasn't come back, but I'm not risking my neck on those steep-as-fuck stairs unless I have to. Until then, you can stay in here."

That option would be great if a fresh fear hadn't reared its ugly head. I'm less afraid of the power outage than the way I feel now that I've seen the moonlight gliding over his muscles. I consider asking him to close the curtain, but that wouldn't erase the overpowering manly scent or the warmth radiating from his body. He folds his arms over his broad chest, and the shift in his stance highlights the package in his boxers. The moon literally sends a beam of light right along the edge, outlining his bulge in 4K clarity. My mouth waters and my nipples press against my cami. I fold my arms over my chest so the moonlight can't betray me as well.

What the fuck is wrong with me? I'm like a bitch in heat. I should be focused on ensuring my safety, not eye-fucking my chauffeur.

I clear my throat and set the knife on the side table beside the bed. "Sorry it's so hot in here."

He sits beside me, and the mattress sinks from his weight and pushes me closer to him. Our shoulders are nearly touching. "It's not your fault."

His body heat courses over my arm. He's a furnace, and I want to burn alive.

I need to stop. "Maybe I should just go downstairs and check the breaker myself." I get to my feet, but my shitty ankle gives way and sends me sideways . . . right on top of him.

He grips my body with his hands to keep me from rolling to the floor, and I'm draped across his lap like a naughty schoolgirl who's about to get a paddling from the headmaster. Now instead of seeing the outline of his cock, I feel it pressing into my ribs. And it's so much bigger than it looked. And it's hard.

I get to my feet, but he keeps his hands on my waist as I stand in front of him. His warm grip runs down to my hips, and I don't stop him. I absolutely should, but I don't. I'm too shocked. All this time, I thought he hated me—I thought I hated *him*—but I guess the animosity between us has been some weird form of foreplay. That's the only way I can rationalize the electric heat between us right now.

"What are you doing?" I ask, but it's a stupid fucking question. I know what he's doing, and I want him to do it.

"Shh."

His fingers sink into my sides, and he pulls me closer. After raising the hem of my cami with his teeth, his lips move along my stomach, his tongue spinning warm circles across my skin. I allow my hands to move to his biceps, to feel the taut muscles tensing just beneath the surface. Ridges ripple under my fingertips. I can only assume these are more scars. He's covered in them, but I somehow find them more of a turn on than a turn off. This man has survived something horrific. He has beaten something with his spirit instead of his fist.

A shiver runs through me as his hands explore beneath my shirt. He teases me with his tongue and teeth until he brings a moan from my lips.

Then he stops.

He fucking stops.

"I think it's been fifteen minutes," he whispers against my flesh. Warm breath brushes across the wet lines left behind by his kisses, and I want to melt. But why did he stop? What sort of cruel game is this? I'm ready to pounce on him and ride him like I'm going for the eight-second bell, and *now* he wants to check the breaker box?

He rises to his feet, and it takes everything in me to stop myself from yanking down his boxers and begging him to stay with my mouth. The rustle of fabric fills the silence as he puts on his pants and leaves the room. Once the door closes behind him, I pace beside the bed. No matter how I sort through this weird situation in my mind, it doesn't make any sense. He wanted me—I *felt* how much he wanted me—and even though I don't know why, I wanted him.

My foot collides with something by the bed. Nylon fabric wraps around my ankle. I kick it free, and something hard skitters across the floor. Feeling around, I realize the strap of his bag wound around my foot and I've knocked something out of it. I'll have to clean it up before he gets back so he doesn't think I was snooping. God, how embarrassing.

The ceiling fan whirs to life, and the gentle buzz of electricity fills the house once more. Whatever was wrong, Ambrose has fixed it. Now I just have to figure out how to fix whatever the fuck is wrong with me. I reach for the cord on the ceiling fan and light fills the room. This cabin has been empty for so long that the breakers probably—

Ice fills my veins, turning my blood to sleet. I can't breathe. My heart is the only functioning organ in my body, and it pounds a rapid beat in my chest. My eyes register what I knocked out of his bag, and my brain finally processes the chilling truth.

Ambrose is my stalker.

Chapter Eighteen

Ambrose

My plan didn't go as I expected. Well, it did, but I'm still struggling with doubt. She wanted me, but I wanted her too. I can't deny the way my body reacts to her. I stop at the bottom of the stairs and grip the railing. A crossroads waits before me, and I still don't know which way I should turn.

The risers creak beneath my feet as I climb toward the awaiting juncture. If I go in that room and fuck her the way my body begs me to—the way *her* body begs me to—I don't know if I can live with myself. It goes against everything inside me. She didn't want the man at the club or the dirty vagrant outside the gas station, but she would allow a scarred street fighter to get between her legs. A man other women look at with a disgust they can't hide. She might be a choosy whore, but she's still a whore. She's still too much like my mother.

I reach the top of the stairs and pause. Something thuds inside the bedroom, and the sound of a whimper follows. What is she doing? I rush to the door and open it in time to see her wide green eyes outside the window, her fingers gripping the sill as she dangles above the sloping half roof. Then she drops. I rush toward her, and my foot slams down on something hard. Cursing beneath my breath, I lift my foot and watch as a single acorn rolls beneath the bed.

God. Fucking. Damnit. She knows.

She won't get far in bare feet and on a busted ankle, so I grab my shoes and slip them on, then throw on a sleeveless t-shirt before I follow her. The knife I gave her lies on the small table beside the bed, forgotten. How unfortunate. I tuck it into my pocket so it can't be used against me later. I look out the window and see her running toward the woods. By the time I catch her, I'll be so amped up I won't be able to control myself. But that might be a good thing. I feel for my knife and lean through the open window as her pale skin disappears into the trees. "There's no need to run, Oaklyn!" I yell, but she doesn't even spare a glance behind her.

I drop from the window and land on the half roof with a thud, and I almost worry I'll sink through the shingles and land on the hardwoods covering the floor on the lower level. Instead, my sneakers grip the roof and guide me to the edge. My second descent is a bit more graceful. I sink into the soft ground and turn to face the trees.

"Oaklyn!" I scream into the darkness. "Stop running and face your tormenter. You're braver than this." The sound of bare feet tromping through dry leaves greets my ears, but it's growing more distant. I race into the forest to catch up with her.

Thorny vines scrape my skin, but the marks they leave behind only blend with my scars. These shallow wounds will fade, unlike the deep cuts my mother drove into my skin.

My eyes adjust to the darkness as much as they can. It helps me see the disturbed brush a little better, but not much. The leafy canopy diffuses most of the moonlight. I'm mostly guided by adrenaline and the scent of her fear, but this internal bloodhound serves me well. I rush forward until I spot her ahead, her body puncturing the forest, twisting and contorting through the trees in ways I can't. I'm too big for that. I expected her to be piss-poor prey, but my tragedy has surprised me again. At this rate, there's no way I'll catch up to her, and I desperately need to catch her. If she escapes me, she's sure to turn my ass in to the police. She knows too much now.

My heart races against my chest as I close the gap between us. She's slowing, a limp growing more obvious on her right side. Her injury rears its glorious head to cripple her and give me the advantage. It ruined her life once, and it's fully prepared to do it again. This time more permanently.

"Your ankle is giving you trouble, isn't it?" I shout toward her.

She curses and stumbles against a thin trunk that nearly cracks beneath her insignificant weight. Her gait grows more ragged. The pain coursing through her leg and foot must be terrible, because she's struggling to keep herself between the trees now. She stumbles into them like a pinball thrust into a rectangular box filled with branches and bushes. I slow down a little, enjoying her desperate attempt to escape. The ghosts of her past have wounded her as much as mine have wounded me. Unfortunately for her, my wounds spur me on while hers slow her down.

Even though I'm no longer running, I'm drawing closer

because she's fully limping at this point. I'm near enough to hear her strangled whimpers and each gulp of air she fights to take in. As the trees grow thinner and we near the edge of a meadow, I see my opening and rush forward. My shoulder collides with her back, and I wrap my arms around her as I spear her toward the ground. The soft earth spreads beneath us, and her scream punctuates the silent woods.

"Please, don't," she gasps, pleading to any light inside me, but it's too late. This all-consuming darkness has overtaken my eyes, and I see nothing else.

I flip her onto her back, raise my hand to her throat, and enjoy the desperate movement of her skin beneath my palm as she tries to swallow. Her hands wrap around my wrist. Nails claw at my skin, tearing and biting, but I won't be deterred.

"Why did you run from me?" I ask, putting weight into my hand.

"You know why," she chokes out. She kicks her legs, flailing the way I longed for in her bedroom.

"Because I fucked you?" My cock hardens in an instant at the memory of defiling her as she slept.

She squirms beneath me again, gripping my wrist with renewed strength, but she doesn't answer the question.

"You ran because you didn't like what I did to your whore cunt."

She stalls beneath me. "I'm not a whore." That single word weighs her down more than I do. Rage replaces the panic in her eyes, laying a speed bump of doubt beneath the fiery chariot racing toward her.

Some women don't like to be called a whore, even when the ugly shoe fits, but her disdain for the word is . . . different. I still can't decide if she's delusional and wants me to use more politically correct terminology or if she really doesn't believe she's exactly what I say she is. Maybe she needs a refresher.

"Do I need to show you the video, Oaklyn? Show you how much of a whore you are?"

She grits her teeth and stares into my eyes. "Do I need to show you a dictionary? I'm not a fucking whore."

That's enough of that. I adjust my grip on her body and flip her onto her belly, pinning her down with my crotch against her ass. Pulling my knife from my hip, I bring it to her throat and press the flat side against her skin so she can fully grasp what she's up against. Her fingers grip the sparse meadow grass and sink into the earth. It's the only movement she can make with a blade so close to such a vulnerable part of her body. I brush tendrils of sweat-soaked hair from her cheek, and my fingers slide through a river of tears. I absorb the liquid hurt into my skin, letting it live there. With my free hand, I yank down her shorts and rub her tears between her legs.

So soft.

So warm.

She strains against me as I work open my jeans, but she can't free herself from my need. Her thighs clench. It's meant to keep me out, but it only makes it easier to guide myself to the heat between her legs as I push inside her. So deep in her struggle, she feels incredible. So fucking tight.

I lean down so that my mouth hangs just beside her ear, then I curl my hips forward until I feel her end. Turning the blade in my hand, I press the thin edge against her throat. "I'm going to give you your finale, my tragedy."

"No, no, please!" she begs.

I move my free hand to her hip to give myself more leverage, but I stop. My fingers run over something I know all too well. Lines of raised flesh. Several of them. A mosaic of familiar marks.

"What's this?" I ask, tracing the ridges along her hip.

"You aren't the only one with scars," she cries.

It's the first time she's mentioned my scars. How long has she been holding on to her opinion of them? I halt the straining motion of my hips, keeping flush against her ass.

"I don't know if you noticed them before," she pants, "but feel my hips. My thighs."

I saw the scars on her thighs in the car and when I fucked her. But I didn't see her hips.

"Are these from your accident?" I ask.

"Some of them," she says, "but I put most of them there myself."

"Then we aren't the same."

"Someone caused your scars. Someone caused mine too. I just held the blade."

Her words outline a painful story, and that bothers me. I don't want to feel sympathy for her. I don't want her to become a person. I want to use and discard her. That's it.

Unwilling to let her confuse me further, I harness as much anger as I can and push the blade against her neck again. But something stops me. It *can't* stop me. I've gone too far. With my cock buried in her unconsenting cunt, I'm *still* going too far.

"Please don't kill me yet," she begs. "Give me a few days to show you who I am, then you can decide. Please, Ambrose."

When she says my name, doubt sinks its teeth into my gut and rattles my bones in a death roll. And I hate it. I should end her right now. Here in these woods, deep in the middle of nowhere, I could commit the perfect crime and exact my long-awaited revenge. I could finally free myself of these violent thoughts and cleanse these scars with blood.

So why can't I do it?

Her warmth pulses around my cock. Maybe it wouldn't hurt to give her a few more days. A short stay of execution in exchange for something I need just as much as revenge. "You want to live, tragedy?" I ask.

She nods and the blade strains against her neck. "Yes," she whimpers.

I ease the knife away from her and replace it in its sheath. "Then let my come be the only thing that can save you."

I pull back and push into her again. She becomes a small and complacent thing, letting out pained groans as I grind her into the dirt and fuck her harder. Selfishly. Though she tenses and tightens around me, she doesn't try to get free. She consumes every inch I give her and clutches the wispy sprigs of grass in her clenched fists.

"Raise your hips a little. Let me go deeper," I growl.

She does as I command, arching her back so that I can push further inside her. I draw closer to my release with each thrust, but her hair has fallen over her cheek again. I want to see her face. Leaning forward, I grind against her ass and pull back the red curtain to reveal her green eyes. Her full lips. Her fear.

It's enough to send me over the edge.

"Take my come like a good whore," I growl in her ear as I fill her. I bask in her warmth for several more thrusts, then I pull out of her. Her body relaxes, and she doesn't make a move to run as I ease away from her. Good. "You can get up now."

She gets onto her knees and raises her shorts without bothering to clean up the mess between her legs. As she struggles to her feet, I fight the urge to help her. It's her own fault. All of this is her fault.

I fold my arms over my chest and study her. "Don't try to run again. It won't end well for you."

She nods her head without looking at me and rubs her arms with her hands. She must be cold.

I turn and motion for her to follow me, and like a whipped dog, she does. "We should get back to the house. The play is almost over, but I'm willing to see what surprises you have in store for the final act."

And it will be the final act. There will be no encore. When the curtain falls in a few days, this traveling show will come to an end. I refuse to back down next time, no matter how the uncertainty rallies against my purpose. After all, a tragedy can't have a happy ending.

Chapter Nineteen

Oaklyn

I limp through the woods on the way back to the cabin, keeping some distance between me and my attacker. My stalker. What the fuck have I gotten myself into? I nearly fucked him willingly. Had he not stopped to check the breaker box, I would have allowed him between my legs.

The breaker box. He cut it off.

I fight the urge to repeatedly slam my palm against my forehead and rave about what an absolute moron I've been. Though I've never considered myself a genius, I at least counted myself among the intelligent—an egocentric distinction I can no longer claim. It doesn't take Sherlock fucking Holmes to put the pieces together now. The way he always seemed to show up at the club when I finished my shift. The fact that only my stripper clothes were destroyed when my line of work disgusts him. His willingness to drive me, a complete stranger, halfway across the country. It's so obvious.

But not all of it was so clear, I remind myself. How had

he recorded the video in the private area? How had he plastered pictures all over the dressing room and left an acorn and some jizz in my shoes without drawing any attention?

Maybe I shouldn't be so hard on myself.

A sharp pain cuts a path from my ankle to my knee, and I stumble against a tree. Rough bark scrapes against my cheek. I try to keep from making a sound, but a whimper squeaks out of me. Ambrose keeps going. He's walking pretty fucking proud of himself while I'm absolutely crippled. He wouldn't have caught me if it wasn't for this damn ankle. Just one more way my injury has affected my life.

"Keep up," he calls over his shoulder.

I stare at the back of his tousled hair. It's not brown. Not blonde. Somewhere in the middle. I've sat beside him several times now, but I haven't really studied him like this. Inching through the forest, I have nowhere else to look.

"My ankle hurts," I say, dropping to the forest floor to rub away the ache in my useless limb.

He stops and turns to face me, his brown eyes narrowing. "Your ankle wouldn't hurt if I had killed you like I was supposed to. Would you like me to remedy that?"

Maybe that would be better at this point. I'm returning to my parents' cabin with a man who plans to use me for several days before ultimately ending me. I stupidly asked for more time because I hoped it would give me a chance to prove my life is worth living. But is it? Now that I've been placed outside the normalcy of everyday life, I can look through the window and see my existence for what it really is. I don't like what I see, so why would he? I'm prolonging my suffering at this point, but the human need to keep sucking air won't allow me to give up just yet.

So I don't answer him.

My silence doesn't seem to sit well with him, because he

stalks toward me with clenched fists and a set jaw. I tremble harder with every crunch of the leaf litter beneath his shoes. When he reaches me, I clench my eyelids shut and await the moment he unleashes his frustration on me. Well, I wait for him to do more than he already has. Then his arms wrap around me and . . . I'm rising?

He cradles me against his chest and takes a step forward. While allowing him to carry me would be of benefit to my busted leg, the warmth of his hands on my bare skin makes me uncomfortable. I wriggle in his grasp and try to free myself, but he stops and clutches me tighter, his fingertips digging into my muscles.

"Do you want help or do you want to keep walking on your crippled ankle?" he snaps, his muscles straining to contain me.

I don't want his fucking help. I don't want his hands on me. He's the reason my ankle feels like I've taken a jack-hammer to the joint. But I *can't* keep walking on it. The metal plate grinds beneath my flesh and sends a bolt of pain into my hip with each unstable step. So I stop squirming. I relax every muscle in my body, hoping he enjoys carrying my dead weight.

Asshole.

The foliage thickens around us, and we reach the part of the woods where the thorny vines run rampant. They shredded my skin on the way in, and I brace myself for more of the same on the way out. With the way he's holding me, I'll bear the brunt of it.

Seeming to realize this, he stops and sets me on my feet, then gives me his back and squats down. "Climb on."

Allowing him to pick me up was one thing, but will-ingly draping my body over him and pressing my boobs into his back is another. I go to take a step, determined to do this on my own, but my body refuses to cooperate. My arm flails for a nearby tree trunk, but I only succeed in slicing my palm on a vine. "Fuck, fuck, fuck," I whisper as I pull my hand to my chest.

"Would you stop being so stubborn and just get on my goddamn back? I'd like to make it to the cabin before next week."

"Fuck you," I say under my breath. If he hears me, he doesn't react.

But he's right, as much as I hate to admit it. Getting myself through the tangle of branches, bushes, and vines will take forever. The cabin might only be one hundred yards away, but that's miles on this ankle.

Closing my eyes and heaving a sigh, I step closer and position myself against his back with my arms wrapped around his neck. I'm braless, and I can only hope he doesn't feel the hard points my nipples have tightened into. It has nothing to do with him and everything to do with the chill in the air. He hooks his powerful arms beneath my thighs and rises with little effort, then releases his hold once he's standing.

"You'll need to hook your legs around me," he says. "I can't move shit out of the way without the use of my arms."

I hate the way his deep voice vibrates through his back and sinks into my core, but I grit my teeth and do as he says. As we weave through the compact forest, I duck my head and press my cheek against the back of his neck to shield my face. His leathery scent rushes into my nose. Part of my body recoils with disgust, but the other part—namely my lower half—wants me to keep breathing in that glorious smell. I try to appease the opposing sides of my brain by sniffing, just not as deeply.

Lights glimmer in the distance, filtering through the

leaves and dispelling the darkness. We break through the tree line, and he slows to a stop. As he squats again, I ease off his back and steady myself by gripping his shoulders. I go to take a step forward, but pain rockets up my leg and I let out a yelp. Cue an Ambrose eye roll. I want to scream into his face and remind him once more that this is all his fault, but I don't have the chance because I'm swept into his arms again as he carries me toward the house. He brings me in through the back door and sets me on the couch. I bat his hands away the moment my back hits the thick cushion, but he grips my wrists and pins my arms above my head. Leaning down, he places his face against my neck.

And he inhales.

"What are you doing?" I ask, panic climbing up my throat on a wave of bile.

He stops. "The same thing you did to me." His warm breath glides over my skin and brings goosebumps to the surface.

Now I'm just mortified because he knew I was sniffing him the entire time I rode him like a pack mule. I can't get a word out, even if I wanted to. I'm ashamed because of this undeniable attraction I feel for the man who has been tormenting me for weeks. The man who drugged me and took what he wanted. What I would have willingly given him had he asked.

None of it makes sense! He's not unattractive. He's scarred, sure, but there's an undeniable handsomeness beneath those scars. Why the fuck would he need to stalk and assault me?

He releases my hands and goes to the kitchen. He rifles through the cabinets and drawers, finds what he's looking for, and begins filling whatever it is with ice. He wraps it with a dishrag he pulls from a drawer, then brings it to me.

"Put this on your ankle," he says, wiggling it in front of my face. "It'll bring the inflammation down."

I take the baggie of ice from him and apply it to my ankle with a wince. I almost thank him, but then I remind myself that this is. His. Fucking. Fault.

He disappears into the pantry and reemerges with an economy-sized jar of peanut butter. As he bends to look for a spoon, his white undershirt rides up his muscular back and reveals even more scars. My breath hitches. His face, head, arms, and back are covered in them, so I can only imagine where else they mark his skin. What the hell happened to him? I know he fights, but those aren't from fighting. When he turns around, he catches me gawking.

"Want a closer look?" He abandons the peanut butter and spoon on the counter and walks toward me. As he nears the couch, he grips the hem of his t-shirt and lifts it away from him. "Maybe looking isn't enough for you." He grabs my hand and runs it along his abs. Along the scars. There are so many.

I don't try to pull away, and that seems to bother him more than if I struggled to free myself from his skin. If he expects me to be repulsed by these marks, he's setting himself up for disappointment. Am I intrigued? Absolutely. But I'm not disgusted.

He drops my hand and returns to the kitchen for his peanut butter without another word. It's almost as if he's looking for a reason to fly off the handle and attack me, and now he's annoyed that I didn't fulfill my side of the bargain. I won't give him a reason to kill me.

I wrack my brain, trying to figure out why he's chosen me as his target and why he feels like he has to end my life. If he's worried I'll rat him out now that I've seen his face, he doesn't have anything to worry about. No one would believe me. He's not the only one who views me as a worthless whore. If I say he assaulted me, he'll just claim it was consensual. That I asked for it. No one believes the woman.

"You don't have to do any of this, Ambrose. You could leave. I didn't call the police after what you did to me, and I won't call them now. Just go. Please."

He stops the spoon before it reaches his mouth, and he tightens his lips as if he's considering it. The spoon lowers. "Why didn't you?"

I can't answer that. He doesn't need to know why; he just needs to know I didn't. I shake my head and focus on the ceiling. "Why are you doing this to me?"

"That's a complex question with an even more complex answer," he says, then he finally shoves the spoon into his mouth. He has no intention of elaborating any further.

I turn away from him and lie on my side, exhausted after my late night hike through the woods. The chill from the ice burrows into my bones and creates a new ache, but I leave it there. That pain is more tolerable than the alternative. I begin to doze, but I snap awake when I hear him rinsing the spoon in the sink. Then he comes closer.

"Time for bed," he says as he scoops me into his arms.

I push against him and try to free myself, but his hold is too strong. "I'm not sleeping in a bed with you."

A smirk slides across his face as he looks down at me, and a shadow darkens his brown eyes. "Oh, you absolutely are. I won't risk you slipping out the window again. Only one of us will leave here alive, tragedy, and I'm not ready to drop the curtain just yet."

The stark realization stares me in the face, and I can't hide from the truth. I'm going to die. I'm going to be murdered because I got into his Jeep. Because I hitchhiked.

As he climbs the stairs with me in his arms, I can only

imagine what I'll have to endure before I draw my last breath. It doesn't help that he's so fucking attractive. If my stalker had been someone like Jake, I would only have to endure situational fear and panic. Now I have to deal with confusion on top of that.

He's a killer, Oaklyn! Think with your head and not your hormones!

"I have to use the bathroom," I blurt.

He lowers me to my feet at the top of the stairs, and I hobble toward the first door on the right. He stays close behind me. I fear he'll demand to watch me relieve myself, but he only wants to check the bathroom to ensure I can't escape. Satisfied with the useless miniature window that only a child could fit through, he leaves and closes the door behind him.

I lower my shorts and sit on the toilet, running through ways to save myself as I piss. There aren't any weapons in here. There aren't even any items that could be repurposed into weapons. The most dangerous item is the seashell soap dish, and that won't do me any good. He looks like he takes harder hits to the head than what I could ever muster. I stupidly left the knife in his room when I panicked and flew out the window. He's probably hidden it now. Without any options—or brilliant ideas—I grab a washcloth from the shelf above the toilet and clean myself as much as I can. As I rub the dirt from my face and rinse it down the drain, I sense him out there.

Listening.

Waiting.

When I exit the bathroom, he's standing there with his arm above his head, resting it against the door frame. That pose would be panty melting if he wasn't such a psycho. He pulls a flask from behind his back and offers it to me.

"For your pain," he says.

How fucking sweet.

I scoff. I'm not taking anything from him. He doesn't have a good track record with mixing drinks.

His hand drops to the handle of his knife and I sigh. I take the flask from him and unscrew the top.

"Good girl," he says with a smirk. "Only take a sip, though. That shit is potent."

With a roll of my eyes, I tilt the flask and let the flavor-less liquid wash over my tongue. It tastes like water, and I consider guzzling a bit more. I'm fucking thirsty. I listen to his advice and take the smallest sip I can, though. The memory of the two shots of vodka isn't that far removed from my mind.

I hand over what I can only assume is night-night juice and allow him to lead me to my bedroom. He checks the window as I sit on the edge of the bed, and I hope he'll allow me to sleep alone once he sees no easy way out of this room. He crushes that hope beneath his ass when he walks to the other side of the bed and sits down.

I'm not sleeping with this man. Nope.

I clamber out of bed, leaning my weight on the night-stand as the pain shoots through me again.

A strong hand reaches out, grips my arm, and drags me back to the mattress. "Where do you think you're going, tragedy?"

"Why do you keep calling me that?" I exhale a defeated breath and lie back, scooting as far from him as I can.

He rests his head on his hand. "Because you're going to have an unhappy ending. I knew this from the moment I met you." He turns off the bedside lamp. "Go to sleep. Tomorrow, we begin act three."

Chapter Twenty

Ambrose

S he doesn't relax as she lies beside me. Each rigid muscle tightens with tension because she's in bed with the thing of her nightmares. Instead of waking up and escaping the monster in her bad dreams, she'll wake up next to it. And I'm enjoying that way too much. I listen in the dark, and her ragged breathing eventually shifts to something soft and even. It was only a matter of time. She didn't get the heavy dose she took from the vodka bottle, but a sip will be enough to keep her knocked out for a while.

Now that she's asleep, I'm left with my thoughts. I had one goal in mind when I agreed to drive her out here, and that was to end things. The perfect opportunity presented itself in the woods, but it only showed me how weak I truly am. Instead of digging a deep grave to hide my unleashed vengeance, I'm lying beside her to ensure she doesn't run off. I keep coming up with excuses to keep her alive, but I can't continue to do this.

Even though I know how this has to end, I want her

around for a few more days. I want to experience more of her. But I'm afraid of what I'll find within her. What if I start to like everything I've hated? I worked too hard and nursed my hatred for too long to let that happen.

It doesn't help that she's trying to find similarities between us. She fails to see that her scars aren't mine. They're hidden in private places, not showcased for the world to see. She doesn't have to wear a leather jacket in the summer heat to keep people from openly staring at her. She may think she understands me, but she has no idea.

The knife on my hip calls to me. I could cut her up and help her understand. Slice her face so she can feel a shred of the shame I've known my entire life. She'd hate who looks back at her in the mirror. Like I do.

I pull the knife from its sheath and shift onto my side. Bringing myself closer to her body, I hold the blade so that it hovers just above her pale skin. I mimic dragging it down her arm and creating a red fissure that would take time to heal. But that flesh would never be as it is now. Pure. Unblemished. A blank canvas. It would become like mine. Ugly. Destroyed. Disgusting. I brush the hair from her face and press the knife against her cheek. The soft skin sinks beneath the weight, and it would only take a little more pressure to bring a line of blood to the surface.

But I can't.

I slide the knife into its sheath and grit my teeth. Why can't I do this?

I reach out and rub my hand down her side, feeling her in ways she won't allow when she's awake. Well, she would have allowed it if she hadn't discovered the acorns. She wanted it. Her soft moan as I kissed her stomach told me so, and that's why I had to stop her. It proves she's the whore

I've made her out to be. Only a cumslut would be so willing to sleep with a scarred monster.

Thinking about the soft sound that rolled from her lips hardens me. It shouldn't, but I can't deny the way my body begs to use her again. I band an arm around her waist and pull her against me so that her ass presses into my pelvis. She doesn't stir. Her heat melts into me, and the scent of soil and sweat reaches my nose. She doesn't smell like the club now. She smells like my untamed thing. Mine.

My hand moves to the front of her neck, and heavy thoughts of squeezing her throat creep into my mind. Instead, I move lower and free her breast from her camisole. The natural curves of that soft mound call to me, begging me to touch. To taste. To enjoy. This would be easier if she had those super-fake tits. I wouldn't be so tempted by her. It's a temptation I shouldn't give in to, but my cock aches for her. Once tonight wasn't enough.

I remove her shorts and rush to release myself from my jeans because this girl has occupied every waking thought I've had since the night she got into my car. I put my cock against her, then slide it between her warm thighs. I'm still haunted by the memory of how it felt to slip inside her. I need to feel it again. Selfishly. Her days are numbered, which means I can only relive this moment so many times before I never feel her around me again. A countdown hangs above her head, the seconds ticking down, and I *have* to fuck her until detonation.

I draw my hips back and spit in my hand, then coat my dick with saliva. Gripping her full hip, I push inside her. A muffled whimper sticks in her throat. She stirs against me, but I won't stop. I can't.

"Shh, tragedy. I'm just taking what I decided was mine the moment I set eyes on you. Go back to sleep."

Her face settles against the pillow, but I doubt my words have relaxed her. She's lost to the gentle hum of a dream-inducing cocktail.

I ease out of her and glide through her warm center, my movements controlled and gentle. It's almost as if I don't want to wake her. Because I don't. I just want to use her.

With every pulse of my hips, her wetness grows. She'd never get wet like this if she were awake. I'd probably be forced to listen to fake moans as she pretended to enjoy it, and I don't want that. I want her exactly as she is right now —slippery and compliant. She's fun when she's feisty and full of fire, but I like this just as much. Maybe more.

My hand rises to her chest as I push inside her again, and I find the hardened tip of her nipple. I hold that perfect point between my fingers, rolling it around as my palm fills with her full breast. She stirs again and her back arches. Am I pleasing her? The whimper transforms into a soft moan, and now I'm certain she's enjoying this. I'm also certain she's imagining someone else inside her mind. Someone she likes. Someone who isn't covered in scars. Someone who isn't me.

My hand rises to her throat, and I push into her as I keep time with her pulse against my fingertips. I pull her warm body closer to mine. Everything about her teases my senses. My eyes feast on her slightly parted lips, and I imagine pushing past them with my cock. The scent of her berry shampoo cradles me as I bury my face into her hair and increase the tempo of my hips. I lick the crook of her neck, and her fear-laced sweat dances on my tongue. Each soft whimper and moan elicits a rush of euphoria in my brain. And the touch. Oh god, the touch. She's so soft she doesn't even feel real.

She grows silent, her mind crossing the line between

semi-conscious and unconscious. I lower my hand and put it between her legs, exploring until I find her swollen clit. But she doesn't respond.

How very disappointing.

I roll her onto her back and hover above her. A veil of red hair obscures her face, but I want to see those closed eyes. I brush the hair away and am rewarded with a sight that makes my balls ache. Her eyes are closed, her lips moving only when a puff of breath whispers past them. Fuck Sleeping Beauty. My tragedy is a sleeping *goddess*.

I'm overcome with the need to be inside her again. I spread her thighs and rub my thumb against her clit. She's so slick and warm. When I still don't get a reaction, I move closer and push my cock into her until I can't go any further. That brings another moan past her loose lips.

"Shhh. Let me fuck your pretty little pussy while you sleep," I whisper. "Just let me use you. I'll be done once I've given you every last drop of me."

My hands move to her waist. I pull her against me with each forward thrust, driving into her harder and faster. She moans again and the headboard bangs against the wall, over-taking her sensual sounds.

"God, you are *such* a good whore." The last word changes on my tongue. It sheds its cocoon of disgust and undergoes a metamorphosis, shifting into something vestal and precious.

I part her thighs further and push deeper. I can't hold out any longer. I wanted to squeeze her throat and feel her come around me, but I'll have to wait until she's awake. When she's more conscious, I can force her sweet little cunt to spasm for me. Even though she hates me, I'll make those green eyes come to life before they roll to the back of her head. And then I'll rip that life away.

For good.

My hips stall, and a deep groan rolls from my chest as I fill her. She'll be pissed when she wakes up and feels my come between her legs again. When she realizes I took advantage of her once more, that will only add to the anger. But how would she feel if she knew how she'd moaned when I fucked her? Too bad I didn't record it. She'll never believe me if I tell her.

Sated, I climb off her and ease her legs straight, then cover her with the blanket. I don't bother putting her shorts on because it's not like I'm trying to hide what I've done. On the contrary. I want her to know. When she wakes up tomorrow, I want to watch her face fall when she realizes I've defiled her.

I roll onto my side and close my eyes, refusing to fight with myself over my realization: When she wakes up tomorrow, I want to defile her again.

Chapter Twenty-One

Ambrose

Morning sun fills the room, and I wake to Oaklyn huffing up a storm. She tosses my arm off her with absolute disgust because I somehow turned over and held her while I was asleep. It's a small fucking bed. I'm surprised we didn't wake up on top of each other. Her slender fingers lift the blanket and she peers beneath it, then she reaches down and touches herself. If she didn't realize I fucked her before, her soaked pussy would definitely clue her in now.

Her haunting green eyes meet mine, and she releases the blanket. Instead of panic, a level of brokenness masks her face. It's a look I've never seen on another person . . . besides myself.

"Just get it over with and kill me, Ambrose. You've done enough to me. Stop playing this cat-and-mouse game and just take the final bite already." Tears well in her eyes, and she tries to blink them away. "I can't do this anymore. You act like I had some life I loved before you came and fucked it all up. You think you're causing me so much agony, but I was in agony long before I met you."

I shake my head. "I'm not done with you yet. You don't get to decide when it's time to end the show."

She looks away, her jaw tensing as her teeth clench together, and before I can react, she's on top of me. I don't expect her speed or agility, and that lapse in judgment will be my undoing because she's reaching for my knife. I expect the blade to sink into my skin, so I close my eyes and grit my teeth against the incoming assault. She'll bury it in my flesh, just as my mother did. She'll prove that I've chosen the perfect representation of the woman I hate.

But she doesn't do any of that.

I open my eyes. She's kneeling on the bed, the knife clasped in her shaking hand, but the blade isn't aimed at me. It presses against her own throat.

"If you won't do it, I will," she says through gritted teeth. Her green eyes have taken on a feral glint. She's a cornered animal, fully prepared to gnaw off her own limb to free herself from the hunter's snare. I know this look because I've been there myself.

"Give me that," I say, reaching for the blade.

She leans back, pressing the knife into her skin until a thin line of red appears just below the razor-sharp edge. "My life ended months ago. You can't kill something that's already dead." Her nostrils flare wildly, and something tells me this is much more than an act meant to push me to release her. She's not bluffing.

I spring forward and grip her arm, twisting her around and putting her back against my chest while keeping the knife away from her throat. An inhuman scream erupts from low in her gut. She struggles to break free, slicing my forearm as she bucks and writhes against me.

"Give me the goddamn knife." The words bite out of me, ripping through my throat. I have control of her wrist and I'm not trying to stab her, which is comical considering I had fully intended to do exactly that. It's my entire reason for being here.

She wiggles free and sends a parting kick into my groin. I drop to the floor. Gripping my stomach in a breathless heap, I'm useless to stop what happens next. I can only watch as she retreats to the door, but I don't panic. If she runs, I'll catch her.

But she doesn't run. She stops at the door and turns to face me, an untamed electricity pinging through her eyes. Her chest heaves with each breath she takes. Her nostrils flare. With a scream, she thrusts her arm in my direction and drags the knife down her forearm. Right up and down the road. She looks down at the wound, a haze of disbelief crossing her face as the blood funnels through the gash and drips onto the floor.

Fuck me.

Air rushes into my lungs, and I'm on my feet. I rip the knife out of her grasp and toss it away as she begins to sway against the wall. I wrap my arms around her and carry her to the bed, setting her on the edge and gripping her shoulders to keep her upright. Warmth slaps against my foot, and I look down. A crimson ribbon slides from her and pools against the hardwood. I have to stop the bleeding.

When I release her shoulders, Oaklyn lies back on the bed, her eyelashes fluttering. I tear the shirt from my body and wind it around the wound until I've run out of fabric. It's not enough. Blood crowds the cotton fibers, turning it a deep shade of vermillion.

"Stupid girl," I snarl, even as her eyes shudder closed.

Blood coats my fingers, leaving them tacky as it tries to dry. I have to stop the bleeding, but a hospital isn't an option. I press down on the wound, mentally urging the fucking fountain to shut off before it kills her.

Why?

Why the hell am I doing this?

If she wants to die, I should let her. This ending wouldn't be as beautiful as the one I planned in my head, but it's still a tragic way to go out. If I release her arm, she'll bleed out before long, even if she missed the radial artery. I just need to let go. I loosen my grip, and a trickle of blood snakes down her arm and spreads through the blanket beneath her.

I can't do it.

My hands seize her arm again, applying more pressure than before. "Oaklyn," I shout, lifting one hand long enough to smack her sweat-coated cheek.

She doesn't respond. I want to tell her I'm not ready for her to die. I'm not ready to let her go. Once she's gone, what do I go back to? She gave me something worthwhile to focus on, even if the focus was only harnessed hatred. Now, that hatred has morphed into something foreign. Something I can't explain or understand. The scales stand even, with disdain weighing down one side and admiration on the other.

And I do admire her, especially considering what she's just done. It was something I wanted to do countless times. Hell, I even tried once, but I only ended up adding more scars to my body.

No one was there to beg me to stay, though.

I only survived because I hadn't driven the blade deep

enough. She might have accomplished what I couldn't, and the thought terrifies me. No one is exempt from the wake of destruction she's left in the path to her end, and I've been caught in the fallout. Even if I can't explain it, even if I don't yet understand it, I have to save her.

Chapter Twenty-Two

Oaklyn

A thick fog obscures my eyes, and I don't recognize the hard feeling beneath me. This isn't a mattress. It's wood. My fingers move along the surface, gliding until I reach an edge, and I realize I'm on a table. *What the fuck?* I bring a hand to my head, then lower it to my aching wrist. I graze taut, sticky skin and a seam in my flesh.

Memories rush back, and the fog over my eyes begins to dissipate. I'm at the cabin. I ran from my stalker. My stalker is Ambrose. He threatened to kill me, and I . . .

I touch my wrist again, unable to admit what I've done.

A bottle of super glue sits on the shelf beside me. I feel my arm again and note the hard line that runs through the wound. He pushes me to this and then saves me? Why? So I can play more of his little game? The cat has stepped on the mouse's tail and pulled it back toward its teeth.

Footsteps come toward me, and his warm hand grips my wrist. "You're lucky you had super glue here. Otherwise, I was about to have to stitch you with some needle and thread," he says, examining his handiwork. "Superglue is a fighter's best friend."

"Or you could have just let me die."

He shakes his head. "You wouldn't have died. Once the bleeding slowed, I could see that you didn't go deep enough. You nicked some blood vessels, but you missed the important ones. You'll be woozy for a while, but you'll live."

I sit up and immediately regret that decision when the blood rushes from my head and the haze returns. Blinking back the fog, I steady myself and take a deep breath. "I don't understand," I whisper. "You say you want to kill me, but you went out of your way to save me. You should have just let it happen or helped me along."

"You aren't ending this on your terms."

"Let me go or end me, Ambrose." I turn to face him, but he refuses to look me in the eye.

He pats the wound. "It's dry. Go shower," he says, and I realize he already has. Who showers while someone is unconscious on the dining room table? I guess the same person who fucks someone while they're unconscious.

Fucking Ambrose.

"I'm good," I say. If I'm stinking and covered in blood, maybe he won't keep having his way with me.

___ "Now, tragedy," he says, raising his voice.

My eyes narrow on him. "Or what?"

He fists my hair and draws my lips toward his mouth. "I'll fuck you right now. I know you'd rather die than have my scarred body all over you again." He breathes against my lips. "Right?"

Double A right I would, but it has nothing to do with his scars. I won't explain that to him, though. Let him think whatever he wants. "I'll shower," I say, and I hope my decision drives a dagger through his heart.

As I drop my legs from the side of the table, the weight of the world assaults me. A dizzying buzz knocks me off balance, but a strong arm catches me before my ribs collide with the table.

"Slow down," he says. "You've lost a surprising amount of blood. I wasn't even sure I could get you closed up."

"My hero," I say as I push his hand away.

A smirk creeps onto his lips. I grip the table to balance myself, and my skin sticks to my shirt. I look down. Dried blood cakes my clothes and skin. Yeah, I need a fucking shower, not only to clean up but to rid myself of all traces of Ambrose on my body. In my body. A wild shiver runs through me.

I limp to the downstairs bathroom. He knows I have nowhere to go, so he doesn't follow me. Warm steam rises as I turn on the shower. I undress and step inside, averting my eyes from the rust-colored water circling the drain. A crust clings to the edge of the shampoo bottle from years of sitting on a shelf, and I flick it away so I can squirt some into my hands. I work up a thick lather in my hair, closing my eyes as the sweat eases its grip on my scalp and floats away on the suds. Using a washcloth, I scrub my skin until it's pink. I don't use as much effort around my wrist, only pressing hard enough to release the dried blood. A deep ache claws through my arm. Flaming fingers drag glass nails through the muscles. I really did a number on myself.

Stepping out of the shower, I release a deep sigh. It feels so fucking good to be clean. Renewed. More hell awaits me when I leave the bathroom—more Ambrose—but I can't think about that right now. I wish I was back at the club, bitching about my life. At least I could dance. My ankle sings when I put weight on it, and I'm not sure I'll ever dance again. In any capacity.

I reach for the towel hanging by the sink, and I'm annoyed to find it wet. We usually bring our own towels when we visit because moths always seem to eat up any we've left behind. This one already has holes in it and was probably abandoned because of it. My lip curls as I wrap it around myself. I don't want his body against mine in any way, shape, or form. I also don't like that I enjoy the scent he left behind.

My foot brushes against my shirt on the floor. It's a grotesque reminder of waking up with my shorts off and my pussy full of *him*. Again. I lift the shirt and a groan rises into my throat. The blood will never come out of it. Yet another article of clothing this man has destroyed.

With a sigh, I pull the towel closer and step into the hallway. My ankle cries as I hobble toward the kitchen and look around. I expect to see Ambrose, but he's gone. Maybe he thought better of everything he was doing and left. I'd be forced to limp for miles to the nearest sign of life, but I don't exactly hate the prospect, especially if it means I'm free of him.

But no. He comes through the front door with a plastic bag clutched in his fist. He says nothing as he goes to the fridge and begins placing things inside. Vodka. Ginger beer. Limes? It's everything I'd need to make my favorite drink, but how the hell does he know what I drink?

Realization smacks me and reminds me he's been stalking me, and it's clearly gone on longer and with much more attention to detail than I expected. My brain struggles to wrap around the thought of him sitting in the shadows as I ordered a Moscow Mule and drank it, blissfully unaware.

It's gross.

It's weird.

So why am I the tiniest bit intrigued by it?

He isn't the first man to obsess over me, but I can't remember the last time someone studied things that mattered to me. Usually it's my bra size or how flexible I am, not something so inconsequential as what I order at the bar. A pit forms in my stomach. Instead of being repulsed, I'm bordering on insane because I'm actually a bit touched. Then I think of everything else he's done to me and yep, there it is. The repulsion returns.

I shuffle toward the stairs and grip the railing, but he's at my side before I can take the first step.

His arm winds around my waist, and his warmth presses against my back. "You need to sit down. Those stairs are steep, and you're still weak."

"My clothes are upstairs in my bag."

He guides me to the couch and pushes me onto the cushion, then he heads upstairs. When he returns with my bag, he holds it toward me. "You don't have much in there."

"Yeah, some asshole cut up most of my clothes." I snatch it away, not wanting his hands on my things for a moment longer.

His lips twitch. "Maybe it was an asshole who didn't want you parading around like a whore."

"What's your issue, dude? Whore this. Whore that. Who are you trying to convince? Or are you just struggling with the fact that you're attracted to me?"

A growl leaves his throat, and he's on me before I can blink. He places his hands to either side of my head on the back of the couch, bracketing me between biceps cut from marble. "I'm not attracted to you. I'm not attracted to women *like* you," he snarls. Lies weave between his angry words, tied off with a knot of fallacy. His own voice box doesn't believe the words he speaks.

I look into his dark eyes and steady myself. "Whatever you say."

He leans closer and his warm breath rushes over my cheek. When he speaks, it's all gravel and tempered frustration. "Don't tempt me, tragedy. I'll end the show right now. Break your little neck. Show you just how unattractive and worthless you are to me."

I want to laugh in his face with each new lie he tells. I've struck a nerve, and the way his dick strains against his jeans tells me everything I need to know. He can say he isn't attracted to me all he wants, but his body betrays him. He's very much attracted to me, and I'm far from worthless in his eyes. You don't stop a worthless woman from killing herself.

My body betrays me as well. With each breath that caresses my skin, my core clenches a little tighter. Goosebumps pebble my skin. Confusion overwhelms me as thoughts scrabble for purchase in my mind. I don't want him inside me again, but I don't know if that's because I genuinely don't want it . . .

Or because I'm not *supposed* to want it.

No woman deserves to have her consent stripped away from her, and I'm not advocating for assault here, but what if a woman discovers she doesn't mind if it happens again? I'm sure the first person who voiced their love for being tied up and flogged got some weird looks too. It's not anything I've fantasized about, but now that it's happened, I can't deny that I'm open to being used by him again. I won't lie to myself about that. I won't be like him.

But I won't admit it to his face, either. Admitting it to myself is enough.

I clutch my bag to my chest and duck under his arm.

This close proximity is too dangerous for a number of reasons. I'm losing my fucking mind, for starters. Clutching the scratchy towel to my body, I head for the bathroom to change into something comfortable. Once I'm behind the closed door, I dress in a pair of jean shorts and a tank top. My reflection catches my eye. Bruises still stain my neck, and I got some gnarly scratches from running through the woods. An ashen cast to my skin makes me look a bit tired, but I suppose blood loss will do that to a person. I study the gash in my arm—a red wound that will become yet another scar.

Why did I do it?

I don't have a good answer. My mindset at the time wasn't fabulous. He dredged up the sunken ships of my past, and it was hard to look at them lying on the shore. Useless. Destroyed. Decaying. He's forcing me to look at what I've become, and I can't do that without glancing over my shoulder at what I used to be. What I'll never be again.

I close my eyes. I don't want to look anymore.

My line of work doesn't bother me, and I'm not ashamed of what I do. Strippers get slapped with all sorts of unfair labels, but that doesn't mean we're any of those names they call us. It's not the job that I can't bear to think about. It's the daily reminder of my loss. If an up-and-coming neurosurgeon had a horrific accident that disfigured their hands and prevented them from pursuing their dream, they'd be forced to abandon years of study and a lot of work to shift their trajectory toward another line of medicine. This is no different.

Actually, it is. People would pity the neurosurgeon instead of degrading them.

I grab a brush from beside the sink and drag it through my hair. I may feel like a drowned rat, but that doesn't mean

I have to look like one. Ambrose will do what he wants whether I look like heaven or hell, so I might as well do something for myself.

Once I've done what I can with my red locks, I turn to face the door. I don't want to go back out there. I don't want to face him again. I don't want to deal with the confusing feelings he stirs inside me. But I must.

I grip the handle with a sweaty palm and open the door.

Chapter Twenty-Three

Ambrose

The bathroom door clicks shut, and her bare feet pad down the hall. I turn to give her a snide remark, but my words tangle in my throat when I see her. I choke on them. She's brushed through the snags in her hair, and that vibrant red color accentuates her green eyes. Her white tank top hugs her body, revealing every delicious curve. Long, toned legs work beneath her in a way that swings her full hips when she walks. I bite my lower lip because what I really want to bite is too far away.

I turn away from my greatest temptation and pull the ingredients for a Moscow Mule from the fridge. There aren't any copper mugs here, so I search for something comparable in the kitchen cabinets. I pick up and put down several old family mugs with pictures of a young Oaklyn plastered along the sides. Pictures of her dancing with a wide, young smile on her face. I'm sure she never expected what she would become. How does a cute little dancer like her become the whore she is now?

179

I pull one of the picture mugs from the cabinet, knowing it will hurt when she's reminded of her past, but I put it back and choose a plain green one instead. I don't know why, and I'm not in the mood to dig too deep into the meaning of that decision. The answers would probably piss me off.

"When did you have time to go to the store?" she asks as she drops to the couch. "It's miles away."

"You were out for a while. I figured you wouldn't get very far if you woke up while I was gone."

She offers a scoff.

I twist the cap from the vodka bottle, breathing in the strong scent. I miss alcohol. It had a way of numbing the hurt, but the numbness never lasted long enough. My pain is a needle, driving deeper than the lidocaine can reach. It surpasses the numbness and digs until it finds an awakened nerve ending.

I finish preparing her drink and bring it to her. She's placed the bag of ice onto her ankle again—or what's left of it, since most of the ice has melted by this point—so it must be bothering her. I hold the mug toward her, intending to make up another ice pack once she takes it from me, but she just looks at the drink and turns up her nose.

"I'm not drinking anything from you," she says.

"I literally just opened that bottle, tragedy. Stop." My eyes rove down her body. "And besides, I don't *need* to drug you if I want to have my way with you."

"But you like it that way," she quips.

I shake my head. "I do, but I like it when you fight me, too."

Her eyes narrow. "What's wrong with you?"

I set the mug on the coffee table and sit down on the

chair beside it. "How much time you got?" We'd be here for a month if I tried to unload every piece of baggage.

"Not long, I guess," she says, turning her face away from me.

It takes a moment for my brain to register her meaning, and that's a fucking problem. My plan to kill her stays at the forefront of her racing thoughts, but that dark horse has fallen back a few furlongs in mine. I should be more focused than ever on how I'll take my revenge, especially when I've been handed the perfect scenario on a silver platter.

She sighs but she keeps quiet, which is probably a good thing. A headache has been building behind my right eye since her stunt this morning, and I could use some silence. I get these wicked migraines sometimes. Probably from all the head trauma over the years. It feels like a vise has clamped around my skull. Squeezing, squeezing. Usually I sequester myself in a dark room, but I don't have that luxury right now. I don't even want her to know I'm in pain. I can't allow her to see any weakness. As a fighter, weakness makes you prey, and I'm not the one who'll be hunted.

A bullet of nausea pierces my gut, and I adjust in the chair to find a more comfortable position. I have to get a handle on this pain. "Do you keep any ibuprofen here?" I ask. It won't get rid of the migraine, but sometimes it can take the edge off.

"Yeah, in the medicine cabinet upstairs. Why?"

"Just figured it might help your ankle," I say as I rise to my feet. On my way through the living room, I close the blinds and flick off the lights that are driving a nail through my eyes and into my brain.

In the bathroom, I find a bottle of ibuprofen with a faded label, but the pills aren't set to expire for a few more months. I toss back four and sip water from the sink to wash them down. Placing two in my palm, I return to the living room. I hand them to Oaklyn and offer her the mug again, but she shakes her head.

"Thanks, but I'd rather choke while dry-swallowing," she says as she knocks them back.

And I'd rather choke her with my cock, but she doesn't see me spouting off every sarcastic remark that springs into my head.

Gritting my teeth, I head back to the kitchen and prepare another bag of ice for her ungrateful ass. The heat of her skin has reduced the first one to water. When I return to her side, her eyes are closed and her hands are folded over her chest like she's a kitten taking a catnap in the sun. Her shirt has risen a little, revealing a thin strip of skin above her shorts.

That's where I place the bag.

She bolts upright, sending the bag to the floor, then turns to me with a scowl. "Why, Ambrose? Are you insane?"

What more do I have to do to show her just how insane I am? Cut off her face and wear it? Because I will. "My diagnosis or lack thereof is none of your business," I say. I lift the bag of ice and place it on her ankle with a smirk.

Dropping into the chair once more, I try to relax the tense muscles in my neck as I close my eyes. Sweat coats my skin, but I manage to keep a straight face as the migraine rips through my skull. I lift my fingertips to my right temple and press. It eases the pressure in my brain, but only slightly.

A warm rasp of fingertips brushes against my shoulder, and I jump. Oaklyn stands beside me, the bag of ice clutched in her hand. She holds it toward me.

"What's that for?" I ask.

She jiggles the plastic, then places it against my head. "I know a migraine when I see one. You wince every time you walk by a window, and you're sweating like a whore in church."

"You'd know what that's like," I say as I clutch the bag to my scalp.

She's only being nice to me for one reason: freedom. She thinks I'll let her go if she's the magical wonder girl who shows me kindness when no one else has, but this isn't some cheesy Hallmark movie. There are only three options in our scenario: kill, keep, or let go. Letting go is off the table, but I struggle between the other two options. Getting rid of her would be the smart thing. It's easier to get away with murder than kidnapping. Fewer risks involved. This isn't a decision I have to make right now, though, so I don't.

I tip back my head and rest the cold bag over my right eye as she retreats to the couch. "Being nice to me won't get you what you want, you know."

"Probably not, but that's not why I did it. Despite your low opinion of me, being a halfway decent person just comes naturally to some people."

"Halfway decent people don't strip."

She scoffs. "You don't know anything about us. A lot of us are just trying to make ends meet, and some of us even enjoy the work. What makes your career choice different from mine? You're still selling your body for entertainment."

Her words suck because they're partly true, but I'm not selling my body for sexual pleasure. I'm selling it for gory pleasure. For bloody entertainment. I'm not using my assets to titillate grown men. I'm using my strength to tap into their bloodthirst. We are *not* the same.

"Fuck off, tragedy," I say, completely done with the

direction of this conversation. I won't allow her to lump us into the same industry in her warped little mind. We're entertainers, sure, but one of us has no dignity. No shame.

I've spent my whole life trying to find something I'm good at and a crowd I fit in with. My mother demolished my dream of a normal life when she sliced and diced me. Oaklyn demolished her own dreams, then danced naked in the ashes.

"I wish you'd stop calling me that," she says.

"Why? Because you don't like being reminded of what an absolute disaster your life has become?"

When she doesn't answer, I turn to look at her. Her chin quivers below her full lips, her eyes locked on the ceiling. A glaze of tears covers her eyes, but she doesn't allow them to fall.

"Yes," she finally says, "but it's not because I strip. It's because I long for things I will never have. It's because no matter what I do, no matter how hard I work or how much I strive, I will never reach my goal. This situation has made me realize that I have been extending my arm toward a brass ring that will forever be out of reach."

The headache begins to ease as the ibuprofen kicks in, and I pull the bag of ice from my face. "All this drama about a car? Yeah, they're fucking expensive these days, and even a used hunk of junk will cost you a fair bit, but it's not that far out of reach."

"It's not about a car, Ambrose." Her voice is barely above a whisper.

"What sort of goals do you have?" I ask, genuinely curious.

She shakes her head. "I've said enough. Probably too much. It doesn't matter."

"I want to know, so I guess it sort of matters," I say.

"No," she says, getting to her feet. "You've used information against me already, and I refuse to give you more boulders to hurl at me. I've never shared my silly pipe dream with anyone, and I don't plan to do so anytime soon, especially not with you. It can be buried alongside me. It's been dead for a long time anyway." She heads for the back door, but she's not exactly a flight risk, so I let her go.

It bugs me that she won't share this secret with me. I'll have a hard time silencing her forever without first hearing about her hidden dream. I don't think it's a ploy, but if it is, it's a damn good one. I haven't exactly built a good rapport with her, though. I would normally just take what I want, but this isn't something that can be manhandled out of her. If I want her to expose this private part of herself, I'll have to earn her trust.

But how?

Chapter Twenty-Four

Oaklyn

Brown water laps at the rusted metal bracings around the dock. Mussels and algae cling to the pilings, only visible when the water eases back to reveal them. I stare across the lake, my chin resting on my knees. So many memories reside in this place. Times when my parents and I played games in the water. Times when we had picnics on the shore. Times when I still had my whole life ahead of me and hadn't yet put a voice to the decision that would prove bigger than our bond.

I blink away a heavy tear and wonder what they're doing right now. Probably blissfully living their lives while I tread water. I'm in my self-loathing era. I've been here for a while.

Footsteps crunch through the grass behind me, but I keep my eyes locked on the glimmers of light in the water. A flash of tan skin slides past, and I venture a glance to the side.

Ambrose walks to the edge of the dock, wearing only a

pair of shorts. The sun kisses the light sweat on his skin. I've seen his muscles before, and I've certainly felt their power, but I've never seen them in broad daylight. And never this close. Everything ripples and glistens.

I mentally wipe a runnel of metaphorical drool from the side of my mouth and beat back my hormones with a broom. This man has done horrific things to me. I'm not allowed to admit how insanely attractive he is. I should be locked in a mental health facility for the insane urges rolling through my core.

He rips down his shorts, revealing a perfectly toned ass. I never realized how attractive a man's backside could be until this moment. As he walks closer to the water, his muscles tense and tuck, creating lines that draw my eyes and refuse to let go. He always harps about his scars, but doesn't he realize how his natural physique overshadows them? He's beautiful.

I take a moment and openly study his scars in a way he wouldn't otherwise allow. Unless those street fights involve knife-wielding maniacs, I don't think they came from his fighting career. They're too numerous. I wish I could ask about them, but I don't want to draw his anger. We've kinda hit an impasse. He doesn't seem in a rush to kill me at this point, so that's good, I guess.

He dives into the lake and sends a spray of cold water over me, soaking my white tank top.

"Really?" I yell as I cover my chest.

He pops up at the surface and flicks his head to get his hair out of his face. "Get in here, tragedy," he yells.

That's a hard no. "I don't swim."

"Don't or can't?" he asks. He glides to the edge of the dock and places his forearms on the aged wood. Fuck him for looking like a scarred sculpture as he stares up at me.

He pulls himself onto the dock and kneels in front of me. His cock rests against his thigh, and I steal a glance at his piercings for the first time. My eyes widen. How dare he assault someone with *those* decorating his dick. Ribbed, but not for her pleasure.

He smirks. "So which is it? Can you swim or not?"

My eyes narrow and rise back to his face. "Why does it matter?"

"Fine, don't tell me." He leans forward and drags me into him, lifting me as he stands.

I flail against him. "Don't, Ambrose!"

"Sink or swim, tragedy."

He tosses me into the lake. Cold pressure squeezes me as I sink through the murky water. I stay down for a moment, listening to the quiet. The nothingness. I haven't felt the comforting embrace of open water in a very long time. I'd forgotten just how peaceful it could be to float through silence. Sunlight filters through, breaking into diamonds as the ripples cut through the sunbeams.

A shadow blankets the water, sending a muted crash toward me as it breaks the surface. A muscular arm bands around my body and pulls me upward. Holding me against him, Ambrose brings us toward the dock.

He came to save me.

Not that I needed it. I'm a perfectly good swimmer. I just didn't feel like getting in the water today. I would have resurfaced. Eventually.

His hands grab my sides, and I try to push him away.

"I can swim, dude," I say. He looks so fucking handsome, all heroic and concerned, and it pisses me off. "Get off me!"

He releases me. "I thought you were drowning."

"Maybe I was enjoying the quiet down there. Ever think of that?"

He grips the dock and wipes the water from his face. "Suicidal again, are we?"

"Fuck you!"

I slap him. I hit him so hard I swear the sound crosses the entire lake. He has *no* idea the anguish I've endured since my accident. Since before the accident, if I'm being completely honest. I lost my family. I lost everything. And he's forcing me to face it. He can't see the panicked thump of my heartbeat as the memories swirl around me. Even if he could, would he care?

I go to slap him again, but he catches my wrist and spins me around, pulling me against him. His chest warms my back. "You need to calm the fuck down," he says. His words race across my skin, and I shiver. "You also need to trust me."

"Trust you?" I wiggle against him, trying to break free, but he has all the control. By bracing himself on the dock, he can easily stay afloat and hold me as tightly as he wants. I stop struggling and just allow him to hold me. I'll use my words instead. "Why the fuck would I trust someone who pretended to help me while simultaneously causing me so much pain? Why the fuck would I trust someone who plans to *kill* me, Ambrose?"

He releases me, then turns me again and pulls my body against him. My legs wrap around his waist, and I'm breathless as he stares into my eyes.

"I haven't killed you, have I? I've had enough opportunities, but I haven't done it. You're supposed to use this time to convince me that I shouldn't do it at all, but you're wasting it." His hand goes to the top of my head, then slides down my hair like he's petting me. He leans closer, his lips only a breath away from mine. "Suck me, tragedy."

His hand closes around my hair, and I'm dragged beneath the water. I don't have time to think, let alone stop my descent. His powerful grasp guides my head toward his cock, and I put my hand up to stop my face from colliding with it. My fingertips meet his hard girth. Instead of feeling appalled or afraid, I'm disgustingly turned on. The water dilutes my anger and inhibitions until they dissolve into nothing.

He wants my trust. So I give it to him.

I open my mouth and bring him past my lips. His piercings graze my tongue, and I don't know how I never noticed these inside me.

Probably because I was asleep most of the time.

I push that rational voice from my mind and take his cock fully into my mouth. I swirl my tongue around the tip, and my chest tightens. I need air.

He grips my hair and pulls me to the surface. I pant for a moment, then I'm forced beneath the water again. I take him to the back of my throat, and his piercings wrench a gag from my abdomen. I close off my throat to prevent lake water from sucking into my lungs, but now my organs are screaming for oxygen. I can't surface on my own, and the thought makes me panic. My lungs clench.

But I have to trust him.

I keep going until I feel like I'm about to pass out. Seconds feel like hours, but I don't stop. I suck him, gripping the base of his dick as a black haze crowds my mind. My grip loosens. I'm fading.

He yanks me to the surface.

"No more," I gasp, coughing and spitting water.

He pulls me to him and presses his lips against my ear. "One more," he whispers.

I'm driven down again, and he pushes my head toward his cock. He takes control and moves my mouth along his throbbing length, and I willingly extend my tongue against his heated skin. Moving back my head, he lines himself up and pushes into my mouth, gliding over my tongue until his pulsing head hits my throat. He comes, and I don't know what to do because my mouth is full of water and now his jizz. He snatches me to the surface, then pulls my back against him so he can grip my jaw, holding my mouth closed.

"Swallow all of it," he growls.

Tainted lake water and come slide down my throat. When he's certain I've done as he commanded, he releases me. I scramble up the ladder and race to the grass, where I fall to my knees and retch. Everything comes up, and I'm forced to taste it a second time. I gag again, caught in a wave of dry heaves. I'm so fucking disoriented.

He eventually joins me and kneels beside me, placing his hand on the back of my neck. He's taken the time to put on his shorts again. "I expected a whore to take my come a bit better than that," he says with true disappointment in his tone.

"Maybe it's time to consider the possibility that I'm not a whore, asshole," I snap. I drop to the grass and roll onto my back, my chest heaving as I take in the glorious air.

His fingers trace the outline of my nipple through my shirt. "Until I'm done with you, you're my whore. I own you and every breath you take."

Instead of feeling offended, I feel oddly protected. Safe. The tiny feminist voice inside me shouts that I should buck the ownership of the man, but I'm getting a little sick of these rational thoughts telling me what I *should* or *shouldn't* do. Sometimes it's okay to be a little irrational.

I close my eyes and allow myself to let go. I may only have a few more days to live, so I might as well give him what he wants. And what he wants is all of me. If he chooses to kill me at the end of this, I can die knowing I did what I could to save myself.

"Okay, Ambrose. Let's talk."

Chapter Twenty-Five

Ambrose

The sun's rays kiss my shoulders, burning my skin with their fiery lips. This place is beautiful. So vast. The water seems to go on forever. But despite the vastness of the scene in front of me, I can only think of the brooding heat beside me, almost stronger than the sun itself. Oaklyn went from being a whore to being *my* whore—my slutty actress in this fucked-up play I've cast, produced, and directed. And now she's ready to talk.

My trust exercise went better than I anticipated. I figured I'd have to work a little harder to show her she could open up to me, but it only took controlling her need for oxygen while she sucked my cock. Holding her underwater might have been enough, but I couldn't allow her to become complacent or think she was safe from my selfish desires. Best decision ever. I can't begin to explain how it felt to fuck her face beneath the water, where her fear tensed every muscle in her jaw. I lived for it. While my dick was buried in her throat, I wanted her to feel the fear of suffocation before I brought her up for air. She needed to understand the complete way I own her now. I think she does.

"A dance studio," she says, interrupting my thoughts as she sits up.

"What?"

"That's the end goal for me. I want to open a dance studio." She picks at the grass near her thigh, pulling the green strands between her fingers until they snap. Her head turns, and her gaze focuses on something in the distance. "My silly, unattainable dream I've never spoken aloud."

I don't know how to respond to her. Her goal does seem very unattainable, but I don't want to say that.

Why not?

I've gone out of my way to wreck her for weeks, so why do I care about her feelings now? It would hurt her if I said that, which is what I'm supposed to do. I'm supposed to open old wounds and dig until the pain blocks out everything. But I can't, so I say nothing.

"What about you?" she asks. "What's your end goal?"

This isn't about me. I have zero desire to talk about myself or my dreams, so I shift the conversation back to her. "Why can't you just teach at a dance studio in town? Do you have to own it?"

She shrugs and brushes her fingers against the grass to get the dirt from her hands. "There aren't any studios in town. Or anywhere nearby, for that matter. I checked. Despite what you think, stripping wasn't my first choice."

I drop my gaze for a moment, finding the change in her features almost uncomfortable. She's nearly expressionless, aside from an unreadable emotion on her face. It reminds me of burned-out anger. Like when I'm in a fight and I get exhausted to a point where it feels as if I'm punching in slow motion. The anger is still there, crawling inside me, but my body is too tired to feed off of it. My mind can't keep up with the intense emotion worming through my muscles. My body is tired, but my mind is raging. That's what I see on her face now. A tired anger. An exhausted fighter.

"What about your family?" I ask. "They won't help you?"

She looks at me with a deadpan stare. "Even if my family would have helped me before, I doubt they will now that someone sent them a video of me shoving my tits in a stranger's face."

I almost laugh. It's fucking hilarious. But I don't. I keep a straight face and just listen as she continues.

"I'm well aware you feel like I deserve my mother's wrath because of what I do for a living, but she hated me long before I ever shed an article of clothing in a club. She wanted me to be a doctor like my father. She didn't think pursuing a career in dance was worth my time or her money. I put myself through school and honed my craft on my own."

"Your mom hated you because you wanted to dance?"

She doesn't meet my gaze, but she nods.

I look away and toss a nearby twig toward the water. "Well, your mom's a bitch," I tell her. What more can I say? So was mine. We have that in common.

"Do you have parents?" she asks, and it draws my eyes back to hers.

"Everyone has parents."

She scoffs. "You know what I mean."

I do. But I really don't want to talk about this.

Then again, does it matter now? She won't be able to use what I say against me when I leave this place alone. The dead can't speak.

I sigh. "I don't know who my father is. And my mother . . ." Even though it doesn't matter, the words stick in my chest.

Warmth encases my hand, and I look down. Oaklyn has placed her hand over mine. Instead of shying away from the scars on my skin, she's touching them. Willingly. Her gesture gives me the strength I need to continue, but I still can't say it, so I gesture to the scars on my face and chest.

Oaklyn's eyes widen. "Your mom did that to you?"

"I lie and say they're from fights, but a few people in town know how I got my scars. Those that were around back when it was all over the news, anyway." I listen to the waves crash against the dock, hoping what I've said is enough. I don't think I can say much more.

"Why would she do something like that?"

My shoulders lift in a shrug. "I don't know. I was a baby at the time, and I never gave a fuck about the 'why' once I was old enough to question it. Whatever her diagnosis or reasons, it doesn't matter. The institution notified me when she killed herself in their care, and I'm certain it wasn't because she was plagued with guilt for stabbing supposed demons out of her baby. So I didn't ask questions I don't fucking care to know the answers to."

She plays with the hem of her shirt. "And your mom was a dancer?"

I nod.

"Is that why you hate me so much?"

I gnaw the inside of my cheek. I don't hate *her* specifically. I hate all that she represents. She was just the unlucky one to get into my car.

"I hate me too," she whispers, and I almost don't hear it.

Can she not pull on my heartstrings, please? I don't need to be played like that. And she *is* playing me. Her response isn't genuine. She's merely adapting for survival.

It's an innate instinct. That's all. Anything else is contrived from that adaptation.

So why don't I believe what I'm telling myself?

"I don't hate you," I murmur.

She lets out a soft laugh. "You don't try to kill people you like."

I shake my head. "Murder happens all the time between people who don't hate each other. Some people even kill those they love."

"Then why haven't you done it?"

That's a great fucking question. Why haven't I?

Because I'm being stupid and weak. The thoughts of killing her were once a constant in my mind, but they've become sporadic at best, overtaken by thoughts of fucking her. Using her. Keeping her. But it can't be that way. It's impossible and impractical.

She wanted to know my pipe dream, and now I have an answer. Keeping her alive is my pipe dream. Ever since I pushed inside her, I sealed our fates and wove our futures together. Now I'm stuck on this road, kicking a can without an end in sight. I want to keep her alive, but I can't.

"How's your ankle?" I ask.

"Don't change the subject, Ambrose. Why haven't you killed me?"

Frustration brews in my gut. Her desire to die almost takes the fun out of killing her. Like handing her a gift instead of a disservice.

"Don't ask me that question, tragedy."

"Why?"

"Because I know you want to die. Or you think you do, at least. When the blade is against your throat, you'll change your mind."

She scoffs again. "Stop acting like you know what's in my head. You have no idea."

I turn toward her and fist her hair, pulling her near my mouth. "Stop acting like a pretentious bitch and I'll think about it."

I inhale every breath she exhales, and fear laces each one. But it tastes . . . different. Now there's a hint of something else. Defiance? Anger? It probably isn't desire, but that might be what I taste on my tongue.

Is she curious about what it would be like to give in and allow me to fuck her? It's human nature to seek pleasure. I don't need to force her every time. She can let me bring her to heaven before I send her to hell.

Her green eyes gloss over, and I can't pull away. Every breath I inhale makes me want to take one more from her lungs. Not just want, but need.

I lean down and kiss her. It's the first time my lips have grazed hers, and I'm lost in the warmth of her mouth. I seek her tongue and—

And she bites the ever loving fuck out of my lower lip.

Pain sears through my face, and a low growl erupts from my chest as I get to my feet. She scoots backward and spits. I run my tongue along my lip, tasting the blood and feeling the bite mark in the tender flesh. Fuck. That's hot. Irritating, but hot. She looks up at me with a doe-eyed stare, probably wondering what my next move will be. Fuck if I know. I can't decide between wrapping my hands around her throat or fucking her absolutely senseless. Maybe both. I stare her down as the battle rages inside me.

"Why the fuck would you do something so incredibly stupid?" I ask.

She licks her lips and shakes her head as she stands. "Because I'm fucking confused! My body wants one thing, but my brain says it's a horrible idea, and I don't know what the fuck is going on anymore. Stop fucking with my head!"

I know exactly what she means. "It's the same for me. I shouldn't want to fuck a whore, but I can't deny how much I want you."

"What? No," she says. "It's not the same because I'm not who you think I am. I'm not a whore, but you are undeniably a stalker-slash-murderer! I can't keep playing this cat-and-mouse game."

Cat and mouse, huh? She should really be more careful with her words.

"You don't know how much fun a cat-and-mouse game can be, but I can show you. Should I show you, tragedy?" I ask, brushing my hair back and spitting blood on the ground.

She shakes her head, but the wild look in her eyes tells me she's waging her own war in her mind. She's curious.

I fold my arms over my chest. "I'll be nice and let you decide. You can go inside the house and we'll continue chatting over drinks if you want." I pause and smirk. "Or you can run. I'll even give you a head start so you can find a good hiding place. If you choose to run and can remain hidden until nightfall, I'll drive you back to New York and let you go. But if I catch you—and I *will* catch you— you're going to spread your whore thighs for me. You're going to *let* me inside your pretty little cunt. When I catch you, you will give yourself to me and fuck me like you like me. Your stalker. Your future killer. Choose wisely."

She looks toward the house, the wheels spinning in her mind. I've placed the deal of a lifetime at her feet. The odds may not be in her favor, but I'm betting on her need to cling to the small chance that she can evade me.

"Do you promise you'll let me go if you don't find me?" she asks, her chest rising and falling.

"Do you promise to let me inside you when I do?"

She closes her eyes and nods.

"Then run," I say.

A fleeting moment of indecision flits across her face before she turns toward the woods and bolts forward. Her hair trails behind her like a red banner in the wind. That—coupled with her white shirt—will make spotting her pretty easy. I walk to the front of the house and flop down in a chair to watch her until she disappears. The head start is the least I can do, especially considering how she's still limping on her right side. The odds are stacked against her in so many ways.

I begin a countdown in my head, working my way backward from one hundred. When I hit zero, the game will truly begin. And I won't be denied my prize.

Chapter Twenty-Six

Oaklyn

This fucking sucks. The woods go on forever, and I'll never find a place to hide. We're in the middle of nowhere, my ankle hurts, and I just need to find a place to lie low. I duck behind a rock and pant as I peek over the edge. I don't see him. I don't hear him either. But I know he's coming, and he'll definitely find me if I stay out in the open like this. Watching the woods with wide eyes, I recall memories from my childhood as I search for a forgotten place to hide. We never played hide-and-seek when I was little. If we were in the woods, it was to—

I mentally snap my fingers. The treehouse.

My legs shake as I take off again. My father built a large tree stand for hunting whitetails in winter. Not a fan of the cold, he included walls on all sides, as well as a roof. When my mother began complaining and saying he needed to be more present for us, he gave up hunting and converted the stand to a treehouse for me to enjoy when we summered here. Ambrose will be searching the ground for me. I can only hope he won't think to look above eye level.

The old treehouse comes into view. Branches snake through the windows, and the camouflage paint has faded from years of neglect. The forest has tried to reclaim it, but it still sits on a sturdy branch, its rear wall securely anchored to the trunk. Well . . . it *looks* secure. If it's not, I'm sure I'll find out when I plummet to the ground.

My fingers grip the wooden blocks my father repurposed into a ladder. The rusted nails poking from the wood don't reassure me. I lift my leg as high as I can, testing the strength with my weight. I hop on my good ankle, trying to gain momentum. It takes all my strength to hoist myself up, and a splinter goes through my finger as I nearly slip. I grit my teeth and look up at the warped floorboards fifteen feet above me. The steps aren't even the sketchiest part of this thing.

When I get to the top, I wiggle the wooden boards and test their strength. They don't give way, so I hoist myself into the death box with a grunt. I freeze, listening for an inevitable creak of wood. The floor holds. Scooting backward until I reach the rear wall, I look around for any weapons, but the only thing left in this treehouse is the table. It's bolted to the wooden beams beneath it, and it looks sturdier than the fucking floor. It won't be of any use to me. With a sigh, I close my eyes.

And I wait.

Bushes eventually rustle outside, the sound somehow so far and too close at the same time. I bite my lip to keep from whimpering. I'm so torn. My mind is split in half. I don't want him to find me, but is that because I fear what he'll do to my body? Or because I fear I'll enjoy it? I don't want to know the answer. He can't find me.

"Tragedy?" Ambrose yells, and I throw my hand over my mouth to stifle the scream that begs to free itself from my lungs. He's near the tree. It sounds as if he's directly beneath it.

Blood rushes in my ears, and I can't hear a thing aside from my pulse pounding away inside my skull. How can I listen for receding footsteps when my eardrums refuse to work properly? Seconds tick by. A cramp ratchets through my leg, and I squeeze my eyes shut. I need to readjust, but what if he's still standing below me?

Enough time has passed. He wouldn't stay in one spot for this long.

I take a risk and lean forward to massage my convulsing calf. The wood groans beneath me.

"Ah, there's my little disaster," he says below me.

Fuck.

My eyes widen with rabid fear as I look around for an escape, and only then do I realize how royally I have fucked myself. I'm trapped.

His steps thump against the ladder, and the sound tells me he felt so confident in his ability to find me that he took the time to put on shoes. I never should have made a deal with the devil.

Fingertips curl over the wooden ledge, and his face rises into view. My heart clenches, struggling to find a steady rhythm as I stand. With minimal effort, he brings his massive form over the edge and sits there, his legs dangling below him.

"Did you miss me, tragedy?" He turns toward me. "You must have, since you picked such an obvious hiding spot. Almost as if you wanted me to find you."

"Fuck you," I grind out through clenched teeth.

He gets to his feet with a devilish smirk. "Yeah, you're

205

gonna fuck me. You lost our little version of hide-and-seek, so that's exactly what you're gonna do. I guess it wasn't a very fair game, though. I expected more from a resourceful whore like you."

"I'm not a whore!" I charge toward him, ready to push him through the opening in the floor and go down with him, but he braces himself and spins me around, pinning my back against his bare chest. He's so goddamn strong.

His mouth lowers to my ear as he takes a few steps forward, moving us away from the only way out. "If you keep fighting me, you won't have the option to give yourself up anymore. I'll take that choice from you." Warm breath slides over my neck. "Now . . . do you want to come?"

His question is so out of place that it puts me into a state of shock. Why would he ask me that when everything feels so hopeless?

"What?" I ask.

He smirks against my head. "I asked if you want to come."

I don't even know how to answer him. I don't even know if I *can* come right now. Shifting in his grasp, I rub my thighs together and sense a wet warmth between my legs.

Okay. Maybe I can.

I relax in his arms, and he releases me. "Get undressed for me," he says, his voice low and deep. "Don't forget our deal. You agreed to fuck me like you like me."

I reach for the hem of my shirt and begin to lift it, but he shakes his head.

"Slower, tragedy. Like I'm paying you for it."

My lip curls. "Do you want me to do it like I like you or like you're paying for it? Because those are *not* the same thing for me."

His lips draw into a smirk. "Like you like me."

I raise my shirt, nice and slow like he wants, and drop it to the floor. A decade of dust rises in a plume around it.

"Yeah, like that," he says.

I step into him. If he wants a believable show, I'll give it to him. I do this for a living. This is no different. Even when I felt sad or hopeless, I flashed a smile that sold the show. The only difference is what I'm hoping to earn this time; instead of money, I want to walk away with my life.

I lift his hands to my chest, and his hungry fingers explore my skin. His calloused touch brushes over my nipples, hardening them and sending a rush of heat between my legs. And I hate that. I shouldn't be so turned on by his touch. He pulls me into him and takes a hardened peak into his mouth. His tongue swirls over the sensitive skin, then he sucks and bites down. I whimper when the bolts of pain and pleasure collide.

"You like that, huh?" he whispers before moving to my other breast and repeating the motions. Lick. Suck. Bite.

I cry out and pull his head against me, unable to split my arousal from my fear.

"Yeah, you like that," he growls. "Take off those shorts. I want to see all of you."

My fingers hook into my shorts, and I peel them away. With a greedy hand, he reaches between my legs and cups my warmth with a groan. I close my eyes, ashamed of the wetness he finds there. He pushes me to my knees, and the dry wood bites at my skin. He doesn't need to tell me what he expects next. I know what he wants. And goddamn me for wanting it too.

Instead of unfastening his pants, he steps away from me. He backs up until he's on the other side of the treehouse, then he stops. His hard glare never leaves my face.

"Crawl to me," he commands.

His voice demands obedience, and I drop my hands to the floor and do as he says. The wood scrapes my knees. Splinters prickle against my palms. But I don't stop. I crawl to him until I'm inches from his legs, then I rest on my knees in front of him.

Without being told, I undo his pants and release his hardened cock. Velvet warmth caresses my palm as I wrap my hand around him and feel his length. With my thumb, I toy with the barbell at the tip, and my mouth waters prematurely as I mentally prepare myself to suck him again. I lick my lips, then spread them to take him inside. The piercing clacks against my teeth, and when I ride down his shaft, my lower lip snags on the piercing right before his balls. He moans, wrapping my hair in one hand and putting his other on the ceiling, bracing against the pleasure.

"Fuck," he whispers. "Such a good whore."

Instead of angering me, his words make my core clench with need.

He grips the base of his dick. His hand guides my head away from him, then he pushes his fingers into my mouth. "You have a great mouth," he growls. "Too good. I want more than just your mouth this time, though."

He grabs the back of my neck and forces me to my feet as he releases the pressure on his cock. His body presses into me, forcing me backward until I hit the rough wooden wall. His hand races to my throat, and the look in his eyes worries me. He's struggling with some internal thought, some mental war, and my life hangs in the balance. I feel it in his tightening hold that only allows me the smallest gasp of air.

He leans against my mouth, and each breath I take belonged to him first. "I hate that I find you sexy, you know that? I fucking *hate* that I want to keep you alive so I can

208

fuck your slutty cunt until it milks every drop of come from me." His grip loosens and slides to my breast.

"You can fuck me all you want. I want you to fill me." I reach out and wrap my hand around his hard cock. "You don't have to threaten me to get that."

His eyes narrow. "I don't believe you, Oaklyn. I don't think there's a single fiber of your being that wants to let me inside you. Now or ever." He takes a sharp breath. "I really hate liars, but even though every motion you make is fake and every word you breathe out is a lie, I still have this urge to make you come before I get rid of you."

His sexy words mix with deep threats, and my stupid body responds to all of it.

He leans down and nips my neck, his fingers twisting my nipples and sending jolts of heat to my throbbing clit. His mouth moves to my ear. "Let me make you come with my mouth," he says, his voice all gravel.

I don't know how to respond. My body wants what he offers, but it feels so wrong. My brain can't let go of everything he's done to me. "You haven't given me a bit of pleasure any time you've been inside me, so why do you think you can get me off now?"

"I can make you come, tragedy, whether you want to or not. Give me your pleasure," he growls, "or I'll take it." He lifts me and sets me on the old wooden table, then grips my knees and parts my legs. "Keep those thighs spread for me."

"Please," I beg.

He shoves two fingers inside me, and I gasp. "Your dirty little cunt is dripping for me. Stop acting like you don't want it. Now come on your *evil* stalker's tongue. Come for the man who ruined you."

He's on me. His tongue swipes across my slit, and he licks me down to his fingers before rising upward again. His tongue spreads my lips until it collides with my swelling clit. An earthquake rips through me, the epicenter putting dangerous pressure on the most sensitive part of me. As much as I hate him, the touch of his tongue blows up the fucking Richter scale. My back lifts from the table as a moan erupts from me.

His lips wrap around my clit, but the intense pleasure is replaced by pain as he bites down. I yelp and try to close my legs, but he pushes them apart. His lips wrap around my clit again, but instead of biting me, he sucks. Intense pressure grows beneath each quick lash of his tongue. His fingers piston inside me, drawing up more pleasure with every thrust. My chest rises and I can't even think about the wood scratching at my ass any longer. I can only think of his violent tongue stroking my clit. I can only think of that warm, wet muscle bringing me dizzying pleasure instead of hurling insults at me.

I'm going to come.

I feel it in every tight muscle in my body. In every jerky movement I make. I'm right there. I'm so close. I couldn't stop it, even if I wanted to. Not as long as he keeps licking me like that and fucking me with his fingers.

Then he stops and sits up, and an emptiness engulfs me.

"I don't want to feel you coming around my fingers," he says. "I want to feel you coming around my cock."

Any inhibitions I would have felt at the thought of allowing him inside me have been thrown to the wind. My orgasm is so close, and I *want* to come.

"Fuck me, Ambrose," I beg.

He notches the head of his cock at my entrance, then he sinks inside me with a wild groan. Each powerful, rhythmic thrust of his hips bolsters my building pleasure. I moan as his cock stretches me. His first piercing rubs against sensitive places inside me, and the second grazes my skin whenever he drives deeper.

"Fuck, I want to come," I pant. No, it's not even a want anymore. It's a need. I'm past the point of no return. I haven't just allowed my pride to jump to its death; I've pushed the mother fucker off the cliff myself.

Ambrose's hand slips between us, and he rubs my clit as he gives me every inch of him, harder and faster. His free hand grips the edge of the table, and both of mine reach back to brace my quivering body as he pounds into me. I squeeze the rough slats of wood as my thighs tremble. It's been so long since I've felt something like this.

"Come, tragedy. Come on your tormentor's cock."

If I wasn't so fucking hard for this orgasm, I would have told him to stop right then. But I can taste it on my tongue. I'll let him say whatever he wants as long as he continues to rub me and fuck me like this.

My body shudders, and I slip into an orgasm that silences my brain. My eyes close, and I cry out. Before I can suck in a single breath, Ambrose's hand wraps around my throat.

"Keep your eyes on me. Don't you look away while I'm balls deep in your cunt."

My eyes roll back in my head as I ride out the waves he's caused inside me, but I keep them open. I don't want this to stop. Apparently, I'm much more pliable after I come. Reckless. Naïve.

"That's my good whore," he groans. "Keep those eyes open."

"Come, Ambrose. Fill me," I whisper over his grip on my throat.

His thrusts grow erratic, and he throbs inside me. His eyes stay on me, never leaving mine until he's sated and ready to pull out of me. This time I *let* him fill me with all that hatred, and I hate that I enjoy that anger dripping from me as he steps back.

"Sexy fucking whore," he growls. His fingers stuff his escaped come back inside me, then he pulls them out, licks them, and draws me toward his face. "Open your mouth for me."

I shake my head. No thanks.

"We're having such a nice moment," he says. "Don't make me hurt you now."

I swallow hard and spread my lips.

He grips my chin, tilts back my head, and gathers spit beneath his tongue. He leans over me. His lips pucker before releasing the warm, come-laced saliva onto my tongue. It startles me, but I keep my eyes on him as I swallow the salty mixture.

"Good fucking girl, tragedy," he growls.

The amount of feral joy on his face from that little gesture makes me feel something I can't explain. He looks almost . . . proud of me? It's been a long time since I've had anyone take pride in anything I've done. It seems I've only managed to produce one disappointment after another in every other aspect of my life. But right now, he's looking at me like I'm a racehorse that's just won the Triple Crown. That look shifts something inside me, and it scares me.

I'm letting him get too close to me. And I don't know how to stop.

Chapter Twenty-Seven

Ambrose

W e reach the cabin just as the sun has begun to set through the trees. I want to go inside and rinse off the sticky residue of lake water and sweat, and I figure Oaklyn wants to do the same, especially after having me inside her. She surprises me when she says she wants to sit on the back porch and watch the sun go down.

"Can I trust you to stay put?" I ask. I'll take my keys with me, and I don't think she'll try to make a run for it, but I need to be sure.

"I guess I'm not the only one who needs to build a little trust in someone, hmm?" She shakes her head and looks out at the water. "I won't go anywhere, Ambrose."

Something in the defeated way she speaks tells me she's being honest. If I leave her sitting on the porch, that's where I'll find her when I return from my shower.

A thread inside me pulls tight and snaps. I've wanted nothing more than to break her since this entire ordeal

213

began, but now that I've done it, I'm devoid of joy. A sick urge engulfs me, and I want to grab her and hold her against me until she's whole again. For the first time in weeks, I don't want to hurt her anymore.

I want to be the one who stops the hurt.

Before the urge can overtake me, I turn and go inside. A shower will clear my head and remind me why I'm here and what I have to do.

But it doesn't. As I scrub and rinse my body, I imagine choking her. It only hardens my dick. I envision gripping her hair and pressing a knife to her throat, but the Oaklyn in my mind just smiles and licks her lips, enjoying it. The signals have crossed somewhere in my head. I still want to hurt her, but I want to bring her to the edge of pleasure at the same time.

I still want to hurt her, but I no longer want to break her heart.

My palm slams against the shower wall, but it isn't enough to vent the frustration brewing inside me. I've fucked this up. The universe gave me the vessel for my revenge on a silver platter, and I'd rather play with it than destroy it. I have to kill her. When I leave this shower, I have to end her life before this goes any further. Before I reach a point when I can't bear to say goodbye.

I turn off the shower, dry myself, and walk to the bedroom to dress. Tucking the knife into the sheath on my belt, I steel myself and head downstairs. As I near the back door, I freeze. Voices drift through the wood, muffled but discernible. Oaklyn is speaking to someone.

"I needed some time to think," Oaklyn says, "and I figured you wouldn't mind."

"Who else is here, Oaklyn?" a female voice says.

"Mom, it's just me. I told you."

My fists unclench and I can't breathe. She's been given the perfect opportunity to cry for help, but she hasn't. She's . . . protecting me. She's protecting her stalker, her future killer.

"Then whose car is in the driveway?" her mother continues. "I know you didn't scrounge up enough for one while being a dirty little slut. How much do those men pay to look at your breasts? A dollar per nipple?"

"Mom!"

"Who is here? Tell me now, or I'm going to the police and have you charged with breaking and entering."

Oaklyn pauses. I peer through the gauzy curtain beside the door and watch as she nibbles her lip, thinking. "A friend let me borrow their Jeep."

"What friend? Did you trade your body for a ride? God, you disgust me. I never imagined my daughter would become a whore."

Tears well in Oaklyn's eyes, and her chin wobbles beneath her lips. When I call her a whore, it usually pisses her off—or turns her on—but when her mother says it, a knife sinks into her heart and twists.

I've seen enough. My hand shoots toward the doorknob, and I yank open the door. "I drove her here. I'm her fucking friend, and no, she didn't trade her body for a ride."

The breeze catches her mother's short gray bob and sends strands into her gaping mouth. "Excuse me? You can't talk to me that way on my property. Do you know who I am? I babysit the governor's Shih Tzu!"

I clamp my teeth on my inner cheek to keep from laughing. "Even if you suck the governor's dick every Sunday after tea, lady, I have no fucks to give. What I do give a fuck about is the way you're speaking to her." I point a finger toward Oaklyn.

"Do you know what she does for a living? You must not if you're willing to shack up with her. You might want to get tested for STDs." She turns up her pointy nose, and I clench my fists to quiet the growing need to punch it.

"I know exactly what the fuck she does," I say through gritted teeth. "She dances."

Oaklyn's eyes widen. She stares at me as if my face has changed and she no longer recognizes the man in front of her. Fucking same. I no longer recognize myself. I never thought I'd defend her and her career choice, but I can't stop myself. The look on her face when her mother berated her made me sick.

Her mother throws her hands into the air and starts toward the front of the house. She digs in her purse, then raises her phone in the air as she walks, growing more frustrated by the second when the signal bars don't materialize. "You're all crazy, and I'm driving to town so I can call the police. Dancing isn't a profession. It's a hobby! And taking off your clothes always makes you a whore. As her mother, I just wanted better for my daughter." She tosses her phone back into her purse.

"You're no mother," I seethe.

She stops walking and turns to face me.

Before she can speak, I charge toward her and grip her arm. "You haven't been a mother to that woman since you pushed her out of your life because she refused to live *your* dream. I may not know what a good mother looks like, but you sure as shit ain't it." I snatch the designer purse from her arm, find her flashy phone, and throw it to the ground. The heel of my shoe slams down on it, shattering the case and sending a spider web of colors across the screen.

"What are you doing?" she wails.

"Giving us a head start." I toss the purse to her feet and

turn to Oaklyn. "Get your shit and get to the Jeep. Our fun family vacay has come to an end."

Oaklyn rushes inside without a glance behind her. I turn back to her piece of shit mother.

"If you *ever* contact Oaklyn again, I'll smash more than just your phone. You have done more than enough damage to her, and I refuse to let you hurt her any more than you already have. As far as you are concerned, you have no daughter. Don't even think about contacting the police, either," I add. "If you bring any trouble to our fucking doorsteps, I'll bring some to yours. Got it?"

She sucks in a breath to say something stupid, and my hand goes to my knife. Her eyes follow the movement, and she stops.

"Yeah, you got it. Have a nice trip home." I turn and head toward the cabin before she can say anything else.

When I get inside, Oaklyn stands at the foot of the stairs with our bags in her hands. The neck of the vodka bottle peeks from the top of hers, meaning she even took the time to pack up the stuff I bought to make her favorite drink.

Tires rake across the gravel outside, and Oaklyn's attention shifts to the front door. "Is she gone?" she asks.

I nod.

"We'd better hurry," she says, rushing toward the door. "If she gets to town before we're gone, she'll send the cops for sure. She'll—"

I grip her arm and stop her, looking down into her frantic face. "She won't call the cops, tragedy."

She struggles, trying to pull away. "You don't know her. She will. We have to leave."

"Come here." I pull her into me, wrapping my arms around her and keeping her still. The bags drop from her arms, and her heartbeat gallops against my skin. My hand goes to my knife, but I stop. I can't kill her here. Not now. Not after her mother saw my face.

A sob bursts from Oaklyn's mouth. She cries against my chest and relaxes in my arms until I have to hold her up. No one has ever leaned on me like this. I've never comforted someone, and no one has ever comforted me. I don't know how to do it. So I just do what feels right and hold her up. I won't let her fall.

We stay like that in the dark room for what feels like hours. When her sobs quiet to sniffles, I let her go and look into her eyes.

"Why didn't you run?" I ask. "Why didn't you tell your mom the truth?"

She swipes at her puffy eyes and shakes her head. "I don't know. I just couldn't."

This woman is just as confused as I am.

I lift the bags to my shoulder and move toward the front door. "We'll head back to New York, but I don't want you to get the wrong idea," I say. "I'm not ready to let you go, and I don't do anything I don't want to do. We'll stay at my place until . . ."

Until what? I almost said until I figured out what to do with her, but I don't want her to realize how undecided I am. So I leave the sentence hanging. Let her think what she wants.

"Until you kill me," she whispers.

I don't answer her. We walk to the car in silence, two paths converging on our way toward the end of the line. One way or another, decisions must be made. Soon.

Chapter Twenty-Eight

Oaklyn

A painful silence wedges between us as we push toward New York. I watch the side mirrors for the glint of blue lights, but I never see them. Whatever Ambrose said to shut my mother's mouth has worked.

I watch him as he drives, remembering the first day I sat in this Jeep and stared at him in a similar manner. It feels like years have passed since that moment. In a way, they have. I'm no longer the same person I was that first night. I'm confused as fuck. I don't understand why my body responds to a monster like him. He should disgust me, but I find myself drawn to him.

"Why do you keep staring at me?" he asks, shifting in his seat.

Because he's so attractive. Because I like his dark eyes and the way the little ball of muscle tenses at the back of his jaw when he's thinking. Because instead of scaring me, his scars excite me.

But I can't say any of that, so I say the only other thing that comes to mind. "Tell me more about what happened to you."

He doesn't look at me. He just shakes his head and keeps his eyes on the dark road.

"It's only fair," I say. "You got to witness my train wreck of a mother firsthand. Thanks for that, by the way."

A deep sigh rolls from his nose, and his grip tightens on the steering wheel. "My mother had some kind of break-down when I was a few months old. Thought I was possessed or something. Took a knife to . . . Well, she took a knife to all of me. Somehow, I survived, and now I have to look like this for the rest of my life." He glances out the window and lowers his voice to a whisper. "Sometimes I think I'd have been better off if I hadn't survived the attack."

"Why? Because you have scars?" I reach toward his face and run my fingers over the raised flesh.

He yanks his head out of reach. "Don't pretend I don't disgust you. That I didn't have to make a bet to get you to sleep with me."

I guess I'm not the only one in a self-loathing era.

Ambrose is a piece of shit—there's no denying that—but as mentally ill as he is, he isn't ugly. He's a solid sculpture of carved muscle. A slew of cracks run through the exterior, but despite the damage, I still see the beauty in him.

"You aren't ugly, Ambrose," I whisper. I reach for his face again, and he doesn't pull away. Instead, he only flinches as I graze his scars. "Would I have gotten into your car if I thought you were ugly?"

His eyes soften, rounding a pinch. He's trying to figure out if I'm lying. This time, I'm not. I have scars too, so I don't judge him for his. If he had come to the club and bought me my favorite drink, I'd have danced for him for free. If he had asked me out on a date, I'd have said yes. He's the one sabotaging his own self-worth.

My thoughts bring me to another question. "Why'd you pick me? I know your mother was a dancer, so that has something to do with it, but why me specifically? What do you hope to accomplish by killing me?"

"I don't know why it had to be you, but I have to kill you because it's the only way I can make things right. I couldn't end my mother, and someone has to pay for what she did."

I turn to face him, eyes wide. "Do you . . . Do you fucking *hear* yourself? How does ending my life make things right?"

His fist collides with the steering wheel, and the Jeep jerks across the center line. "I don't fucking know, but it does! Don't make me question this shit more than I already do, tragedy."

"Who makes things right for me when I'm gone?" I ask, my voice just above a whisper.

He grits his teeth and doesn't answer me, so I answer myself. No one. Not a single person will fight for me when I'm gone. When my dead body—or body *parts*—are discovered in some desolate area twenty years from now, no one will even know who I am.

The silence answers another question as well. He still plans to kill me. If he didn't, he would have said he'd changed his mind. I thought maybe we'd turned some kind of weird corner when he'd stood up to my mother and defended me, but it seems this was just another level in his fucked-up little game.

"Try to get some rest," he says. "We've got a long drive ahead of us."

My body aches from all the running, and exhaustion weighs me down, but it's pretty hard to close my eyes and drift off to dreamland when my death looms just over the next hill.

My stomach growls, and the silence in the Jeep only amplifies it. I wrap my arms around my stomach to muffle it, but it still draws his attention. He only looks. He doesn't ask if I'm hungry or offer to stop. I guess we're back to Asshole Ambrose. It's probably better this way. It's easier to remember how much I should hate him when he's being a jerk.

He yanks the wheel toward the offramp and sends me into the door. The tires squeal and the rear end fishtails, but he manages to straighten out before we spin into the guardrail.

"What the fuck?" I scream. "Are you trying to kill *both* of us now?"

He sets his jaw and doesn't answer.

I look behind us, expecting to see blue lights or hear the wail of sirens, but it's all darkness and headlights and tires on pavement. What was the big fucking hurry to pull off the interstate?

A few minutes later, he brings the Jeep to a stop in a parking lot, and my anger evaporates. We're at the diner.

"Don't even think about ordering that fucking drink again," he says as he gets out of the car.

We go inside and sit at the same booth we chose last time. The waitress is different, and so is the mood. On our way up to the cabin, I was blissfully unaware of all the surprises fate had in store for me. I thought I was running toward safety when I was really running into the arms of my stalker. Now my brain has been ripped in two directions, with one side wondering how he'll kill me and the other hoping he'll fuck me again before he does it.

Sitting in a diner full of people could be my way out of

everything. I only need to call out for help. Ambrose doesn't have a gun, but I have a feeling the long-haul trucker seated at the bar might. That bulge on his hip sure as shit isn't his dick.

But I don't. I keep quiet. The thought of someone hurting the man across from me should fill me with joy, but it only makes me feel sick. I've seen too much of the good in Ambrose to want him taken out, even after falling prey to the dark parts of his soul.

We order our food, and it arrives at our table a few minutes later. As we eat in silence, my mind keeps circling something he said earlier about revenge. It bugs me that I have to be the sacrificial lamb to pay for someone else's sins. I consider asking why he can't just take one of the other girls and let me go, but that isn't fair either. Some of them have kids. Some have families that care about them, even when they don't agree with what they do for a living.

I have nothing.

Maybe he chose correctly after all.

His jaw slows as he studies me, then he stops chewing altogether. "What's bugging you now?" he asks.

I shake my head and slide another fry into my mouth. There's no point in circling the same mountain or asking the same questions.

He slides his plate to the side of the table and leans forward. "You can either tell me what's on your mind or I can take you to the bathroom and force it out of you. Your choice."

God, I hate the way his threat makes my stomach clench with excitement instead of fear. "I don't know. Maybe it's knowing I'll be dead this time tomorrow. Tends to put a damper on things."

He looks around to be sure no one heard what I said,

then pulls a twenty from his wallet, slaps it on the table, and slides out of the booth. He stops beside me, leans near my ear, and whispers, "Let's talk about this outside."

I lower the last bite of my burger and leave the booth. As I follow him to the car, I feel like a naughty child being escorted out of a store for screaming in the toy aisle. It was his fault. He pressed me to answer him.

We near the Jeep, but he doesn't go to the driver's side. He turns and pins me between the car door and his body instead. His hands go to either side of my head as he looks into my eyes and leans closer, daring me to move away from him or fight him off.

"Let me try to help you understand." His breath rolls over my lips. "Do you know what it means to be obsessed, tragedy?"

I shake my head. I know the definition of the word, but I don't know how he defines it.

"It means I can't let you go. It means that even if I don't want to kill you, I don't have a choice because the thought of another man touching you sends me into a blind rage. Even if you run to a convent and become a fucking nun, it won't be good enough because I don't even want some *god* to see your naked body if I can't. It means that the only way I can ensure you stay mine until your last breath is to be inside you when you take it."

Words tangle around my tongue. I have so many thoughts, but they fly too fast to catch hold of any of them. Pinned beneath his body and his gaze, I can only listen.

"This started as a way to get revenge on my mother," he continues, "but it has become something bigger than I can control. You are my ultimate obsession. I don't want to kill you, but I don't see another way this can end."

He presses his lips to mine in a rough kiss, and his hand

moves to my throat and squeezes. Instead of pushing him away or biting him again, I relent and let him explore my mouth. I give in to the tightening hold around my neck, trusting he'll let me breathe again. Even now, when he's confirmed my definitive end, I want him.

There is no escaping what will eventually happen to me, but if no one can avenge me once I'm gone, maybe I can avenge myself before I leave.

Chapter Twenty-Nine

Ambrose

She's in my apartment. This moment seems so surreal. Her eyes dart around as if she's expecting plastic curtains draped over my walls and floors for easy cleanup. Her gaze lands on the computer on my desk, and I wonder if she realizes that's where I sat and looked up all the information about her. Where I sent an email to her mother and exposed her in more ways than one.

She lowers her bag to the floor and rubs her hands against her hips as she glances around one more time. "So this is where I die, huh? I mean, it's nice, don't get me wrong, but—"

I grab her bag and walk to the kitchen before she can finish. I feel jilted that she's snatched away the fun of killing her. She ruined my plan by kissing me like I don't disgust her. She sucked all the wind from my sails when she made me *like* her. But I can't show her that, and I can't let her go.

My tragedy has to meet her end, or she was never my very own disaster to begin with.

I set the bag on the counter. All the drink ingredients wait on top, so I pluck them from inside and make a Moscow Mule for Oaklyn. Her favorite drink can be her last drink. It's the last kindness I can show her. She watches every move I make as I mix it and pour it into a coffee mug. I'm not trying to drug her again, if that's what she's worried about. I want her awake for the play's denouement.

I hand the drink to her. She goes to the couch in my humble living room and sinks into the cushions, balancing the mug on her knees. She hasn't looked me in the eye since we kissed.

"What did I do to make you hate me so much?" she asks.

She didn't really do anything. I hate what she does and what it makes her. But I don't hate *her*. Not anymore. Not now that I've glimpsed the sweet dancer inside her.

Her eyes finally rise to meet mine. "I think I deserve to know."

I run my hand through my hair and pace in front of her. Frustration simmers just below my skin. Talking isn't my thing, and working through *feelings* sure as shit isn't either. Whenever I need to let off some steam, I do it in the ring. There's no crowd here, though. No cocky opponent to pour my rage into. It's just me and her.

I stop and face her. "I don't hate you. I hate dancers. Not the dancer you were before, but the one you became. I hate women who flaunt their tits in men's faces in exchange for cash. I hate people who remind me of the woman who ruined my life."

"Sacrificing me won't somehow right your mother's wrongs, Ambrose. You have to see that." Her eyes plead for me to hear her words, and her voice wavers when she speaks again. "Killing me doesn't wipe the scars from your body."

"I have no choice now! I've done far too much to let you live. I barreled past the point of no return when I spread your legs and took your cunt when you didn't want it. Even if I trusted you to keep your mouth shut, I can't let you go because I'm too obsessed with you. I would always be in the shadows, watching and waiting. Is that how you want to live?"

She shakes her head and looks at the mug in her lap.

"There's no other end for you, tragedy. I wouldn't have named you that in the first place if there was."

Her thumb clicks against the mug handle, then stops. "Can I make you a drink at least?"

Her question takes me off guard. "No, I don't drink," I tell her as I sit beside her.

"If you're going to kill me, the least you can do is have a drink with me," she says.

If that's her dying fucking wish, so be it.

"Go on, then. Make me a drink."

She gets to her feet and walks to the kitchen, only slightly favoring her ankle now. A bag of ice is good enough for me after a rough fight, but she needs something softer on her delicate skin. I make a mental note to buy gel ice packs from the store, then scratch through it. She won't be here with me the next time I go to the store.

The thought that once brought me so much excitement makes me feel sick.

I drape my arm over the back of the couch. "Make it strong," I yell toward the kitchen.

She returns after a few minutes and sets a drink in front of me on the coffee table. I stare at it. It's been so long since I've tasted alcohol. She's prepared my drink in a mug identical to hers, and I almost smile. This is the sort of cute couple shit I've never known. That I'll never know. Even once she's gone, she will always be my obsession. No one will ever satisfy me like she does.

I lift the mug and swish the liquid around. The acrid scent of vodka wafts up to me, and the hairs on the back of my neck stand. Drinking this feels more taboo than the murder I intend to commit, but maybe it will drown out the doubt bubbling low in my gut. It's called liquid courage, after all.

I throw back the drink, and the liquor singes my throat. She really took "make it strong" to heart. I look over at her, and she's back to balancing her glass on her knees again. She picks it up and takes a swig before lowering it. She drinks much slower, savoring the flavor. I tip the mug to my lips again and finish mine off. I'll let her take her time. A few more minutes won't hurt anything.

I yawn. The drive has taken more out of me than I realized. "Thanks for the drink," I say.

She nods and takes another sip of hers. "Thanks for drinking with me," she says with a smile.

Oaklyn

AMBROSE RELEASES ANOTHER YAWN, this one much heartier than the last. His lids close over his brown eyes in a slow blink, and he shakes his head. I can't help but wonder if he knows he's been drugged. Can he feel the heavy blanket of dysphoria covering his mind like I did when he did the same to me?

I tap my fingers on the mug and hope he doesn't go into

the kitchen. I took a big risk by putting his flask of sleepy-time juice in my bag before we left the cabin, and I don't want my plan blown now. My heart had nearly beaten out of my chest while he was making my drink. I'd tucked the flask into a side pocket in my bag, but I wouldn't put it past him to snoop. Thankfully, he only went for the bottles on top.

Another yawn. And another.

It seems to be working pretty quickly. Remembering how a small sip had affected me, I only put a dash into his drink. Unlike Ambrose, I don't have murder on my mind.

"I don't know why I'm so tired," he says, his voice low and groggy. He tries to stand up, but he stumbles backward.

I fight back a smile as he falls onto the couch.

"Shit," he groans. "What did you do, tragedy?" His words meld together. He lifts his hands, but they flop back to the couch before his head follows. Wordless whispers leave his mouth. His eyes close, and the whispers stop.

I peer down at Ambrose as he sleeps. A ribbed sleeveless t-shirt hugs his muscles. Jeans ride low on his hips. I trace my fingers over the scars on his face, then move to the soft pink lines lacing his chest. So much damage to one body. No wonder he's so angry at the world.

He's not the only one dealing with a lot of emotions, though. I'm angry. I'm frustrated. I feel trapped. The unlocked door calls to me, but running isn't the answer. Even if I run to another country, he'll find me.

You're making excuses. Stop lying to yourself.

And it is a lie. I can't run, but it's not only because I know he'll follow. It's because for some insane reason, I have come to care about this man. He's more than his gruff exterior and unhinged decisions. I'm drawn to *him*. I see past the scars, both literal and figurative. If he could just get over this stupid idea that he has to kill me, I could show him what it means to be cared for. We're two untethered ships, attached to nothing and no one as we sail through a storm. If we could only find a way to sail side by side, we could put all of our hurt behind us and weather the waves together.

But that's just another pipe dream to add to the list.

I pull the knife from his hip and put the tip of the blade against his neck. For once, I have all the power, and I want to know what it feels like to hold a life in my shaking hands. I freeze in place before I can pierce his skin, as if an invisible barrier stands between me and the unthinkable. It's probably my moral compass—an internal guidance system Ambrose clearly lacks.

"Fuck!" I scream, and even the piercing frustration in my voice doesn't wake him.

Harnessing that anger, I try to push it through the blade. I don't want to kill him. I just want to leave a mark he'll never forget. The wires in my brain are still firmly connected to my conscience, and I can't take the life of this man, even though he plans to take mine.

And he will take my life when he wakes up. I'm pretty sure about that. I just need to think of some way to get my own vengeance before he does. Something that will show him he's not the only one with a score to settle.

My gaze falls to his lap, and I get an idea.

I drop the knife to the coffee table and step out of my shorts. I unfasten his jeans, nearly ripping off the button in my frenzy, then I snatch down the zipper. Without even bothering to warm my cold hand, I sink my fingers beneath his boxers and pull out his limp cock.

"Get hard for me, asshole," I say through gritted teeth. I wrap my hand around him and squeeze. Even though I stroke him with the rough, callous, painful touch he deserves, his cock begins to harden. It swells and grows until he fills my hand. Wetness drips down my thighs at the thought of what I plan to do to him.

I'm going to use him like he used me.

I'm going to pull all my pleasure from his lifeless fucking body. He's my toy, rendered down to nothing more than a doll with a dick.

I straddle his lap and grind my pussy along his length. The piercings send a satisfying shiver up my spine. The memory of the pleasure his cock gave me is not a distant one. I hate that I liked how he made me come, but I love that I'm taking it again—this time, on *my* terms. He can't judge me or my career. He can't call me a whore or a slut. He can't do anything but lie there while I use his cock.

I lean back and bring his head to my entrance, watching for any reaction as my warmth presses against him. He doesn't move, and the power makes me ache. I lower myself to his pelvis, and a moan leaves my lips as I rock on his lap. With my hands on his chest, I ride him hard. Up, down, up, down, with a scoop of my hips between each motion so my sensitive clit can brush against his pelvis as I force his cock to please me. For a moment, I miss the feeling of hands touching me elsewhere, but then I remember that dolls don't touch you. They just lie there and get fucked.

I moan as I drop back my head and keep driving my hips on his lap. An angry energy surges through me, and I put my weight into my hands again. I hate-fuck the person who ruined what little of a life I'd gotten back. The man who has wrapped an invisible chain around my heart and won't let me go.

I draw back my hand and slap his face hard enough to make my palm sting. "Fuck you!" I scream as I drop my weight onto his lap. "Fuck you for what you've done to me when I've been asleep *and* awake. You evil . . . fucking . . ."

My angry words morph into moans, and my abdomen clenches. Sweat drips down the small of my back as I increase the tempo and pressure in time with my selfish desires. The hairs of his pelvis give me that last bit of friction I need.

With his cock impaling me and every muscle in my body quivering and tense, I come so fucking hard. I cry out and continue to use him until my clenching core begs me to stop. I drop down, lying on my chest with his hard cock still buried inside me. He won't get to reach his climax. This was all about me getting mine for once.

Full and stuffed, I pant against his skin, but I don't want it to end quite yet. I look up at him and bask in the remnants of my orgasm. His head lolls to the side, and my eyes focus on the soft pout of his lower lip.

"I like you, Ambrose," I whisper, "but I *really* like your dick." I grip his hair and turn his face toward me. "You're my little plaything now, aren't you? Useful for nothing more than my pleasure. You can't talk or move, but you can lie there and let me fuck myself with your cock, huh?"

I grip his chin, open his mouth, and gather spit beneath my tongue. Leaning over him, I drip the spit into his mouth. It's my turn to have control and do what has been done to me. He gets to be blissfully unaware of the degrading piece of me I left inside his mouth, but that's okay. This is enough.

Now I know why he did this to me. It's like I own his body. His cock. Like I can use him without having to worry about getting him off or pleasing him. It's intoxicating, and I'm drunk off his helplessness.

But now the fun is over and I have no idea what will happen once he wakes up. I wish he could see this as a fair trade. I wish we could come to some kind of fucked-up truce. You assaulted me. I assaulted you. The playing field is leveled now. Maybe we can play a new sort of game?

I sigh and turn my head toward the door. The only game he'll play is one where he makes the rules. If I knew what was good for me, I'd grab my shit and never look back.

I return my attention to his face. Will he really kill me? Am I the only one who feels this magnetism pulling us together?

Probably yes on both counts.

I close my eyes and drop my head to his shoulder. He'll be out for several hours at least. I still have time to decide what I'll do.

Chapter Thirty

Ambrose

I wake up on the couch, confused as fuck. My heavy lids struggle to rise enough for my glassy eyes to focus on the room. I don't know where I am or what day it is. I feel as if I've slept beneath a two-hundred-pound blanket for a week.

After a quick survey of my body, concern wraps a twine around my heart and squeezes. Wrinkles and stretched fabric mar my sleeveless t-shirt, as if someone gripped the fabric between clenched fists. Was I in some kind of fight? I rub my hand over the front of my pants to make sure I didn't piss myself or anything. My jeans are buttoned but not zipped. Well, they're half zipped. I sit up and look around.

Oaklyn! Shit.

I rise from the couch, then drop back to the cushions. My head spins and the floor rolls beneath my feet. She fucking drugged me.

The empty mug stares up at me from the coffee table, and I curse under my breath. I struggle to remember what happened. I made her a drink in the kitchen, then she asked me to drink with her. She fucking *insisted*. This bitch. She probably drugged me so she could escape.

I reach for the knife on my hip, but it's missing. Glancing around, I spot it on the coffee table and snatch it up. She must have thought about killing me but chickened out before she could go through with it. After everything I've done to her, she still couldn't do what anyone else would have done in her situation. Now she'll pay for her mistake. My fingers curl around the weighted handle, and visions of what I'll do to her flash through my mind.

But first, I have to find her.

I storm toward my bedroom, eager to change into some fresh clothes. As I barrel through the doorway, my feet refuse to take another step. Red hair drapes over the white pillowcase, and the thin sheet rises and falls in a slow pattern. She's right in front of me, asleep on my bed.

Okay, now I'm really fucking confused.

She turns over, still fast asleep, and the sheet falls and wraps around her waist.

"What'd you do, tragedy?" I whisper as I step toward the bed.

Nothing makes any sense. Why drug me if she didn't plan to kill me and escape? Even if she couldn't kill me, she still had a golden opportunity to get away from me, at least for a little while. But she stayed.

I step closer and study her face. Memories flicker in my mind like a strobe light, only granting brief flashes of what happened last night. Her hand on my cock. The weight of her on my lap. She slipped me inside her. She drugged me and rode me like a madwoman.

I rub my hand against my crotch, and a deep ache

burrows through my pelvis. She rode me hard enough to leave bruises.

More memories flicker through the haze. She lay on my chest with my cock still buried inside her. I bet she'd come by then. I vaguely remember a few of the words as her tits pressed against me.

"I like you, Ambrose, but I really like your dick . . . You can't talk or move, but you can lie there and let me fuck myself with your cock, huh?"

Jesus Christ in hell. I wish I could remember more. I wish I could have felt that whole scene play out. Did I even get off? I undo my jeans and pull out my cock. Remnants of dried come cling to my skin, but I don't think any of it belongs to me. Two bruises mark my junk, probably from her banging up and down on my lap like I was a fucking Hopper Ball.

For a fleeting moment, I feel used. It's just a drop of water in the ocean compared to how I've made her feel, though. It's not even the same, really. Knowing she fucked herself with my cock turns me on to the point of being painful, and I worry I'll bust while just thinking about it.

I grip my hard cock, unable to deny the urge clawing through me. Stroking my dick, I step closer to the bed and ease her head around so she's facing me. My mind clings to those fleeting memories of how she used me, and my balls throb with an ache I need to quell. My erection aims toward her mouth. I stroke harder and faster, keeping my eyes on those full lips that released such hate-filled words as she came on my cock. It's enough to push me over the edge, and I come, shooting ropes of pleasure across her lips and cheeks.

Her eyes fly open as soon as the warm beads hit her

skin. She opens her mouth, and some slides onto her tongue. "What the fuck!" she screams.

I lean over and gather the come with my fingers, then push it into her mouth. My fingertips curl at the back of her tongue and she gags, straining against my hand.

"This is for using me last night," I say, fucking the back of her throat with my come-coated fingers. Not wanting her to puke, I pull them out and get into bed with her before she has a chance to run away. I crawl between her legs, and she kicks at me. Avoiding her flailing feet, I hook my arms around the backs of her thighs and draw her knees upward. I pull her shorts aside and expose the pretty little cunt that left the bruises on my dick.

"What are you doing?" she says while trying to pull her legs out of my steadfast grasp.

I growl in response and bury my face in her pussy. She already pleased herself plenty with my dick last night, but she deserves to come again. I like that she stooped to my level and used me the way I used her. It was beautiful. Her need for vengeance spoke to me in a language I understood very well.

Her struggle ceases as I tongue-fuck her pussy, licking upward and teasing her clit. Instead of pushing me away, her hands relax and pull me closer.

"You liked raping me, didn't you, tragedy?" I stuff my come-coated fingers inside her, and she gasps as I sink them up to the knuckles. "You came from it, didn't you? Tell me." I swivel my hand so I can curl my fingers toward the front of her pelvis, dissolving her anger.

Her back arches and her thighs tremble. "I liked . . . using your cock . . . while you were asleep," she pants.

I slam my fingers into her as she admits what she did.

"Did you come?" I ask. I want to hear her say it. I want her to tell me that what I found on my dick had been left by her alone.

"I . . . came," she moans, the sound amplifying as I curl my fingers inside her. "I came as I rode your dick, Ambrose, then I told you how much I hated you as I lay on your chest."

She's so pliable when she's on the tip of an orgasm. So much more willing to bend to me. I don't even mind that she's lying about what she said.

"Do you hate me right now, when I have you hanging off the edge of an orgasm?"

"Yes," she pants. "I fucking hate you."

God, I love that. I think I like it more than when she said she liked me. Let her hate me if she needs to. I had no issue coming when I hated her.

Hated.

Why is that past tense? As her slick, wet pussy drips from my touch, I struggle to harness the hatred I once had for her.

I sit up on my knees, keeping my fingers inside her, as I lean over and lick my come from her cheek before kissing her. As I thrust in and out of her cunt, she slowly welcomes me into her mouth.

Kissing her is something else. I sense the need and hunger in every movement of her tongue. She doesn't shy away from the salty taste of my come, and her throat moves as she willingly swallows me. My compliant little whore.

"Come for me, tragedy," I growl against her lips.

She tenses as if she expects me to threaten her life with the next set of words that leave my lips, but I can't find the desire to kill her anymore. I want to make her come for me again and again, and I can't do that if she's dead. Instead of a threat, I let my new truth fall from my lips.

"Be a good girl and come."

She does. I have to pull away from her mouth as her moans grow and rise to a trembling crescendo. Her body quivers beneath me, and her eyes roll to the back of her head. My hand goes to her throat, and I put pressure on her neck as her orgasm wanes. She accepts her fate, ready to die if I don't let her draw air. This would be the perfect moment to take her life, but whatever stayed her hand last night has chosen to affect me as well. I can't do it.

I release her throat and brush the hair from her face as she pants. "I don't want to be without you," I whisper.

"Then don't," she breathes.

She makes it sound so simple. She doesn't understand that I stand to lose her either way. If I kill her, she's gone forever. If I let her live, she'll leave.

"You won't choose to stay with me," I say. "You and I both know that, and I can't be without you."

Her eyes flutter as they rise to meet mine. "Haven't I chosen already?"

I can't deny the veracity of her words. She had every opportunity to take off after she drugged me. When I realized what had happened after I woke up, I expected to have to hunt her down. I was prepared to travel across the country to find her if I had to. When I found her in bed, I was too distracted by what happened while I was drugged to think about what didn't happen. The magnitude of what it means didn't hit me until this moment.

She could have killed me. She could have escaped. She could have turned me in to the police. And she did none of those things. She made a choice, and she chose me. My little tragedy stayed.

But what could we ever be? Enemies born from my obsession couldn't possibly become lovers. Can't she see that?

"How can this work?" I ask. "After everything I've done to you, how can you stay?"

Her hands brush against my cheeks, and her soft touch glides over my scars. I don't pull away. For the first time, I don't feel the need to hide my disfigurement like a dirty secret or wield it like a weapon to induce fear. I allow her to see these marks and touch them in a way no one else has. No one else has even tried.

She licks her lips, and her eyes meet mine. "When you pushed my head below water, I had to trust you to let me up for air. When you give me pain, I have to trust you to follow it with pleasure. Now it's your turn to trust me." She pulls me closer and kisses me, then speaks against my lips. "If I run, just let me run, Ambrose. But if I stay, don't push me away."

I nod. It's the best I can do because I can't make a promise I can't keep, but for her, I'll try.

Chapter Thirty-One

Oaklyn

He posed a good question. How *can* this work? I'm not entirely sure, but I can't walk away. I proved that last night when I had the chance to leave and I chose to stay.

"Having doubts about sticking with me, tragedy?" he asks.

I must look doubtful. I'm not *doubtful*, per se, but I am confused as fuck. Why does my body respond to a monster like him? Why does it betray me when he touches me? His touch should disgust me, but it has the opposite effect. He's an expert with my body, despite having abused it so much. I guess that's what I should expect when fucking my stalker. He knows me in ways no one else has taken the time to notice, like how I like my favorite drink or how to turn me into a quivering mess on his lap by rubbing me a certain way.

His hand rises to my face, and his ginger touch lands on my cheek. "If you expect me to feel remorseful for the things I've done, you'll have to wait forever. I'm not sorry for what I've done to you, because I wouldn't have seen you as more than a whore destined for death at my hands if I hadn't."

I sigh. Threats dilute each compliment that springs from his mouth. Can't he just say something nice without it preceding something about murdering me? And that brings me to another concern.

I'm attracted to Ambrose, scars and all, but I don't feel *safe* with him. While I trust him to protect me from others, I don't know if he can protect me from himself. I'm still unsure he can triumph over his desire to kill me.

My stomach grumbles, and he looks down at it with a smirk. "Looks like I haven't fully satisfied you after all." He rises from the bed and goes to his closet. "We'll have to do some shopping later, but I'll go grab a quick breakfast to hold us over this morning."

I almost laugh at this. A few days ago, I was running through the woods to get away from him. Now we're planning a shopping trip and breakfast. Life has thrown me some hellacious curveballs over the past few years, but this one has beaned me right between the eyes. I'm almost dizzy from all the changes.

His phone rings in the living room, and he goes to answer it once he's dressed. I close my eyes again, happy to sleep a little longer after Ambrose relaxed me, but his voice rises and reaches me from the next room. Wondering what has him so heated, I slip out of the bed and tiptoe to the doorway, keeping myself out of sight should he pace past the hall.

"I fucking told you," he says. "The reason doesn't matter, so stop asking. I'll come back and fight when I'm good and goddamn ready. If you want me in tonight, either pay more or book me for a double."

He's speaking with his boss, which reminds me I have to call Jake and let him know I'm back in town. I haven't even considered how my return to work might affect Ambrose. He doesn't like what I do, but I'm not willing to stop doing it. I want to dance, and I want to earn my own money. I'll need to broach the topic before he leaves, but the thought sends a rock rolling through my gut.

"If you've already blasted promos for tonight, that sounds like a you problem. Either book me twice or pay more for the last fight of the night." He pauses. "I don't give a fuck. Make it happen or find a new headliner."

The phone clatters onto a hard surface. I scurry back to the bed and situate myself beneath the covers before he can return and catch me eavesdropping. He comes toward the bed and sits on the edge with a sigh as tension weighs down every muscle in his body. Leaning forward and placing his elbows on his thighs, his hands curl into tight fists, and the muscle in his jaw contracts and relaxes in a rhythm that scares me. Unable to fight this confusing urge to comfort him, I reach toward him and rub slow circles on his back.

The muscles begin to relax.

"I might have to fight tonight," he finally says. "I don't know how I'll get through the night when I don't know if you'll be here when I get back."

I shrug. "I need to get back to work too. You can pick me up from the club when—"

His attention snaps to me. "I don't fucking think so."

I knew this wouldn't be easy, but I didn't think it would go south quite this fast. The anger raging in his eyes reminds me to choose my words carefully, but I can't just roll over and agree to stop dancing.

"We have to find a way to work through this," I say. "I'm not willing to give up my dance career, even if you don't agree with it."

"I can provide for you, so there's no reason to go back to that shit hole. Yeah, I can't buy you a Tesla or put you in a mansion with a pool, but I'll make sure you have everything you need and as much of your wants as I can afford."

I shake my head. He doesn't get it. "It's not just about the money, Ambrose. You say you'll provide for all of my needs, but I *need* to dance. I'm not asking you to like it, but you'll have to learn to deal with it."

"Fuck no." He gets to his feet and paces at the foot of the bed. When he stops and grips the railing, I fear it will snap in his tightening grasp. His dark eyes meet mine, but I refuse to cower under his glare. "Your body is for my eyes only. Don't you get that? If you want to be mine, you can *only* be mine. You'll have to make a choice."

His words are a slap in the face. Haven't I made enough choices already? "That isn't fair."

"Don't talk to me about fair, tragedy. Don't you fucking dare."

There has to be a solution to this. A compromise lies somewhere, but he has to be willing to see it. "What if I stop doing private dances? I can tell Jake I'm only available for stage time and nothing else. That way, I can keep dancing and you're the only one getting a private show."

"No," he says, leaving no room for compromise.

I fold my arms over my chest and look away, unwilling to continue this conversation. If he can't see how irrational he is, rubbing his nose in it won't help. It's already right in front of his face.

He releases the bed railing and stands upright, his muscles tensing beneath his shirt as he comes toward me. I flinch when he reaches my side, expecting him to grab my throat or fist my hair, but he does neither. He leans forward and kisses me hard. His fingers rake my scalp, and he grips the red tendrils tightly enough to make it hurt while sending a shiver through my core. He made me come only minutes ago, but I'm already hungry for another mind-blowing orgasm only he can provide. When he pulls away, I'm breathless.

"The bus stop is two blocks down," he says against my lips. "If you're gone when I get back, I'll respect your decision. I can't promise you won't see me in the shadows every day for the rest of your life, and I can't promise you won't wake up some days with pain between your legs and the memory of the previous evening erased. I can only promise that if you leave, I will kill you if you ever come looking for me. You can't have it both ways, tragedy, so choose wisely."

He releases my hair and leaves the bedroom. Seconds later, the front door slams and I'm left with an ache between my legs and an impossible decision.

Ambrose

I LEAVE the bagel shop with two orders because I can't stop myself from hoping she'll still be in my bed when I get back to the apartment. Guilt claws at my throat, begging to burst from it in the form of an apology when I return. I'm no better than her shitty family for forcing such a decision on her.

But I won't apologize and I won't change my mind. Sharing her isn't an option.

I meant what I said. I'll let her go if she chooses to keep dancing, but she better not show her face to me again. If I want to see her, I'll find her myself. Probably on a regular fucking basis. I'll continue to take what I want from her, but she'll no longer reap the benefits of an amicable arrangement. Maybe I'm no better than her family, but if she can't choose me, she's no better than my fucking mother.

Pulling into the apartment parking lot, I take a moment to prepare myself for what I might walk into. An empty home never bothered me before, but the thought of it now pulls my stomach to my feet. I want her to be inside when I open the door. I want that more than anything I've ever wanted before, and I don't know how I'll handle the disappointment if she's not there. She came into my life and fucked everything up, and now she holds the final thread of my sanity between her fingers. If she's severed that thread, I don't know what I'll do.

I grab the brown paper bag containing our breakfast and start across the parking lot. Anxiety badgers my brain, and I can't even be bothered to cover my face from the prying eyes that seek out my scars. Let them look. Hell, let them take a fucking picture for all I care. I just need to get inside and learn the answer to the question that's been burning through my mind since I left the house.

Did she stay?

I unlock the front door and step inside. My footsteps brush along the carpet, then shift to a thud as I toss the sack of breakfast on the counter in the kitchen. Her bag no longer sits beside the sink.

Maybe she grabbed it so she could shower and change clothes.

My heart grasps at excuses, but logic shouts the truth over each weak argument. I won't find her in the shower. I won't find her in the bedroom, either. I won't find her anywhere in this apartment because she probably left as soon as I drove out of the parking lot. Silence greets me in every room, and I'm forced to face facts when I reach the bedroom.

She's gone.

My brain tempts me. It tells me I should rush straight to my Jeep and hunt her down so I can put an end to my torment, but that organ fails to realize I'll be tormented either way. She chose to leave, and I have to let her go. Killing her doesn't solve anything anymore. At least if she's alive, I can still watch her. And use her.

I go to the couch and sit down with the breakfast I no longer have the stomach to eat. My tragedy has lived up to her nickname, but not in the way I anticipated when I first coined it. She was supposed to meet her tragic end in the finale, but she turned the tables and brought about my tragic end instead. Fucking plot twists.

My phone chimes, and I roll my eyes when I read the message. Darby caved and scheduled me for two fights. I'll go head to head with Boris for the first bout, then I'll face a newcomer in the final match of the night. I squint at the screen and study the man's name. He must be new to the street fight scene entirely because I've never heard of him, and I know everyone worth knowing. It isn't like Darby to put a rookie in the ring with someone like me, so he must be looking for a bloodbath.

If that's what he wants, that's exactly what he'll get. I have a lot of pent-up frustration to let out.

I try to sit back and get my head in the game. When I have a scheduled fight, I need to warm up my body *and* my mind. The crowd thinks it's all a game of thoughtless jabs and kicks, but there's a lot more to it than that. Sure, all the heavy blows and sprays of blood are fun to watch, but the opponents are playing a different sort of mental chess in the ring. We're searching for weaknesses and exploiting them. We're calculating. It helps when you know your opponent, though, and the unknown elements for the final match are grating on my nerves.

It also doesn't help that my thoughts keep circling back to Oaklyn. I picture her in the crowd, watching me do what I do best. I know what it feels like to hear people cheering me on because they've got money riding on my win, but I've never had someone root for me because they support me. And now I never will.

She made her choice, and it wasn't me.

On top of everything else, my body aches and I'm tired. I'm in no shape to fight tonight, but the money is too good to pass up. My opponent won't care if I'm in top form, though. He won't care that I'm mentally exhausted. He will happily kick my ass with a smile on his face if I can't get my shit together. Most of these fuckers couldn't beat me on my worst day, but I won't risk my winning streak for anything. I have to focus.

I lift my phone and consider telling Darby I can't come in tonight, that I'm sick or hurt or some other fabricated story. But it's no use. Like Oaklyn needs to dance, I need to fight. I just have to make sure I don't lose.

Chapter Thirty-Two

Oaklyn

Dressing for work doesn't feel the same as it did before I met Ambrose. I never considered how much skin I show to the men who watch me dance, but now it's *all* I can think about. Even though I chose to leave, I still feel like I belong to him. It doesn't feel right to give these parts of myself away anymore. They aren't mine to give.

I contemplate tucking my tail between my legs and returning to his apartment. It hasn't even been twelve hours since I last saw him, and I already miss him. That would be suicide, though. He'd make me pay for hurting him, and I'd deserve it. It isn't right to yank around someone's emotions like that, and he was falling just as hard as I was. I'll just have to forget about the devastatingly handsome man who made me come like I never had before. But that task is easier said than done. He hasn't left my mind since I closed his apartment door behind me and shuffled to the bus stop.

Since returning to him isn't an option, I do the only

thing I can and apply a little makeup to hide the red, puffy skin around my eyes. I've been crying all day. If I wipe my eyes one more time, the skin is liable to fall right off. Sick of moping around my trailer, I dress in a baggy t-shirt and some sweats to cover my dance outfit—the only work attire left standing because it was in the laundry room when Ambrose went on his rampage in my closet—then I head for the bus stop.

The sun sinks below the city skyline as I board the bus and find a seat near the back. Vibrant oranges and purples stretch behind the buildings. It's the sort of view I would have used to distract myself from the judgmental glares of my fellow travelers, but now I don't even notice their pretentious eyes. Now I use the sunset to distract myself from yet another impossible dream that has been snatched away from my empty hands.

He asked how we could make this work, and I didn't answer him because I didn't know what to say. I still don't have an answer, but I wanted to find out. More than anything, I wanted to try. But once again, I slid on my dancing shoes and arabesqued my way to the exit. My dream was worth more to me than the family who refused to acknowledge it, but was it worth more than what I could have had with Ambrose?

I'm not so sure anymore.

The bus pulls to a stop near the club, and I trudge down the aisle. Maybe I'll feel better when the music starts and I can put my emotions into movement.

When I enter the dressing room, my eyes land on some-thing beneath my station. It's the acorn from the first night Ambrose started leaving me these twisted little gifts. I'm not afraid of it anymore. Like a psychopath, I get on my hands and knees and retrieve the little nut from the shadows. It's all I have left of him. I slide it into my pocket, then head to the front of the house to grab a drink before my shift officially starts.

A few men sit around the stage, paying more attention to each other than the poor girl grinding against the pole for all she's worth. It's pretty dead tonight, which sucks for my finances but bodes well for my psyche. I don't think I can handle a bunch of drunk idiots pawing at me tonight. Or ever again.

The bartender spots me as I slide onto the stool, and she sways toward me. She asks what I'd like, and I'm a bit shocked by her question. I always order the same thing, yet this girl can't remember something as simple as a Moscow Mule.

Ambrose knew it.

The thought is an arrow to my heart.

I can never tell anyone about my feelings for Ambrose and how they came about. I'd get analyzed to hell and back, which is wholly unfair. Doesn't every relationship begin with a little obsession? Yeah, Ambrose needs a little work in the impulse control department, but we all have our flaws. He just refuses to hide his.

The bartender slides the copper mug into my hands, and I take a gulp. God, I miss him, and now that I've tasted this monstrosity, I miss him even more. He never went too heavy with the lime.

A couple of guys enter the club. Muscles bulge from their too-tight t-shirts, though they don't hold a candle to Ambrose's beautiful build. I don't recognize either of them, and when they sit near me at the bar, I wish they'd chosen a different spot. I just want to enjoy my disgusting drink in peace.

"No, that's the beauty of it," the short blond man says to

his taller, balding friend. "All Marty has to do is take the guy out. After that, he can catch the next flight back to Florida with his cut of the door fee."

I should really stop myself from eavesdropping on this particular conversation. It sounds like these men are talking about a hit. But I'm a nosy bitch, so I keep my ass planted on the stool.

"I don't know," Baldy says. "He agreed to fight dirty and knock the guy down a peg, but now he wants Marty to kill him?"

Yep. Definitely a hit. I pull out my phone and pretend to be very much engrossed in my inactive Facebook account.

"Shhh, keep it down." Shorty looks around, but he doesn't seem to notice me, even though I'm only one stool away. The perks of being a lowly "whore" in this establishment, I guess.

Baldy shifts in his seat. "Look, I'll get Marty to do it, but have you seen the guy he's supposed to fight tonight? I'm not sure anyone *can* kill him. He's never lost a fight, for starters. Then he's got these scars all over. He's been through some serious shit."

I nearly drop my drink into my lap. My brain puts all the pieces together, and I don't like the picture it shows me. A fighter who never loses. Scars.

They plan to kill Ambrose.

"No one is invincible," Shorty says. "Look, just send Marty the text. Darby says this guy has gotten too big for his goddamn britches. While he was away for a few days, the fights only brought in half the revenue. Now that he's back in town, he's threatening to find somewhere else to fight if Darby doesn't pay more. He's bad for business. If Marty can dethrone him and shed more blood than this place has seen in a while, we'll kill two birds with one stone. The fighters will realize how expendable they are and won't bitch about their pay, and Darby won't need that disfigured fuck anymore. The bills will pay themselves."

Disfigured fuck? I nearly lose it. These assholes don't know what he went through to get those scars. But I can't say anything. I have to let Ambrose know about Darby's plan before it's too late. He's scheduled for two fights tonight, and I don't know if the hit is planned for the early fight or the headline.

I switch to my messaging app and shoot a text to Ambrose.

> Don't fight tonight. Darby plans to have you killed.

While I wait for him to see the message, I listen for any more information, but the men have switched to discussions of football as they enjoy their beers. Minutes tick by, but Ambrose doesn't respond. I'll have to go to the fight myself to warn him. When I break the rule and show my face to him, he might kill me before I have a chance to tell him why I'm there, but at least this Marty guy can avenge me if Ambrose is dumb enough to slit my throat before I can speak.

I hurry to the back of the building to look for Jake. He'll have to do without me for one more night, and I imagine he'll be pretty pissed about it. He already gave me an ass chewing for taking off for several days, and I'm scared he'll fire me altogether if I leave tonight. But I don't have a choice. I can't let these men hurt Ambrose.

I enter Jake's office and wince when he eyes me up and down. Even in a baggy t-shirt and some grungy sweatpants, I still feel naked when he looks at me. An oscillating fan blows across the desk, ruffling the stack of comic books he keeps on one corner. I don't think Jake actually reads them. I'm not even sure he *can* read. He probably just looks at the pictures.

"Hey, I hate to do this," I say, "but I have an emergency and I need to leave. I can come in tomorrow and—"

"Hold up," he says, rising from his desk. He walks past me and closes the door, then turns to face me again. "Wouldn't want the girls to hear this, now, would you?"

I shake my head, but the way he stands between me and the door fills me with an uneasy feeling.

"You've already been gone for several days, and I really can't afford to have you disappear on me again. You're one of my best dancers, but I'll have to find someone to replace you permanently if you keep leaving me in the lurch like this." His eyes flick to my breasts. "But maybe we can come up with an arrangement."

A light sweat slicks my palms. I don't like that he's closed the door and caged me in like this. I'm more concerned about that than his threat to hire someone to take my place. I try to push past him. "Never mind, Jake."

His fist closes around my arm, and he swings me in front of him. The backs of my thighs hit the chair, dropping me into the seat. When I try to rise, he grips my shoulders and holds me in place.

A smirk slides onto his face as he leans closer. "Maybe you should stay right where you are and show me how bad you want to keep your job. Then I'll consider cutting you loose for the night."

A strong garlicky odor clings to his breath, and my stomach clenches as the pungent scent finds its way into my nose. I turn my head to escape the stench, and I'm met with a fist across my lip. Warmth trickles down my chin. I touch my fingers to the heat, and they come away red.

"Don't turn away from me, you bitch." He pulls me to my feet and bends me over his desk, slamming my head against the cheap particle board. Stars dance in front of my eyes. "I've wanted to do this since the first night you came to the club, and no one is going to stop me this time. Now stay still and take this like the whore you are."

I don't have time for this, and I am sick and fucking tired of being labeled as something I'm not. The acorn in my pocket presses against my hip, and I know what I have to do. Instead of giving in and taking it, I'll do what I should have done a long time ago. I'll fucking fight back.

As he's busy unbuckling his belt, my eyes search the top of the desk. A pair of scissors and a pen sit in a cup, but they're just out of reach. If I go for them, he'll notice before I can grab them. His zipper falls, and I turn my head to check the other side of the desk. I'm running out of time, but I still don't see anything useful. Then I spot it. A gaudy letter opener with a woman straddling the top sits inches from my fingertips. I ease my hand forward and grab it as he approaches me from behind.

"Just stay like that," he says. "The more you fight it, the worse it will be for you."

His fingertips curl around my waistband, and he's within striking distance. I spin and drive the letter opener into the first thing I see, which happens to be his pasty, flabby thigh. With a high-pitched scream, he releases his hold on my pants and goes for the metal sticking out of his flesh. I don't stick around to deal with the aftermath. I bolt for the door.

I duck through the back hallway and head straight for the dressing room. While grabbing my bag, I catch a glimpse of myself in the mirror. My lip has swollen on the right side and my tears have smeared my mascara. This isn't how I want Ambrose to see me when I go to him, but I don't exactly have time to fix myself up.

My ankle groans with each step as I run toward the bus stop. The overworked joint begs for me to take it easy, but I can't. The bus is already pulling up to the little booth, and it's the last one for at least an hour. I don't have that sort of time to spare.

A loud hiss comes from the massive vehicle as it prepares to resume its journey. I raise my bag in the air and flail it around as I cry at the top of my lungs for the driver to wait. I'm almost there, but I won't make it. It's pulling away.

A flash of color rushes past one of the bus windows, and the behemoth comes to a stop before it's too far off the curb. As I near the vehicle, the woman with the massive carpet bag returns to her seat and eyes me through the window. She stopped the bus?

The doors open and I climb inside as Jake barrels from the building. His waving fists and angry words shrink into the distance as the driver pulls away. I turn and start down the aisle, and the old woman slides her bag into the space beside her on the seat. No words pass between us, but I think I have a better understanding of her now. All this time, I've imagined people were judging me because I was so accustomed to receiving criticism from everyone I let near me. Meanwhile, I've been placing my own misguided judgements on others.

The old woman doesn't have anything against me because of what I do for a living. She just likes to sit by herself.

I have been so blind, but I refuse to keep walking through life with my eyes closed. Maybe throwing away my family to chase my dance dream was the right call, but I never should have walked away from Ambrose. I should have stayed and fought for him, even if it meant fighting with him. If he doesn't kill me when he sees me, I'll tell him how I feel. I'll beg if I have to.

But first, I have to save his life.

Chapter Thirty-Three

Ambrose

I slide from the Jeep and shrug out of my leather jacket. A fresh sleeveless t-shirt clings to my sweat-coated body. I haven't even gotten into the ring yet and I'm already dripping with it. Adrenaline rushes through me like a drug. I've been away from the ring for too long, and I'm ready to get that release I feel when a punch lands with a solid crack.

A few people mill around the parking lot, but most of the crowd waits inside. Their animated voices reach me from here, and each step I take raises the noise level another octave. By the time I reach the door, it's a roar. They came for a show. They came to see blood. And I won't disappoint them.

"Scar!" a booming voice calls from my right.

I roll my eyes and turn to face it. "Darby," I deadpan.

"I tried to call," he says.

My shoulders lift in a shrug. "Left my phone at home. Didn't want any distractions."

He motions me up a flight of metal stairs that leads to his office, and I follow because I don't have a choice. As long as I fight in his ring, he's my boss.

He pulls a cigar from a box on a shelf and pops it into his crooked mouth, then offers me one. I shake my head. I don't put anything other than oxygen into my lungs before a fight. He shrugs and returns the box to its spot before dropping into a leather chair and lighting his cigar.

"About time you show your face around here," he says through a haze of smoke. "I was about to come to your door and drag you back to the ring if you didn't make an appearance tonight."

God, I hate him. "Well, I'm here, so fuck off."

"Word around town is you've been shacking up with some hot little redhead. Since when does scar have a pretty thing like that?"

If his goal is to have me throttle him to death in this office, he's dangerously close to succeeding. "I fight for you. That's the extent of what you need to know about me."

He takes a long drag of his cigar, then studies it for a moment. "You seem to forget what you are, scar. You're a fucking product. All my fighters are like livestock to me. When one strays too far from the herd for too long, its business becomes my business. If you don't want me to track you down, don't leave the pen."

"Maybe if you took better care of the herd, we wouldn't feel the need to run off. Ever think of that?"

His shit-eating grin evaporates, and that's enough for me.

"On that note, I've got a fight to win." I turn and leave his office. I've had enough of his shit.

I make my way down the stairs and push through the packed crowd until I reach the locker room. After wrapping my hands and warming up, I'm ready to take on Boris. I exit the locker room and head toward the center of the building. My eyes focus on the ring, and I roll my neck and work out my shoulders, trying to wake up every aching muscle as I head toward the ropes.

Boris stands in his corner, ready to go. I kind of like that little fuck. Men who fight him often underestimate him because of his short stature, but I know what he's capable of and I respect him. Which means this fight isn't ideal. Fighting someone I respect is worse than fighting someone I hate. He's also a tenacious little shit. He'll fight until he can't stand, then keep swinging while he's on the floor. This bout will be brutal because he almost always wins and I never lose. Good thing I'm in the mood for brutality.

I duck beneath the ropes and approach the scrappy brick house that is Boris. He steps into me and grabs my hand, pulling me into his chest.

"You ready, scar?" he asks, his accent thick in my ear.

"Do me a favor, Boris," I say. "Don't be afraid to tap out if things get rough. I've had one hell of a day, and I really don't want to kill you."

He nods and we both separate with an honest agreement to leave the ring alive tonight. I need him to not be so . . . Boris. In exchange, I agree to not be so . . . me. I strip off my shirt and throw it on the ropes.

The bell rings, and our friendship falls away. Boris and I meet in the center of the ring, and our two sweaty, muscular bodies collide with disgusting force. Fists swing with marginal inhibition on both sides. Exhaustion plagues my muscles long before it should, but I push through it.

Boris sends his signature swing right into my face. For such a compact dude, he packs a nauseatingly strong punch. When he goes for his next move, I block it—a perk to our familiarity. Blood drips from my nose and splatters onto the mat.

I see a flash of red from the corner of my eye, and I'm tempted to look into the crowd for a woman who won't be there. She has no reason to come here, especially not when I made that stupid threat. I did it to protect myself, and I've regretted it more with every passing second. I keep my eyes on Boris because looking for a ghost means risking another jab to the face.

I push forward, sending a hook into Boris' face. The blow stuns him, and I take the opportunity to slam my elbow across his jaw. This sends him to the ground. I pounce on top of him and we lock in a grappling stance. Blood drips from a cut above my eye, blurring my vision in a red haze. I try to wipe it away with the back of my hand, and Boris sees his opening. Using his powerful legs, he flips me onto my back and pins me beneath him. His muscles flex as he strikes me, and I deflect with my forearms.

Blood fills my mouth, and I need to spit it out if I want to draw enough air into my lungs. I turn my head and spew a spray of red onto the mat. My eyes land on the crowd, and time stops.

Oaklyn stands at the front of the crowd like a goddamn angel. I blink to clear the blood from my eyes, sure that I've only imagined her, but she's still there when I focus again. Her makeup runs down her face as if she's been crying, and her bottom lip is swollen to twice its normal side on the right side of her face. Dried blood paints the corner of her mouth. When she realizes I've noticed her, she waves her hands and screams something, but I can't hear her over the roar of the crowd. They're building into a frenzy, and she's in the danger zone.

I have to end this fight right now.

Boris readies himself for another punch, and I slam my head forward so that our foreheads collide. Colors flash behind my clenched eyelids. I flip Boris onto his back again, and I see I've done more than stun him. He's barely hanging on to consciousness at this point, but his fists continue to drive into my ribs. This feisty little bastard refuses to give up, and that's a real problem. It means the only way to end this fight right now would be to kill him.

I could take Boris out with one adrenaline-laced punch to his exposed throat. It would crush the delicate bones and obstruct his airway, which would be one shitty way to go out. He would fight until his last breath, but I need to get to Oaklyn before the crowd swallows her whole.

I pull back my fist, but I can't do it. "Boris, you need to tap!" I shout.

He shakes his head and mumbles something, but I can't hear him.

I move my free hand from the mat and press it on his throat. He'll be disqualified if he's unconscious. Choking him out will take longer, but it beats killing him.

The crowd releases a unified cheer of approval as I push my weight into my hand. This is what they paid to see. Like one cohesive, massive monster, they push forward toward the ring. Everyone wants to be on the front lines to witness this. Oaklyn gets jostled to the side, and she loses her balance, sending her to the floor. Her fucking ankle. They'll kill her if I don't get out of this ring.

So I do the only thing I can to save her.

I release my hold on Boris, and he springs forward. His forearm presses against my neck, and I can only look up at him and smile as I extend my right arm and tap the mat with my hand.

I need to lose.

For her.

The bell rings, ending the match, and I don't stick around to answer the look of shock on Boris' face. I slide under the rope and push people away until I find Oaklyn buried beneath a sea of legs. Pulling her to her feet, I guide her to the locker room. She keeps trying to pull away from me as she screams something, but I can't hear her. Frankly, I don't give a fuck what she has to say until I know she's okay. I also need to find out who busted her lip so I know who I need to murder when I leave here.

"Ambrose, please listen to me," she pleads once the door closes behind her. "I know you said not to show my face, but I—"

My hand goes to her throat, and I force her back against the wall. Fear colors her green eyes, but she's not afraid of *me*. Something else has her spooked. She isn't the only one who's afraid, though.

"You could have gotten yourself killed, tragedy. What the fuck were you thinking?"

"Please, Ambrose, you have to listen to me," she pleads. Tears fill her eyes, and she's shaking. I release her throat, and she falls into me. "I thought I was too late. I thought that man was about to kill you."

My eyebrows pull together. "Boris? He's a beast, I'll give him that, but it would take at least three of him to take me out. I know all that blood made it look like I was getting my ass beat, but I was winning until I had to save you from your own stupidity."

"No, no, you don't understand." She's breathless. Frantic. "Your boss planned to have you killed during your fight. I heard two guys talking about it at the club, but the fighter's name is Marty, not Boris. I know you said to stay away, but I couldn't let them kill you. I couldn't let them . . ." Her words devolve into guttural sobs.

I hold her against me as I try to wrap my mind around what she's just told me. I knew Darby was getting sick of my shit, but I didn't think he'd stoop that low. I'll have to handle him, but right now I need to know who hurt Oaklyn.

"How'd you get that busted lip?" I ask, pulling back her head so I can get a better look at her face. Mascara cuts black tracks down her cheeks, and the lip looks even worse up close. Even her delicate jaw has swollen.

Her chin quivers, and she tries to look away.

"Answer me, tragedy. Who fucking hurt you?"

She meets my gaze. "Jake."

This mother fucker.

"When I found out about the hit on you, I tried to send you a text. You didn't respond, so I went to Jake to let him know I had to leave. He tried to . . . He tried to rape me again, but I stabbed him and got away."

I hate the shame I see in her eyes. She has nothing to be ashamed of. I grip her chin between my fingers and tip it upward. She should hold her head high. "Good fucking girl."

"You have to get out of here," she whispers. "I'll take the bus back, and I promise to stay away this time, but you have to get away from Darby before he hurts you."

So this is what she was so afraid of? She risked her life to get to me so she could save me? My entire life, people have tried to run away from me or kill me. My mother. Women. The men I fight in the ring. Now I have someone who wants to run toward me. Someone who wants me on this earth.

"You'll do no such fucking thing," I say. "You're coming with me." She'll stay right by my side so I can protect her the way she just protected me. I grip her hand and try to lead her out of the locker room, but she digs in her heels and won't budge.

"What about the man who wants to kill you? Shouldn't you handle that?"

With a smirk, I turn back to her and lift her into my arms. If she won't walk, I'll carry her. "I'll deal with Darby later. Right now, I need to get you somewhere safe so I can doctor that lip."

I also need to plan a nice little surprise to thank Oaklyn for what she's done for me today. She needs to know just how much she means to me. I'm not exactly a flowers-and-dinner kind of guy, but an idea takes shape, and I think she'll love it.

She struggles in my arms, but I only tighten my hold as we leave the building. "Put me down," she whispers as people turn to look at us.

I laugh and lean close to her ear. "Let them stare. I'm beginning to like it."

Chapter Thirty-Four

Oaklyn

Ambrose has been gone since I woke up this morning. I'm familiar with anxiety. I've felt its sharp nail gliding up my back before a big performance or when I've waited for a callback after an audition. The anticipation I feel right now is different, though. It tears at my mind in an unrelenting way and refuses to give me a moment of peace. I don't know where he is or what he's doing.

By the time lunch rolls around and he comes through the front door of his apartment, I'm ready to explode. "Where have you been? I was so afraid Darby—"

"I have something to give you," Ambrose says as he drops a bag onto the coffee table.

"What?" I ask.

He motions toward the bag, and I look at him for a moment before opening it. Pink tissue paper fills the inside. I move it aside and find a gorgeous set of green lingerie. The color will complement my skin instead of washing it out like the harsh blacks I usually wore at work. The low-cut thong and silky garter skirt will hide absolutely nothing, but I guess that's kind of the point.

"Go shower and get ready, and I'll show you what it's for," he says, and his words leave no room for argument. His excited expression draws a smile from me, despite my confusion.

I put the lingerie into the bag. "What about the Darby situation? Did you handle that?"

"I put in a call to a couple of brothers who . . . handle things. They fight at the club sometimes, so they already know what a piece of shit Darby is. They're probably in his office right about now, having a nice little *talk*."

That's all I want to know about that. If Ambrose says it's handled, that's good enough for me.

I take a quick shower and dress in something comfortable. I don't know what Ambrose has planned, but I can only hope a pair of shorts and a tank top will be suitable. He doesn't seem like the type to dine at a fancy restaurant, so I'm probably fine. Before I leave the bedroom, I tuck the acorn into my pocket. I've come to see it as my little good luck charm, which I realize is weird since it was once used to terrify me. On our way out the door, he grabs the bag containing the lingerie. I eye him, still confused about what a bra and panty set has to do with where we're going.

"Just wait and see," he says with a smirk that makes me want to strip where I stand.

We get in the Jeep and drive until we hit a familiar part of town. My curiosity shifts to discomfort when I realize where we're going.

"Ambrose . . ." I whisper as we drive down the familiar road toward the club. "If you're going to the club, it doesn't open for several hours and I have no way to get in." It's early afternoon. Jake doesn't unlock the doors until five.

He just keeps driving.

I don't like this. It doesn't feel right. He hasn't said anything more about killing me, but that's what I fear he plans to do. The club would be the perfect place to sacrifice me. It's the reason he chose me in the first place, and it's the fountain that spews forth all his hatred for women in my line of work.

He pulls into the empty parking lot, and my hand trembles on the armrest between us.

"Do you trust me?" he asks.

My eyes jump to his.

"I told you I have something to give you," he pushes.

I rattle the bag on my lap. "Yeah, you gave it to me already."

He shakes his head, and a low laugh rattles his chest. "Oh no, that's not for *you*. That's for *me*."

My leg shakes as anxiety courses through me. Now the bag makes sense. He's going to dress me up like the whore he always says I am, then he's going to murder me in the club. I don't want this to be my end. We've come too far in this fucked-up little relationship for him to kill me in a place we both hate.

"Please don't kill me, Ambrose," I whimper as I look into his eyes.

"Kill you?" he says. He gets out of the Jeep and comes to my side, then opens the door. He leans down. "I'm not going to kill you, tragedy. As much as I'd love the meaning behind ending you in the place where my mother used to work, I have no intention of killing you here. Or at all."

He grabs my hand and pulls me toward the back door. It's propped open with a large stone, which is weird for this time of day. We enter the dressing room, and I glance at my station. My makeup and brush are missing, probably stolen by one of the other girls who considered it abandoned. It was, I guess.

Ambrose removes the stone from the door, and it closes. A scream from somewhere in the club permeates the silent air. I recognize the voice. My eyes roll up to Ambrose, and my head starts to shake before I can even process what I'm hearing.

"What did you do?" I ask, though I really, *really* don't want to know. Even so, I have the terrible feeling he'll show me regardless of what I want.

He pushes the bag into my hands. "Put this on. When you're ready, I want to see you on the stage. I want to see you dance for me, tragedy."

I'm too dumbfounded to speak, so I only nod. He leaves the dressing area, and I pull out the lingerie. As I slip off my clothes and dress in this outfit, I worry whatever's about to happen will trigger Ambrose to do more than he's planned. Another scream pierces the silence as I tighten the bra straps so that my breasts rise and pull together. I close my eyes. I have to trust him. He plans to hurt someone, but it won't be me. I run my hand down the garter skirt and check myself in the mirror.

For the first time in this dressing room, I feel beautiful.

My eyes fall to the heels beside my station, and I slide my feet into them. The final touch.

I make my way to the stage and step onto it. With the lights in my eyes, it's hard to see, but I eventually realize what's happening as my vision adjusts.

A single chair sits in front of the main stage, and Jake is tied to it. Ropes wrap around his wrists, and another set binds his abdomen to the back of the chair, keeping him upright. More circle his ankles and hold his feet against the legs. A pair of panties have been fashioned into a gag over his mouth. When he sees me, he wiggles against his restraints and nearly tips over.

Ambrose strides toward him and pulls the fabric from his mouth.

"Girl, what the fuck have you done?" Jake screams, thrashing against the binds so hard I'm not even sure they'll hold him.

My mouth wordlessly opens and closes. I have just as many questions in my mind as he does in his.

Ambrose's dark eyes burn through me as he takes me in. He looks like his jaw might drop to the floor. I wouldn't let it if I were him; these floors are disgusting.

Ambrose grabs Jake's face and forces it toward me. "Remember what you did to her?"

Jake scoffs. "She wanted me."

Ambrose's eyes flash between us. "That's not the way I saw it. How about you?" he turns his attention to me. "Did you want it?"

I shake my head.

"Two versus one, you sleaze."

"What are you, her boyfriend or something?" Jake says with a sadistic laugh. "You dating a whore?"

Ambrose punches Jake with a ferocity I don't expect. The single blow is enough to rock his neck so hard that I fear his head will snap clean off. With a frustrated exhale, he stuffs the panties into Jake's mouth once again. Jake lets out a tirade behind the fabric, but it's a muffled and word-less mess to my ears.

The anger on Ambrose's face softens as he pulls up a chair and places it beside Jake. "Dance for me, tragedy," he says as he takes a seat. "Eyes on me." He bites his lower lip and pulls a remote from his pocket, then aims it at the DJ booth to start the music.

Sound springs to life. Has it always been this loud? Or is he drowning out Jake's screams and thrashing?

I take a deep breath and let the music guide me. My hips begin to sway, and I glide across the stage before I grip the pole and climb. When I hook my leg around and drop myself backward, I fight the urge to look over their heads the way I normally do when I dance. The way I normally do when I want to pretend I'm somewhere else. Ambrose's words ring in my ears.

Eyes on me.

I focus on Ambrose, blocking out the erratic thrashing Jake does beside him. A confusing twist of emotions rushes across his handsome face as I dance. He's battling between anger and admiration, and I can only hope the latter wins out. As my back hits the cool stage, I tuck my legs under me and sit up, giving him a full view of my ass as I sensually stroke the pole before hooking a leg around it once more. I spread my legs and twist around to face him again.

"Crawl to me," he says.

His stern command overpowers the music, and I can't deny my need to obey him. I get on my hands and knees and crawl to the end of the stage. His eyes ride along each sensual curve of my body as I drop to my elbows and look up at him. He bites his lip again and leans toward me.

He turns to Jake. "She's *really* good, but I don't like that you're getting a chub while looking at my girl." He gets to his feet and sends his foot between Jake's legs.

Jake's eyes bulge and he tries to double over, but the ropes hold him in place. His face shifts from red to purple.

Ambrose turns back to me and walks to the stage. There's no one to tell him he's too close. That he can't touch. Not that I think he'd listen, even if there was. His hand glides down my back until he reaches the bra clasp. He unhooks it in one swift motion, and it slips down my shoulders. Despite the numerous times I've bared it all on this stage, a rush of insecurity floods me. Ambrose lifts me to a kneeling position and brings his lips toward mine.

"My tragic little whore," he growls, and instead of recoiling from the word, I lean into it.

His hand goes to my chest. His touch is firm around the flesh of my breast, but it shifts to something tender toward my nipple. His other hand goes to my throat, and he pulls me into him for a passionate kiss that makes me weak. When he pulls away, I'm a wet mess.

He hops onto the stage and squints as he peers into the audience of one. The bright lights burn into his eyes like they do ours. He walks over to the pole and puts his back against it. As his hands work open his jeans, he doesn't need his words to tell me what he wants.

"Crawl," he says, the word drenched with demand.

I crawl over to him and kneel at his feet as my hands ride up his legs. He pulls out his cock, and the metal studs reflect the strong overhead lights. I take him into my mouth. A low growl rumbles from him as soon as my lips wrap around him. I move along his length until I feel the studs at the base. He puts one hand on the pole above his head to steady himself, then he buries the other in my hair as he fucks himself with my mouth. I love the way the head of his dick twitches as I pleasure him.

He wants my eyes on him, but his are on Jake.

Wearing a menacing stare, he pushes my hair to the side so Jake has no choice but to watch me please Ambrose—the man who bound him to that chair. The man who kept me fucking captive until I captivated him.

"Do you want to see me fuck her?" he yells to Jake.

The dude doesn't even say no. He's gone quiet and almost seems to be enjoying it.

Ambrose pushes me back so I land on my ass on the stage. He drops to his knees and spreads my legs. His hands hover at the shoes before he raises them to my thighs. He pulls my panties to the side, and the warmth of the lights sears through the wetness between my legs. I keep looking at Jake, anxiety tensing every muscle in my body.

Ambrose leans over me. "Keep those eyes on me, tragedy," he growls as he tugs me into his pelvis before pushing inside me.

I gasp as he pushes to my depths and his piercings tease different parts of me. I reach back and grab the bar that sits a couple of inches off the stage floor to brace myself as he fucks me harder. He basks in Jake's increasing anger and jealousy, then pours that high into me as he drives me into the stage. My eyes remain on him, and I try not to think of what happens once he's finished fucking me.

Chapter Thirty-Five

Ambrose

I thought she felt incredible when she fought me, but she feels so fucking good when she willingly lets me inside her. She's truly mine now, in a way I never could have imagined. Like anything that belongs to me, I have to protect her. I have to think about what she needs. I've hurt her too many times, and now I have to make sure no one ever hurts again. I'll take out anyone who does.

Her boss squirms and screams, but his weasel eyes don't leave my tragedy's body. I'll let him watch the way her tits bounce with every thrust of my hips. He's going to die, so he might as well enjoy the beautiful fucking view in front of him while he can. I know I am. Even in danger, he can't help but be mesmerized by her. Like me.

The mirrors surrounding everything make it so much better. I can see every angle of her. The pout of her lips between moans. The fat of her ass cheeks as her legs curl around me. That incredible mane of red hair flowing around her beautiful face. It's enough to make me want to bust. But not yet. I want to fuck her on her hands and knees first. I want that ass up in the air for me.

My cock sheens with her wetness as I pull out of her and flip her onto her stomach. I slide my arm beneath her and raise her hips to meet mine. Fisting her hair, I force her eyes on the writhing, screaming asshole sitting in front of her. I want him to see every ounce of pleasure written on her face as I fuck her senseless.

I push inside her and she gasps.

"I want your eyes on him this time, tragedy. I want you to come while he looks at your face. He needs to see what he could never do to you."

"I can't," she whimpers.

I smack her ass, ignoring her denial. My eyes move to the mirrors, and I twitch inside her as I take in the glorious view. Her ass nestles into my pelvis as I slam into her. Her hair falls down her back and to the side. She's stunning. Mind-bendingly beautiful. A goddess like her could completely ruin a man with just one taste of her incredible body.

And she did.

I hook my arm around her thigh and rub her clit. A soft moan struggles to break free, but she holds it back as she stares at the man who wanted what doesn't belong to him. I tried to take that part of her too, but it only began to belong to me when she offered it freely.

I grind my hips against hers between every thrust, trying to draw those moans out of her pretty throat. I rub circles against her before swiping my fingers over her swollen clit. She finally moans, and the sound invigorates everyone. Her boss strains and writhes more with her increasing pleasure, and she pulls a groan from me as well. It's contagious.

"Come, tragedy. Come on my dick so I can kill your fucking boss with your pleasure staining the front of my jeans."

She squeezes me, clenching almost painfully around my dick. Her thighs tremble in front of me, and I have to hold her up as I keep rubbing her clit. "I'm going to come," she pants, and instead of looking at him, her gaze rises to mine in the mirror. Those bright green eyes don't even look the same as when I met her. They eat through me as my hips stutter against her. She's squeezing me so hard, and there's no way I can stop myself from filling her, but I grip the base of my cock as her spasms try to milk me.

"Get your incredible cunt off my dick and go grab one of those copper mugs from the bar," I tell her, trying to keep from spilling my load as she leans forward and pulls away from me.

She gives me a confused look, but she hops off the stage and hurries to the bar. I like her feisty nature, but I'd be a liar if I said her obedience doesn't do anything for me. She hurries back with a copper mug, and just as she hands it to me, I slide it beneath my dick and shoot my load into it. This is a nice start, but it needs something more. I work up some spit in my mouth and add that to the mug, making it even more watery.

With my cock still out, I hop down from the stage, swirling the mug as if the finest wine resides within it. I rip the panties from Jake's mouth, and curse words fly from him the moment he's free to yell—a whole lot of charming, pretentious things revolving around "Do you know who I am?" and "You just wait until I get out of here."

Spoiler alert, Jake. You'll never leave this place.

I hand the copper mug to Oaklyn, and she stands beside me with her perfect chest bared to the world. I'd drink up just about anything if those tits remained in front of me. An intrigued expression crosses her face as she glances into the mug.

"Don't you do what you're thinking of doing. I'll ruin you!" he shouts at her.

I whip back his head by his greasy fucking hair, and he clamps his mouth tight. He's ruining all the fun by fighting.

"You don't get to boss her around anymore," I say. "You also don't get to threaten her anymore. Now open your fucking mouth."

I raise a fist in the air and bring it down on the bridge of his nose. The cartilage gives way, and a gush of blood fills his sinuses. If he wants to breathe, he only has one option. He shakes his head and tries to clear his airway of blood, but it's futile.

He opens his mouth to take a breath.

The moment his lips part, Oaklyn steps forward and tips the mug on its side, pouring my come and spit down his throat. He gags and tosses his head, then turns toward her. Before he can spit it onto her porcelain skin, I shove the panties into his mouth.

More than anything, I want to torture this piece of shit and then snuff out his existence. I want him to pay for all the pain he's caused my tragedy. But it can't be my decision. If she wants to take revenge, it has to be on her terms. I can't do this for her.

I turn to Oaklyn. "If you don't want to be a part of what happens next, you can leave while I finish what has to be done, but I want you to consider what's best for you. You have an opportunity that I will never know. You can take revenge for everything he's put you through. He dies either way, but I'll handle the torture he deserves if you can't do it."

She tosses the mug to the floor and presses the back of her hand to her mouth as she paces in front of her lecherous boss. This would be the sappy moment in a movie when the heroine chooses to walk away instead of sinking to the villain's level. I never liked those endings. I wanted the revenge. I wanted the depravity. But what does Oaklyn want?

She stops pacing and stares at the man in the chair. Her eyes close, and her fingers move to the slender scab on her lip. Taking a deep breath, she opens her eyes and steps toward him. With her teeth bared, she leans into his face.

"Fuck you, Jake!" She harnesses a feral scream, lifts her leg, and stomps down on Jake's dick with her high-heeled foot. I feel the strength behind her kick through my own dick and zip up my shit so it doesn't have to bear witness to any more of this.

Her boss strains forward, and before I can stop her, she stomps down on his crotch again. And again. She lets out a whole lot of anger on that man's genitals.

I couldn't be more proud.

Now that we've really gotten the ball rolling, it's my turn to play. I can't let her have all the fun. "Give me one of your heels," I say, motioning toward her feet.

She slips one off and hands it to me, then tries to avoid stepping onto the sticky club floor with her bare foot.

"What are you—" she begins, but her sentence stops when I place the pointed tip of the heel against his eye socket and push until it gives way.

A desperate scream rushes from behind the fabric in his mouth, and the sheer force almost allows the words to come through unmuffled. Blood spreads around the clear heel and drips down his face as he continues to writhe in unbelievably delicious torment. I pull the heel from his deflated eyeball and motion for Oaklyn to hand over her other shoe, but she's gone.

I look around the empty club and a slight panic takes hold when I worry this was too much for her. Curb stomping his nuts into oblivion was okay, but maybe cramming the heel of her shoe into his eyeball was too far. Just when I turn to finish the job myself, she appears from the back of the club, wearing her shorts and clutching something in her hand. She's traded the lone heel for her sneakers, and the lingerie bag dangles from her arm.

"I really didn't want to stand on this filthy floor," she says as she slides her shirt over her bare torso. "Plus, I had one more thing I wanted to do."

She steps closer to her panting boss, then opens her fist. A single acorn wobbles around on her palm. With a sadistic grin that almost hardens me again, she grips the acorn between her fingers and shoves it into the gaping eye socket. Her thumb pushes it as deep as it will go.

After releasing a weak groan, her boss finally passes out from the pain. Or shock is taking over. Either way, I don't give a fuck. He doesn't need to be awake for this next part, though it would have been nice.

I walk to the bar and grab two bottles of the highest proof liquor I can find, then return to the chair in front of the stage. I hand one to Oaklyn, and we work together to douse him. I pour it on the floor around him, pull a book of matches from my pocket, and light one. I hand it to Oaklyn. This is her party, and she's the guest of honor. Without a second thought, she flicks it to the ground and it combusts. Flames overtake the carpet and engulf Jake's body before crawling away to attack the rest of the building.

"Burn the shoes. You'll never need them again," I say.

She pulls the heel from the bag, grabs its mate, and

tosses them beneath the flaming chair. The plastic melts in front of our eyes.

Smoke begins to gather against the ceiling. We have to get out of here before someone reports it. I grab her hand and we run for the back door. Before we step into public view, I peer outside to ensure no one will see us leave. I already checked the outside for cameras this morning, and none of the nearby businesses have any that aim toward this parking lot. Finding no one outside, I grip her hand in mine and we bolt for the Jeep.

Once we're inside the vehicle, I use the back exit to pull onto the street, then circle around to park at the nearby gas station so we can get a better look at our handiwork. As the fire overpowers the club, the bright flames dance in her wide, fearful eyes. She doesn't see what I see, though. Watching fire consume the club where my mother once worked is vindicating. Her tortured soul dances above the fire, sexy and sultry, until her damned spirit releases a howl as it's consumed and rendered to ash.

I look over at Oaklyn. The orange hues burn through the green of her irises, and I think it might be a little vindicating for her too. Bittersweet, I'm sure.

In the end, I didn't kill Oaklyn, and I didn't get the vengeance I planned, but destroying Jake and burning the club still felt good. It still feels like revenge. And that's good enough for me.

Chapter Thirty-Six

Oaklyn

As I lie in bed beside Ambrose, every breath I take tastes like the choking scent of the club mixed with cleansing fire. I turn onto my side and look at the man who killed my boss. The man who very nearly killed *me*. I'm now witness to one and a half homicides—me being the half. My mouth waters at the memory of how he looked today. How his thick muscles flexed. How he could have ended me ... but didn't.

When I close my eyes, the flames dance in my mind. It's euphoric. But it's also a little sad. Despite all the pain that building caused me, it was all I had. In the toss of a match, my only source of income is gone. And what about Ambrose? He hired a couple of hitmen to take out his boss, so how will he support us now? It's not like I can be a big help. Even if another club existed in this town, it's not like I could dance there. Ambrose wouldn't want me to, but I wouldn't want to either. I still want to dance, but I don't think stripping is for me anymore. One man's obsession is about all I can handle.

I reach toward Ambrose's face and trace the many scars that line his strong jaw. So much pain etched into his handsome features. He's a fractured demigod walking the earth alongside someone so downtrodden and tired.

Alongside me.

He doesn't stir as my fingertips graze the imperfections running along his neck and bare shoulders. I can see which cuts were the deepest and which were shallow and hurried. Some aimed to kill, while others meant to maim. I can't help but wonder how much he remembers of the incident. If he recalls any of the pain, it's probably not from the actual incident but the aftermath of it. The pain of looking at himself in the mirror and being reminded that he's different. That he's half dead because he's only half alive. But if you put us together, we make a whole.

This new life I've chosen won't be easy. It doesn't fix the rift between me and my family, but I'm okay with that. If my mother couldn't love me because I chased a dream, she never loved me to begin with. All I've ever needed was someone in my corner, and Ambrose has taken that position to heart. Now, he's all I need.

Ambrose

My phone rings, and the blaring sound pulls me from sleep. The only person who calls my phone on a regular basis is Darby, and I know it's not him. The Kursickis never miss a mark. Through eyes heavy with sleep, I grab my phone and bring it up to my face. I blink twice to be sure I'm seeing this right, but the name remains on my screen.

It's Darby.

I answer the call. Instead of hearing the grinding voice of the son of a bitch I'm certain should be dead, the dark, heavily accented voice of Boris fills my ear.

"Did you hear?" he asks.

I wipe a hand down my face as I sit up. "Hear what?"

"Darby is dead," he says with the slightest hint of excitement coloring his voice.

Oh, I didn't just hear it. I set it up. But I can't tell him that. "What? How?" I ask, feigning concern. Of which I have none.

Boris scoffs, and even that has an accent. "Someone found him in his office this morning. They said something about his severed pinky shoved inside his dickhole. It didn't have something to do with you throwing the fight last night, did it?"

I sigh. "Is there a point to this call, Boris? Besides telling me the good news that Darby is dead."

"Yes, yes, I'm getting there." He takes a deep breath. "How would you like to do this fight club with me?"

"You're the one who should take over, not me. I'm not undefeated anymore."

He laughs. "Oh no, that was not a win I can be proud of. You still hold that title to me. I see no better fighters to run the show than us."

I swallow hard, and Oaklyn stirs behind me. She sits up, pinning her ear to my shoulder to try to hear what's being said. I look back at her. Running an illegal fight club turned out super well for Darby, obviously. Is that what I want? What I want for us?

For us.

I've never had to think of another person. I've never been so intricately linked to another person for there to *be* an us. I've always made decisions for myself. For me.

Sick of waiting for my answer, Boris pushes. "You either join, or you quit fighting."

"You'd keep me out of the ring?" I ask.

"If you refuse my offer? Yes. As the true better fighter, my matka would rise from the grave just to slap me upside the head if I didn't at least offer. Don't offend me, bratr."

It's not the first time Boris has called me brother in his native tongue, but the annoyed snap in his tone took the endearment right out of the word. Now it sounds like I'm offending his great-great ancestors by declining.

So I don't.

"Fine, *brother*," I say. "I'll meet you at the ring tomorrow. I have some shit to deal with."

When I end the call and turn toward Oaklyn, her big eyes have lost all their sleepy haze. She looks at me, waiting for me to explain, but I don't know what to say to her. This could be enough to ensure Oaklyn never has to work again if she doesn't want to, but it means entrenching myself further into a dangerous sport built on the backs of my enemies. It could be risky.

I stare into her eyes. It may not be the right call, but it could give us a chance at making something good out of something that started so badly. It's a chance I'm willing to take.

For us.

"You and that guy you were fighting are taking over the fight club?" she asks as she curls her legs under her. "You sure that's a good idea?"

I pivot my body and push her onto the bed. I fall

between her legs and her eyes slowly rise to meet mine. "There's only *one* thing I've ever done that I'm sure was a good idea."

"And what's that?" she asks with a sly smile.

I lean down and capture her lips with mine. "Letting you live, my beautiful little tragedy."

Epilogue

Six Months Later

Oaklyn

A blindfold presses against my eyes as we travel down the road in the Jeep. I tilt back my head to peer around the fabric, but I can only see blazes of light. Every time I lift my hand to my face, he grabs my wrist and moves it away. "Where the hell are we going, Ambrose?" I ask with a frustrated growl. We've been together long enough that I don't think he's bringing me somewhere to murder me.

"You'll see, tragedy," he says, and I can hear the smile in his voice.

"Stop calling me that!"

We no longer live in a constant state of waiting for the tragic final scene. He doesn't need to call me that anymore. But he's never stopped. Being his disaster morphed into becoming his triumph, but I've remained his tragedy. I've also remained his whore, but only when he's about to fill me.

"Never," he says, dropping a warm hand to the back of my neck as he continues to drive.

We finally stop and the engine cuts off, which is good because my patience was about to do the same. Sitting in a loud Jeep when my sense of sight and touch have been disabled frustrated me to no end. I don't like feeling helpless like that.

"Don't take off your blindfold." He gets out of the Jeep and closes the door, leaving me in a stiff, uncomfortable silence. I swivel my head, trying to home in on any sounds outside this metal box, but I only hear his footsteps as he approaches my door.

The door opens and warm air rushes inside. A rope-like handle brushes my palm as he places a bag in my hand. If he thinks I'm going to get dressed in some more lingerie in the middle of the day, he's got another thing coming. That was a one-time deal. I test the weight of the bag in my hand, and I'm happy to find it feels like it holds something a little heavier than some skimpy lingerie.

Ambrose grabs my wrist and dips it into the bag. I expect to feel something . . . wrong inside, but a familiar texture teases my fingertips. Something that feels like home. Even though I feel it, I still can't believe it.

"Take off your blindfold," he says, and I rip it away before he even finishes his sentence.

Just like I thought, the leotard from my final perfor-mance rests on the bottom of the bag. The outfit I kept in my closet as a constant reminder of what my life used to be. The familiarity brings a rush of sorrow with it. It's a reminder of what I'll never have again.

Why the hell would he rub more salt in that very open wound? Why is he being this fucking cruel?

Tears fill my eyes, and I drop the leotard. I don't want to look at it anymore.

His fingers find my chin, and he raises my head so that I have to look at him. "Look around."

My head swivels as I scan the parking lot attached to a small, rundown building. The yellow lines have faded on the cracked pavement beneath my feet, and someone has sent a brick or some other hard object through one of the front windows in the sad storefront.

"What is this?" I demand, the thought of his cruelty sending a crisp, renewed anger searing through my words.

He gives me the smirk that always makes my heart gallop, but right now it makes me want to punch him in the mouth.

"It's yours," he says.

My head shakes. "What?"

"It's your new dance studio." He throws his arms to the side as if to show off some grand prize in a game show. His smile widens when he recognizes my look of disbelief. "I'm not kidding. This is where you'll teach dance."

Even considering the shape it's in, there's no way we could afford this place. We don't ever do without, but we don't exactly have a lot in our savings account. If this is some kind of joke, it's stupid at best and cruel at worst.

"We don't have the money for something like this," I say.

"I do." He puts his arm around me and guides me toward the door, then he pulls out a key and unlocks it.

My eyes dance along the building's interior. The inside isn't in terrible shape, and with a little work, it could be brought to glory. I imagine full-length mirrors surrounding us. I imagine silk outfits and sequins and rehearsals. When I move my feet, I can almost feel the floor's smooth surface and the freedom that every dance move lends my body. I can see how this space could become an excellent dance studio—*my* dance studio—and it's just too much for my brain to handle. It's too good to be true. Things like this don't happen to me anymore.

Ambrose pulls me against his body. "Do you want to know where I got the money?" he asks.

Yeah, I really fucking do, so I nod.

"After my mother attacked me, she ended up in a psych ward. Her parents were too old to take care of me, and since she was an only child, she inherited everything upon their deaths a few years later. That money went into some sort of trust while I rotted in poverty in foster homes. When she met her untimely demise, that trust went to me, her bastard child. I have *never* touched that money because I wanted nothing to do with it. I wanted nothing from *her*." He swallows. "But I know you miss dancing, and I don't mean the way you were dancing when I met you. You miss shit like that." He points to the bag containing my leotard. "I know you can't dance like you did before, on the big stage in front of your permanently disappointed mother, but you can teach others who can one day end up on that stage."

Tears erupt from my eyes, and I cry in ways I haven't in a very long time. This time it's not from the unbearable sadness when the rug is inevitably ripped out from under me. This time it's because for the first time since that accident, I'm able to see a hidden part of myself again. Oaklyn Grey. Me.

Through tear-soaked eyes, I rush forward and wrap my arms around him. His powerful arms encircle me. Arms that do so much damage on a daily basis. They don't hurt me, though. They are my source of comfort.

I wipe my eyes and stand on my tiptoes to kiss him. I'll

be sure to thank him properly later. I'll even let him call me his beautiful tragedy while I'm on my knees.

"There's one more thing," he says as he grabs the bag and pushes it toward me. "Put this on. I want you to dance for me."

Did you like *Driving My Obsession*? Have you read the original dark hitchhiker romance? If you want to know more about Lexington Rowe, check out *Hitched* here: Book s2read.com/Hitched

Want to know more about the Kursicki brothers who took down Darby? Read their story, *Along for the Ride*, here: Books2read.com/MFMHitchhiker

And if you want something even darker, check out *Don't Stop*, an extreme horror hitchhiker novella. Get it here: Books2read.com/Dont-stop

These books are part of Lauren Biel's Ride or Die Romance Standalones. While these stories exist within the same universe, they can be read in any order.

Connect with Lauren

Check out LaurenBiel.com to sign up for the newsletter and get VIP (free and first) access to Lauren's spicy novellas and other bonus content!

Join the group on Facebook to connect with other fans and to discuss the books with the author. Visit http://www.face book.com/groups/laurenbieltraumances for more!

Lauren is now on Patreon! Get access to even more content and sneak peeks at upcoming novels. Check it out at www. patreon.com/LaurenBielAuthor to learn more!

Acknowledgments

Thank you to my readers for making my Ride or Die series of standalones so successful. I wouldn't be where I am without you.

To my VIP gals, I love you so much. I'm so thankful for you all. You've become family! (Lori, Kimberly, Jessie, Nikita, Lexi, Grace)

Special acknowledgement to @mal_reads for bringing light to my darkest books with your reviews! Thank you for being a friend, even when I write the most out-of-pocket things. Yes, spit scenes always make me think of you in a not-weird-but-kinda way.

Shout out to the amazingly talented Brynne Weaver for giving *Hitched* (the book that started this series) an honorable mention in her fantastic dark rom-com *Butcher & Blackbird*. Make sure you check it out!

A roaring round of applause for my husband, who has been my rock on this journey, and for my editor, Brooke, who worked her dark magic on this one.

Thank you to my valued Patrons! Your contribution helped make this book happen.

Lori (special love your way, friend), Michelle M, Tabitha F, Jessie S, Lindsey S, Erika M, Laura T, Marcy S, Kayla W, Venetta B, Jennifer S, Nicole M, Eugenia M, Nineette W, Savannah C, Kimberly B, Jessica C, BoneDaddyAshe, Diana W, Michelle T, Ashley T, Janette S, Kimberly S, Sammi Rae, Sarah J, Stacy B, Kay S, Allison B, Tits, Andrea J, Bethany R, Carla D, Chelle, Gabby S, Hollie P, Jennifer H, Jessica G, Juli D, Rebecca R, Samantha R, Sara S, XynideSuicide, @bethbetweenthepages, Sharee S

Also by Lauren Biel

To view Lauren Biel's complete list of books, visit: https://www.amazon.com/Lauren-Biel/e/B09CQYDK87

About the Author

Lauren Biel is the author of many dark romance books with several more titles in the works. When she's not working, she's writing. When she's not writing, she's spending time with her husband, her friends, or her pets. You might also find her on a horseback trail ride or sitting beside a waterfall in Upstate New York. When reading her work, expect the unexpected. To be the first to know about her upcoming titles, please visit www.LaurenBiel.com.

57401015R00184